Hell Comes Home

Prudence MacLeod

Published by Prudence MacLeod, 2024.

Hell Comes Home
by
Prudence MacLeod
(second edition)

HELL COMES HOME

First edition. April 9, 2024.

Copyright © 2024 Prudence MacLeod.

ISBN: 978-1927478820

Written by Prudence MacLeod.

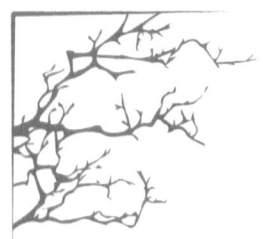

Home

Melanie Rivers sat on her motorcycle, staring at the passing waves as the ferry boat carried her across the short stretch of water to the island where she had grown up. It had been so long ago, it seemed like a lifetime. At length she took out her notebook and pen.

"The endless sea
Washes away the past
Forgiving all sins"

Melanie re-read what she'd written then closed the book and returned it to the pocket of her leather jacket. "Let's hope so," she mused. The boat was approaching the dock; it was time to go. Time to face the music. She pulled on her helmet and started the engine as the ramp touched the dock.

The road rose up a long hill and into the forest. Melanie pulled over to let the traffic pass, then set out slowly for the town a short distance away. An abandoned building caught her eye and she stopped for a moment. Brighton Hotel. It had been a thriving B&B when she was a girl, but it stood empty now, probably had for years, by the look of it. The place had a haunted look to it now and she shivered. She sighed and rode on. Melanie wasn't looking forward to this homecoming.

A small diner caught her eye as she entered the town of Brighton. Candi's Cafe. That wasn't here before. Hungry, Melanie decided to stop and fortify herself. It had been over twelve years, maybe no one would recognize her. Maybe folks had moved on with their lives.

With luck they had forgotten all about her. She hung her helmet on the handlebars and went inside.

The sign said Have a Seat, so she did, taking the only empty table in the room. The buzz of conversation stopped as she walked in, but now it picked up again. She sighed inwardly as she heard the strident voice of the woman at the next table. "It is her; I tell you. That woman is Melanie Rivers. What the hell is she doing back here in Brighton?"

"That's not our business," replied her male companion softly. "Keep your damn voice down."

"The hell I will. I'm not going to stand for this." She turned her full attention to Melanie as she rose from her chair. "What are you doing back here, Melanie Rivers? Hasn't your family done enough damage to the good people of this town?"

Melanie didn't even look at the woman. Sadly, she couldn't even remember the woman's name. She sighed and let her shoulders sag, but her silence gave the woman courage. "Well, answer me, Miss Murderer Rivers."

Melanie's voice was soft as she finally spoke without making eye contact. "Please don't do this. I just want a meal. I'm not here to cause trouble."

"You are trouble, Missy; you earned that nickname Devil from Hell. Your whole damn family is trouble, trouble we don't need. We don't want the likes of you in our town."

That snapped it. There was going to be no way to reason with the woman. Her husband's feeble attempts to shut her up only added fuel to the fire. Melanie shook her head. "It's hard, isn't it?"

"What??? What the hell are you talking about?"

"Not getting what you want. It's hard to want something and not get it. That's how it felt years ago when my family wanted the support of this town, but we didn't get it. Now, according to you, the town doesn't want me here." Melanie rose and faced her attacker. The woman took a step back from the fire in those eyes. "Well this time you won't get what you want either. I've come home to stay. Suck it up and learn to deal. Now, get out of my face."

The woman shrank back into her seat and swallowed hard. "What are you going to do, Melanie? Murder me in my sleep too?"

"Don't tempt me." Melanie sat back down as the young server appeared.

"Please, we don't want any trouble in here."

"Me neither, girl. I just want a burger and a coffee, that all."

The girl searched Melanie's eyes for a moment then nodded her head. "Will that be the deluxe?"

"Sure. Coffee black."

"Coming right up."

"Well, we're not staying here; come along, Marvin." Melanie's assailant stormed out, dragging her husband behind her. No one else had said a word either way.

The server soon returned with the burger and coffee. Seeing the empty table next to Melanie she stomped her foot in frustration. "Dammit, they skipped out without paying."

"It's okay. I'll cover it."

"The hell you will." The deep male voice caused them both to turn to the older man at another table. "I"ll cover it and Melanie's too." He was grinning. "I've waited years to see someone stand up to Janet Carter. It was worth the wait. How you been, Mel?"

"Some good, some bad, Sheriff. Thanks."

"I retired five years ago, Mel. I'm just Hank now."

"Oh yeah? How's that working out for you?"

"Boring as hell, Melanie. I owe you at least a burger for livening the place up a bit."

"I live to serve." Melanie moaned with delight as she bit into the burger. It was delicious and she was famished. Hank chuckled.

"So, how's your mom and dad? You ever see them?"

Melanie nodded then swallowed before speaking. "They're living in the south of France; have been for years. I haven't seen them in a long time, but I hear they're doing fine. Is my grandmother still alive?"

"She is, but she's become a bit of a recluse, as you might have guessed. Folks tend to give Ellen a wide berth."

"She still at the old house?"

"Ah-huh. Melanie, you're not here looking for payback are you?"

"No, Hank, I'm not. Those old wounds are all scarred over; no sense opening them up again."

"So why did you come back?"

"I had nowhere else to go. My job got shipped out to India, the bank took my house, and the dog moved in with the neighbors. Thanks for the burger." She dropped a ten-dollar tip on the table and left the diner.

Melanie turned slowly up the old familiar street. She stopped by the rundown house with the boarded up windows. It was much as it had been the last time she saw it, the weeks after the murders.

Melanie's uncle had gone to the doctor complaining of insomnia. He'd been put on anti-depressants which made him a bit of a zombie. He didn't seem to care about anything anymore. The family convinced him to go back to the doctor. The doctor upped the dosage. On that dose he seemed to turn nasty. One week later her uncle had entered this house with an assault rifle and murdered a family of eight then took his own life.

Melanie pulled out her notebook once again.

"It stands there
cold, empty, and forlorn
Accusing."

She sighed as she replaced the book in her pocket then moved on to the next house farther down the road. This place looked a bit rundown too, but still lived in. She parked the bike then went to knock on the door. A cracked voice came from within.

"Go away and leave me alone. I have a shotgun."

Melanie grinned, her first smile in a long time. "Bet it's not loaded, Nana."

The locks on the door snicked back, and then it slowly opened. "Melanie? Dear god, is that you, Little Mel?" The old woman stepped into her arms and hugged her fiercely.

"It's me, Nana, the one and only." Melanie held the old woman gently, tears of unnamed emotions streaming down her face.

"Oh gods it's good to hold you again, Little Mel. Come inside now before someone sees you."

Melanie allowed her grandmother to drag her inside. "Gees, Nan, I didn't think I was that ugly that you wouldn't want anyone to see me."

"Stop it child; you know damn well what I mean."

"It's okay, Nana; I stopped for a burger at that new diner. Janet Carter was there. She told me to get out of town. I told her to piss off, I'm home to stay."

The old woman turned to gaze into her eyes. "Do you mean that, Melanie? Are you home to stay?"

"Yes I am, Nana."

"It won't be easy, child. People here have long bitter memories."

"I know, Nana. Nothing these folks can do will scare me; not anymore."

The old woman gazed into her granddaughter's eyes for a long moment then nodded. She took Melanie by the hand and led her into the kitchen, depositing her at the table. She stepped to the stove and put on the kettle for tea. "You've seen some hard years, girl."

"Yes I have. I've seen a lot I wish I hadn't, and I've done a lot I wish I hadn't. It's a sick world out there, Nana. I knew it was time to quit and come home when I could no longer tell the good guys and bad guys apart."

The old woman just nodded as she brought the tea to the table. "I suppose you're like the rest of the heathens now, wanting coffee instead of tea."

Melanie grinned as she took a sip from her cup. "I can adapt."

"Will you be staying here?"

"I'd like to, if that's okay."

"Of course it's okay; this is your home too. You know that."

"Nana, my being here won't bring the wrath of fools down on you will it?"

"No more than usual, dear."

"Oh?"

"They claim I'm a witch now. I get the blame for everything from an empty gas tank to the measles." Melanie just shook her head sadly. "It's all right, honey. The best part is some of the come to me for favors, you know, love potions and such. Why, just last week I got fifty bucks for a small jar of orange Kool-aid with extra sugar."

"Extra sugar; you mean pot."

"Ah-huh, the secret ingredient to all my potions."

"Nana, you're a bad woman."

"Girl's got to make a living, Melanie. Geez."

They spent the rest of the day getting reacquainted, Melanie listening, gently prodding for more stories of the old lady's life during the vanished years. For her part, Ellen Rivers was content to talk and just enjoy the nearness of the woman Melanie had become. A woman she had dared not hope to see. To have Melanie home with her was a true blessing and she allowed some of the stress to leave her as she relaxed in the warmth of the young woman's love.

Melanie stopped to gaze around as she entered her old bedroom. It was much as she'd left it over twelve years ago. She sighed and shook her head sadly as she took note that it had been recently cleaned. Obviously, her grandmother had kept it that way all these years in hopes she might someday return. This was the room of an innocent, a girl filled with hope for the future. She would leave this way; maybe some of that past hope would rub off again.

Pulling out her notebook, she thought for a moment then wrote: "Home,
loving, welcoming, embracing, and yet
Foreboding"

Now why had she written that, she wondered, but she could not deny it. She'd had that sense of foreboding since she'd gotten off the boat. Brighton was like a town out of time, lost, alone, and angry. Melanie could no longer stall the inevitable, she had to let her senses explore or she wouldn't be able to sleep.

She sat cross legged on the floor, her back resting against the bed, breathing deeply. As her body sank into relaxation she released herself to the island, to its energy, its living soul. Frightened, uneasy, edgy, these were the emotions that came faintly to her consciousness. Suddenly, there it was, wild, evil, insane, hungry. Whatever spirit that was, it was centered at the abandoned hotel.

Melanie pulled herself back from it, retreating to her grandmother's house. It was calm here, defensive, but calm, and protective. She smiled as she touched her grandmother's energy. Nana had been exploring too.

Melanie opened her eyes and stretched. Whatever that was, it wouldn't approach this house. The old woman's defensive energy was too strong, and now hers was added to it. It was safe to rest. She reached up and pulled a pillow down with her, stretched out, and went to sleep.

The next morning, Ellen Rivers made breakfast then went upstairs to wake Melanie. The room was empty and the bed had not been slept in, however there was a rumpled pillow on the floor beside the bed. She fluffed it up and replaced it at the headboard. "Where have you been, child, and what have they done to you there?"

Returning to the kitchen, she found Melanie at the table eating breakfast. There was also the smell of brewing coffee. "You're all sweaty; were you out for a run?"

"I was, Nana. It's a bit of a habit these days."

"Where did you go? Down by the old hotel?"

"How did you know?"

"You went exploring last night. Whatever that thing is, it knew you were there. Don't stir it up, Mel. It's been there for years. As long as people stay away from it, nothing bad happens. Every once in a while some fool will go exploring there."

"And they die a horrible death soon after, right?"

"Right. You know what that is, don't you?"

"No, but I've encountered them before. It's all right, Nana; I'll leave it alone. I just wanted to make sure it stays put, if you know what I mean."

"I do. Like I said, as long as nobody bothers it, it stays pretty much at the hotel."

"Nana, I'm a big girl now. I need to know what happened here, what no one would ever tell me before."

The old woman gazed out the window for a long moment then spoke softly. "All right, Melanie. It started back in the late sixties. I experimented with a lot of mind altering drugs. One of them opened me to another dimension, a dark place. I escaped, but have been able to see the creatures from there in our world ever since that time. I can see that you have that ability now too."

"Yeah, I do. I came by it differently, but I do."

"How did you come to that, Mel? You're way stronger than I am."

"I was in the military, special training, experimental stuff, and special supplements I'm sure. Now, don't ever breathe a word of that, or men will come and shoot us both. Go on with your story."

"Well, one of those things came and had possessed the manager of that hotel. The drugs they gave your Uncle Gary were making him crazy. I tried to help, but what I gave him, along with what they had given him, opened his eyes."

"So he killed the whole family."

"Yes, and then himself. He was such a gentle soul, but those damned anti-depressants made him violent. Mel, I don't think that one at the hotel is the only one around here, but I can't pinpoint any others. I can feel them though."

"Yeah, there's more of them; I can sense them too. Dammit, I'd hoped to be rid of them by coming home. I guess it was too much to hope for."

"What are they, Mel? What do they want here? Why do they possess some people and not others?"

"I don't know, Nana. I have no answers, only questions."

Just then a car pulled up in the driveway, followed by boots on the steps. "Now what the hell does that moron want?" The old woman rose and went to the door. "Morning, Sheriff, you here for a love potion at this time of day?"

"Really funny, Ellen. I hear your granddaughter Melanie is back in town. Is she here?"

"Maybe. What's your interest in Melanie? You're a married man after all."

"You're a riot, Ellen. Tell Melanie to get her ass out here. I want to ask her some questions."

The man's tone sent Melanie out of the kitchen in a hurry. "What do you want?" She stepped between her grandmother and the police officer. Instinctively he flinched and stepped back.

"I want to know why you came back here, when you plan to leave, and why the hell I can't access your file in any of the data bases."

"This is my home, I plan to stay indefinitely, and you don't have the clearance to see my file. What else?"

"I want you out of town by sundown."

"Won't happen."

"The good folks of this town don't seem to want you here, why is that?"

"You'll have to ask them."

"I did."

"Then you already know the answer to your question."

"I run a quiet town here, Rivers. I want to keep it that way."

"I'm in full agreement with you there, Sheriff. I didn't come home to cause trouble; I came to be with my grandmother. She's all the family I have."

"Just keep your nose clean." He sneered then walked back to his car.

"Dipshit," muttered Ellen as she turned back into the house.

"Second that." Melanie closed the door then turned to follow her grandmother.

"He'll cause you trouble, Mel."

"He can try. Who the heck is he anyway? I don't recognize him."

"Big city detective looking for a soft job. He showed up when Hank retired, got himself elected, and has been a pain in the ass ever since. Come back and have some tea with me."

While Ellen made the tea, Melanie took out her small notebook.

"Authority denied

Angry, confused, vengeful

Frightened"

"He said he can't access your file, Mel. What have you been up to? Are you still working for the government?"

"No, I'm not, but they sealed my file, all our files. We spent years tracking things like what's out at the hotel. We were mandated to find out what they are, where they come from, what they want, and how to stop them. We were a long way from successful. The team was disbanded and sent home, but we secretly kept on hunting them.

Our former boss was reassigned, but we all stay in contact with him, and he helps us where he can."

"So what's the plan? Are you going after that thing out at the hotel?"

"Not if I can help it. Nana, I don't even want to think about where all this will go if somebody starts messing with it. I plan to leave well enough alone."

"Could you get rid of it?"

"Maybe, I have before, but it isn't easy. In fact, it's bloody dangerous. Too many people have died every time we mess with those things."

"Then we'll leave it alone. No sense asking for trouble. Have you any plans for the day?"

"None at all."

"Good, then you can help me in the garden."

Melanie spent the next three weeks helping her grandmother get the old house back in order, doing all the jobs the old woman was no longer able to do. They had just finished the last of the fence painting and were standing back to admire their handiwork when the sheriff returned, a fancy car following close behind.

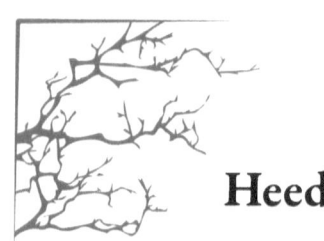

Heed the Warning

"Afternoon, Sheriff."

"Rivers."

The sheriff had a sour look on his face, but he stayed polite. Melanie waited, her attention on the other car. A tall well dressed woman in her mid-thirties got out and approached. The sheriff made the introductions. "Ma'am, I advise you to reconsider."

"Thank you, Sheriff Parker, but I will not. Please introduce me."

"As you wish. This is Ellen Rivers and her granddaughter Melanie Rivers. Ladies, this is Caroline Majors, the new owner of the Brighton Hotel. I will now leave you to it." With that he turned, got back in his car, and drove away.

"It's too hot to stand around out here. Let's got inside for some iced tea while we talk. It's obvious you have something on your mind, Miss Majors, and by the look on the sheriff's face I doubt I'm going to like it." Ellen turned and led the way into the house. Melanie gestured for Caroline to precede her then followed, drinking in the sight of the tall delicious woman ahead of her.

Ellen led them to the kitchen, indicated they should sit, then poured iced tea for all and joined them. "All right, Missy, out with it."

The sheriff had been right about these people. The old woman was an aging hippie, and the granddaughter was something else again. Caroline Majors had made her fortune by reading people accurately. Melanie drew, and yet frightened her. This girl had an edge, and she was dangerous. Ah well, there was no help for it, she was desperate.

"All right, ladies, I won't mince words about this. I need your help. Actually, it is Melanie I came to see, and it is her help I need. Melanie, I have recently purchased the Brighton Hotel with intentions of turning it into a B&B. I'm sick of the rat race, I've made my fortune, such as it is, and now I want to find a slower pace of life. My passion is painting, and that hotel is a perfect place for me to pursue that passion.

"Now, here's the problem..."

"The place is a wreck and you can't get anyone to help you fix it up." Melanie was studying her hands now. "You want to hire me as your helper. I'm sure the sheriff has already told you about our family history. Why would you come to me? Take his advice and go somewhere else. There's a big house on the other side of the island for sale. It would make a great B&B."

"Now what on Earth could make me do that? I got a great price on the hotel." Caroline was smiling wickedly at Melanie now. She had known the girl was watching her from behind. To hell with it all, if sex appeal would turn the tide in her favor she wasn't above taking advantage, besides, the girl was definitely attractive.

Melanie raised her eyes to Caroline's and blushed as she met that mischievous smile. "The place is bad mojo, don't go there, please. Bad things happen to people who go there."

"So the sheriff told me. He also told me the townsfolk think you're behind much of it. Is that true?"

"Lady, you're treading on thin ice here..."

"Hush Mel." Ellen gently patted her granddaughter's hand. "Ms. Majors, about thirteen years ago my youngest son got some bad drugs from the pharmacy. He went postal all over the former manager of the Brighton Hotel and his family. He then took his own life. Since that time this family has been accused of everything from a hangnail to global warming."

"I see. I came from a small town as well. I understand that it's easier for people to blame someone else for their troubles rather than face the truth. Rest assured; I don't give a tinker's damn about your family history. I just want to get the hotel up and running. I will need staff and I can't find anyone to help me. The sheriff said you weren't afraid of anything, Melanie. Will you help me?"

"The sheriff is dead wrong about me, Miss Majors. There are a number of things I am afraid of. Whatever malignant spirit that haunts that hotel is one of them. Please, for your own safety, give up that idea. There's a great spot for sale on the other side of the island. It has a nice house, great view, and is a safe place to live."

"I can't change your mind?"

Melanie was getting lost in those deep blue eyes and Caroline was pouring on the sex appeal. "If anybody ever could, it would be you, pretty lady. No, I won't change my mind, but I beg you, leave that hotel alone. There's something there, something evil. It is best not to disturb it."

Caroline shut off the sexy and rose from her chair. "As you wish. A pleasure to meet you, ladies. Thank you for the iced tea and the chat. Melanie, you know where to find me if you change your mind. Don't bother to see me out, I can find the way."

Melanie was acutely aware of every click Caroline's heels made as she returned to her car. She listened as it drove away then reached for her notebook.

"Beauty arrived

Passionate, bewitching,

Misguided"

"Mel, what do you write in that little book all the time?" Melanie slid the book over to Ellen who read a few pages then passed it back with a quirked eyebrow. "Some of it isn't too bad at all. Why?"

"I have too. I was told that since I won't shave my head and pierce my face to be a real lesbian, I have to write bad poetry just to keep my lezzie card."

"Ah-huh. Sure."

"It's helps me, Nana. I don't even know how, but it does."

"Then keep doing it, sweetie. So, you've got your lezzie card?"

"Does this mean you're going to throw me out of the house?"

"Nope, it just means I'll give up on the idea of great-grandchildren."

"Don't write my future off just yet, Nana. I have found that when I get the world figured out, it all goes to hell on me."

"Yeah, well, I'm glad to see you have a head on your shoulders anyway. That girl was putting the moves on you, but you saw through that."

"I did, but I still enjoyed it. Caroline Majors is delicious."

"She's pretty all right. I doubt she'll stay that way long if she goes poking around that old hotel."

"Yeah, and she will; we both know that."

"Yes we do, sadly. She'll get that damned thing all stirred up and the whole town will pay. That's when they will start blaming us."

"Do you want to move out, Nana? Go somewhere else where nobody knows us? Start over?"

"Start over? Do you have any idea how long it takes to find a place and get a proper pot garden set up? Hell no; I'm not going anywhere."

Melanie just grinned and shook her head at her grandmother. "Nana, you're a bad woman."

Another two weeks went by then the sheriff's car returned. Melanie got a surprise as Hank Doyle climbed slowly out of the machine and doffed his hat. "Morning, Ellen, Melanie."

"Morning, Hank, is that a sheriff's uniform you're wearing? I thought you said you'd retired."

"I had, Mel, but the shit hit the fan two days ago and the mayor asked me to fill in until they can find someone to take over the job. Nobody local wants it."

Ellen turned towards the house. "Come on inside, Hank. It's too hot out here for storytelling." Melanie and Hank found her in the kitchen pouring up iced tea. "So what happened, Hank? Did that foolish woman actually go blundering about in that hotel?"

"She did," he sighed as he lowered himself into a chair. "She hired a couple of guys from the mainland to come over and fix the place up. They lasted about a week before one quit, saying the place was haunted. The next morning she found the other one dead in one of the rooms. The sheriff went to investigate and didn't come back. They found him late yesterday, dead just inside the door. The woman has vanished."

"So why come to us?"

"Ellen, you know damn well why I came to you. I need to know if that woman is still alive. Did she run for her life? Is she dead out at the hotel? What..."

"Easy, Hank, easy. I'll take a look and let you know what I think, but I'm not going anywhere near that hotel."

"Wish I could say the same. Sadly, I have to. Thanks, Ellen."

"Want some company, Sheriff?"

"Melanie!"

"Sorry, Nana, but I owe Hank for getting me out of town twelve years ago. I can't let him go out there alone."

"Dammit, Melanie, you be careful out there. Don't go stirring anything up."

"I'll be careful, Nana."

"All right, Mel; but we have to go back to the office and get you set up."

"What the hell are you talking about, Hank?"

"The deputy took one look at the sheriff's body and ran for his life. He was on the first boat off the island. I need a deputy, Mel, and I get the sense that you are probably better qualified for it than anybody else on this island. How about it, will you help me? Help the town?"

Melanie sighed as she rose from the table. "I'll help you, Hank, but the town can go screw itself for all I care. As soon as the mayor finds a new guy, he's on his own."

"Fair enough; let's go."

Ellen watched them get into the police car. "Don't you go getting her killed, Hank Doyle."

"I'll be fine," shouted Melanie, as the car drove away.

"WELL NOW, MARY JANE'S old uniform fits you pretty good, Mel."

Melanie had just stepped out of the locker room. "Damn, I never expected to be in uniform again. Who was Mary Jane?"

"Mary Jane Willis. She came here from the police academy, worked three years then quit to have babies. She and her husband own the hardware store now. They've got four kids. That's a good luck uniform."

"I sure hope so, Hank, 'cause we're going to need it."

Hank sighed as he put his hat back on his balding head. "And so to work. Emily, we'll be out at the hotel if needed." Emily, the dispatcher, didn't even look up. Her disapproval of his choice for deputy was clear.

Melanie gazed at her sadly for a moment, then followed Hank out to the car. She pulled her notebook from a pocket as he started the engine.

"A uniform

rigid, constricting, unyielding

Demanding"

"Taking notes already, Mel?"

"Sort of." She put the book away and turned her attention to the road. Ten minutes later they were at the hotel parking lot.

"Well, here we are." Hank sighed, but didn't make a move to get out of the car. "Better grab that shotgun from the trunk before we go inside."

Melanie was gazing out the window, checking every window. She thought she saw a quick movement. "Shotgun's no use here, Sheriff. Better to take strong flashlights; maybe a flare gun if we have one with us."

Hank Doyle turned to face his new deputy. "Mel, just what the hell are we facing here? You know, don't you?"

"No, not really. Look, everything I tell you now is classified top secret. If you blab we'll both disappear forever."

"This shit in your sealed file?"

"Yeah, and more. Lots more."

"Just tell me the minimum, Mel. Enough to keep me alive until after the next election. It'll stay inside this car; I swear it."

Melanie sighed then turned to face him. "I don't know what's here, Hank. I mean I don't know what it really is. Could be a demon from hell, a maniacal ghost, or just a curious scientist from another plane of existence. I do know that, by our standards it's evil, completely evil through and through.

"There are a few of them on this island, but this one is a real badass. I don't know what they are, I don't know where they come from, I have no idea why they are here, but I have faced them before and survived. Not everybody does. They're somewhat ethereal so guns are useless, bullets just pass through them. They're more active at night. Strong light is somewhat effective. It confuses the hell out of them.

"Most people can't see them; they just get a feeling of the creeps."

"Can you see them?"

"Yeah, I can. Hank, we stick together in there, no splitting up. If we get separated I won't be able to shield you."

"What would it do to me, Mel?"

"I don't know. I just know you'd go off the deep end and I've have to shoot you. I wouldn't want to have to do that."

"Me neither. Okay, flashlights and we stick close together. Might as well get started while we still have daylight. Since you have some experience here, this is your lead, Mel."

They got out, took strong flashlights then ducked under the police tape the previous sheriff had put up. Climbing the steps they found the door unlocked and a chalk outline of a body just inside. "That's where I found Parker."

"You found him?"

"When he didn't report in, the mayor sent the deputy to look for him. A while later the guy called to say the sheriff was dead at the hotel and that he was quitting. That's when I got pulled in. I came down and found Parker here. He was torn apart from the back, like he'd been running for his life. His reports said they'd found the other guy on the second floor."

"All right, you've been here before, so why are we here now? Don't you have enough for a report?"

"The owner's missing."

"And her car is parked right outside. Okay, Hank, let's take a look. How long has she been missing?"

"Twenty-four hours, maybe more."

"That doesn't bode well. All right, let's start at the top and work our way down."

They took the stairs to the third floor then searched every room as they worked their way back to the lobby. They found the place where the first man had been found, but no trace of Caroline Majors. Once the search of the ground floor was complete, the sheriff faced Melanie. "Okay, are we done stalling now, Mel?"

She grinned ruefully at him. "You're good, Hank. You should never have retired. Yes, I've been stalling, hoping you'd give this up, but I can see you won't. All right, the basement is the best bet. Let's go."

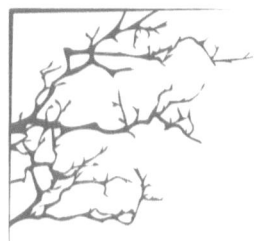

It Begins

Melanie led the way, going slowly and as quietly as possible down the old stairs. They'd barely reached the bottom when her foot hit an empty paint can sending it clattering across the floor. They heard a muffled scream followed by a maddened bellow of rage. It came from behind a door to the right. Melanie spun and lashed out with her foot. The door shattered as it was blasted inwards.

Caroline Majors lay on the floor, slashing at her assailant with an iron poker. He was screaming and stabbing at her with a knife. The man's eyes were wild, uncomprehending, and filled with a maddened rage. Melanie's sudden entrance startled him for a moment and he froze. Mel kicked the knife from his hand then he came back to life.

He threw a pile of rags at her face then disappeared into the back of the room. Melanie gave chase, but stopped at the entrance to the bolt hole. He'd vanished through a jagged hole in the foundation. She shone her light but saw only a dirt tunnel, nothing more. Melanie turned back.

Hank was on the phone with the paramedics; Caroline was unconscious. Melanie was putting pressure on one of Caroline's wounds when he snapped the phone shut. "Did you get him, Mel?"

"No. He had a bolt hole. Did you recognize him?"

"Yes, it was Billy Carter. He disappeared about eight years ago. You see anything else?"

"Did you?"

"No, should I have?"

"There was one of them clinging to his back, the poor bugger. Looks like he's been living here all this time."

"Yeah, it does. I wonder where he was getting food and stuff like that."

"A puzzle for another day, Hank. I hear the sirens. You'd better go up and lead them down here. I'll stay with her."

"Will you be okay alone?"

"I will. It was hooked onto that guy. It left with him. With any luck he'll come back after we've gone."

"That would be lucky?"

"It's way better than having him loose running around town."

"Good point. I'll go bring the lads down to get her."

The paramedics came and Melanie stood back to let them work. "You've seen a lot of this sort of thing, haven't you, Mel?"

"Way too much, Hank." She sighed as she retrieved her notebook from her pocket.

"Beauty attacked
beaten, savaged, tortured
Broken"

Hank had watched over her shoulder as she wrote. "Poetry, Mel, or code?"

"Both, and a habit. If anything happens to me, someone will come who can read this. They will talk to people, go through files, and understand what happened to me, my thoughts and observations. If that happens, Hank, don't get in their way."

"Understood, but nothing had better happen to you. I'm not scared of your spooks, but Ellen is a force of nature I don't want to mess with."

Melanie chuckled at that. "You're a wise man, Hank Doyle." The medics were carrying Caroline up the stairs and they followed. The ambulance sped away and Hank replaced the police tape across the yard then he and Melanie returned to the office.

As they entered the sheriff's office, Melanie stopped to take a good look around. Her glance fell on Emily who suddenly looked away. "We used to be friends, Em, what happened?"

The woman's posture was stiff, defiant as she finally met Melanie's gaze. "You know damn well what happened, Melanie. Your uncle went postal and killed a whole family of people, friends of my family."

"How does my uncle getting bad pharmaceuticals make me the enemy?"

"The same blood runs in your veins, Mel. I remember what you were like just before you disappeared."

The sheriff snorted at that and sank into his office chair. "By those standards you've got the makings of a mass murderer too, Em. We found your cousin Billy Carter at the hotel. He was trying to kill the owner, but Mel stopped him. He's the one who's been doing all the killings this time."

"Billy's alive? How is that possible? Nobody has seen him for years."

"He's been hiding out in the hotel by the looks of things." Hank thought for a moment then went on. "He looked pretty well fed, so somebody has been looking after him. First thing tomorrow I'll be looking into that. Right now we have to build a search party and go find Billy."

Melanie sat at the only other desk that looked used. "I wouldn't, Hank."

"We have to, Mel. He's a killer and we have the evidence as well as a witness, if she ever wakes up. We have to bring him in."

"I wasn't arguing that, Hank. Think about it. You saw the shape he's in. He's been safe at the hotel for years; he'll go back there as soon as he can. Probably there right now."

The sheriff heaved himself up from the chair. "All right then, let's go get him."

"Do we have any tranquilizer guns?"

"The vet has one, Mel, why?"

"This guy won't come easy, and I want him alive. There's been enough killing."

"Agreed. We'll stop off and borrow the gun, but if you fail I'll have to..."

"I won't fail, Sheriff."

Melanie rose from the desk and followed Hank towards the door, but Emily's voice stopped her. "Melanie?" Melanie turned to face her former friend, a questioning eyebrow raised. "Thank you for that, Mel. I'm sorry for my attitude. Want to catch up sometime?"

"Yeah, I'd like that, Em. Thanks."

She followed the sheriff out to the car. They went to the vet clinic and picked up the tranq gun before setting out for the hotel once again. "Hank, swing down by the cliff; see if that old ATV trail is still there."

"It will be. What's your plan, Mel?"

"We don't dare kill him, Hank. If we do, that thing will be loose, and we don't want it running loose looking for another host. Right now we know who it is. If we can take him alive, it will stay hooked to him. If we can keep him sedated, it's rendered harmless. Anything less and he will kill again."

Hank turned down a dirt road leading to the cliffs. He stopped at the gravel parking area and turned to her. "Is there any way to get rid of it permanently?"

"I know a few and hate them all so far."

"Such as?"

"Bottle him up and let him starve to death. If he dies slow, it dies with him. We could also dose him with a slow moving poison. Same result. If we kill him quick, or if he can commit suicide, it can break free."

"Jesus, Mel. Is that the only way?"

"If it was a smaller one I might be able to do more, Hank, but this one is a monster. I can't beat it alone; hell, I doubt my entire former team could take this one down."

Hank had gone pale and turned to look out the window. "Sweet baby Jesus. Okay, so we tranq him and send him to the nut house, right?"

"Yep, that's all I've got, Hank. If you have to shoot him, aim for the knees. We need to keep him alive. Somebody's been feeding him, and I'll bet they came in this way. Give me ten minutes to find his bolt hole; then roll into the hotel parking lot, dig out the bull horn, and make a fuss. With luck he'll run right at me."

"All right, Mel. You be careful. I'll radio when I'm in position."

Melanie watched as the sheriff drove away then turned her attention to the dirt trail before her. She broke into an easy jog, following the well-worn tracks. A few moments later she found another trail, smaller, just a footpath. That led into the trees and then to the mouth of a cave. Her radio crackled. "I'm in position, Mel."

"Same, same, Sheriff. You have a go."

A moment later she heard the siren, then the bull horn. "Billy Carter, this is the police. We have the house surrounded. Come on out with your hands in the air. You're under arrest for the murder of Sheriff Parker."

Melanie settled herself at the mouth of the cave. Aiming the tranquilizer gun down the cavern, she waited. The speed with which he appeared startled her. He was almost on her before she fired, hitting him squarely. A scream of inhuman rage and soul searing pain escaped his lips as he attacked. The drug slowed him down, but it took all her combat skills to keep him at bay. Finally his hands found a hold in her hair. Melanie grabbed his hands then sent a boot at his jaw. Billy Carter sank slowly to the ground.

As he relaxed into unconsciousness, she jerked free of his grasp and leaped away, rolling to her feet. The creature clinging to his back looked like it was made of soot and oily smoke with eyes. It was trying to pull free of the man, but he yet lived, and the creature was trapped. A harsh voice sounded from the unconscious man's throat.

"You will be mine." Melanie's eyes widened as it managed to pull one hooked tentacle free of the man. She whipped a strange glove from her pocket and pulled it on. It was covered in wires and a metallic disc. "Where did you get that?" demanded the voice. "Where?"

Her answer was to suddenly thrust her hand towards the creature, palm first. A bright glow beamed itself at the creature and it hissed in pain before slowly sinking down and disappearing into the man's body, whimpering.

Melanie took out her radio. "He's down, but alive, Sheriff. Come back around and pick us up. Bring the medics."

"Medics? Are you okay?"

"I'm good, but the prisoner is unconscious and I can't carry him. He's a big boy."

"Roger that."

Melanie removed the glove and sat to wait. She reloaded the tranquilizer gun just in case. She didn't need to. The vet had said the load would bring down a horse and he was right. A motor sounded nearby, and she heard someone approach. She was about to call out when a man carrying a small cooler appeared at the entrance to the cave. He took one look at her, dropped his cooler and ran. She reached for her radio.

"Melanie to Sheriff."

"Hank here."

"Marvin Carter was just here, but he ran. He was carrying a cooler of food. He's got a monkey on his back too."

"I see him." The radio went silent, but she heard the siren. A short while later she heard more people approaching. It was the sheriff with the medics.

CAROLINE MAJORS SLOWLY returned to consciousness. She groaned and this elicited a gasp of delight beside her. "Carrie, Carrie, it's Brit, honey. Oh thank god you're alive." She forced her eyes open to see her tearful sister beside her bed. She tried to speak, but could only croak. The girl pressed a drinking straw to her lips and she drank greedily, the water soothing her parched throat.

"Where am I?"

"You're in hospital, honey. They've got you all fixed up."

"Dear gods I hurt."

Even as she spoke a nurse appeared and fussed with the equipment for a moment. "Welcome back, Caroline. Don't try to talk too much, just let everything come slowly. I've started the pain meds for you, and it will only be a minute. I'll be nearby and your sister can buzz me for you if you need anything." With that she was gone again.

"What the hell? I can't move. Brit, I can't move..."

"Easy, Sis, easy, you're all right. They've given you something to keep you still for a while. I was assured it would wear off in a day or two."

"Why?"

"You had a lot of bad wounds, honey. They want to give them a chance to heal a bit more before you start moving around."

"How long have I been out, Brit?"

"A week."

"A week?"

"You were badly hurt, Carrie. They kept you out on purpose."

Suddenly tears sprang to Caroline's eyes. "Oh god, Brit, I remember. Oh god, what he did to me..."

"Hush now, Carrie honey, you're safe. They got the guy and he's locked up. He will be forever. You're safe now."

"Whoops, your monitor beeped." The nurse breezed back into the room. She adjusted the equipment a bit then vanished once again.

Tears seeped from Caroline's eyes as sleep claimed her once again. Brit held her hand until she was asleep, then sighed and rose to stretch the kinks from her back. She left the room and went to the waiting area. The deputy sheriff was there, writing in a small notebook.

"Deputy Rivers?" Melanie looked up. "She's asleep again for a while."

Melanie nodded and rose to her feet. "You look beat. Come on, let's head for the cafeteria. I'll buy you a coffee."

Brit Majors sat at the table where Melanie had put her. She watched as the woman walked away towards the counter. The deputy was an attractive woman. Better yet, she didn't swagger like so many women in uniform. No, she moved with the grace of a hunting tiger. The woman exuded dangerous, but she was so soft spoken and gentle. Brit was definitely interested. She tugged her sweater down slightly to give the deputy a hint of cleavage to look at. That would tell her what she wanted to know.

Brit blushed slightly as Melanie returned with the coffee. Melanie noticed that the girl had offered her a peek at her charms and she took full advantage. Neither did she try to hide her interest. That pink flush at Brit's cheeks brought a rare smile to Melanie's lips.

"Thank you, Deputy. You're the one who saved Carrie and caught the guy who hurt her, aren't you?"

"Melanie, please. Yes, I was one of the people. Yes, I was first in the room where we found her, but the sheriff was there too. It was luck of the draw that the guy ran to my station when we flushed him out."

"Bullshit."

"What?"

"Do you know how I earn my living, Melanie? I'm a gambler. I play poker against stone-faced men, and I can read them pretty well. So, try again."

Melanie was grinning. "Geez, you're tough. Okay, I got her out and tracked down the guy. He's locked away in an institution. He can't hurt her anymore. Now, Lady Gambler, tell me all you know about what went on at the hotel."

"Please call me Brit. Actually, I don't know a damned thing, Melanie. Carrie phoned a couple of months ago to tell me she's gotten sick of the fast lane. She said she'd bought an old hotel and was planning on fixing it up as a B&B. A few weeks later we spoke, and she confessed she couldn't get anyone to help her. She said all the locals were afraid of ghosts, so she was hiring off the mainland. She complained about the cost.

"About a week ago I got a call from this hospital to say she was here, that's about all I know."

"She didn't say anything about the troubles at the hotel?"

"No, I've been on the road a lot recently and we haven't had the chance to talk at length. Now, just what aren't you telling me, Deputy Melanie Rivers?"

"A whole bunch of stuff, Brit. Did you know your eyes change color when you get excited? You might want to hide that from your other gamblers."

"I always wear tinted contacts when I'm sitting at the table. Stop trying to change the subject. Tell me what the hell is going on over on that island."

"I don't dare. You're way too pretty, and if I tell you, bad people will come to make you disappear."

Brit gazed into Melanie's eyes for a long moment. "You're telling the truth, aren't you?"

"I sure am. I've never seen a woman as pretty as you."

"More bullshit, but thanks for the compliment. Have you cleared the hotel yet?"

"What???"

"It's a crime scene. Have you cleared it yet? Can I get a cleaning crew in there to make it all pretty before Carrie goes back."

"She can't ever go back there, Brit."

"Why not? It's her property, and she has the right to..."

"It's not safe to be there. Dammit anyway, why won't you Majors girls ever listen to reason?"

"It's because you haven't given us a reason, sweetie." Brit was smiling wickedly at Mel and pouring on the sexy. "You've given us a lot of mumbo jumbo about ghosts and evil, but nothing concrete. Why isn't it safe for Carrie to go back to her home."

"Pour on the sexy all you like, gorgeous, and I'll love every bit of it, but I can't tell you squat. I just need you to trust me on this one."

"Sorry, honey, but I always call a bluff. Unless you can tell me something that will..." Brit stopped speaking and turned her attention to the nurse hurrying towards her.

"Miss Major's, your sister is awake and asking for you."

"Can she talk now? I promise I don't need much time; I just need to confirm a few details."

"That's fine, Deputy, please just keep it short. She'll tire easily."

Melanie stepped aside to let Brit go first, but the woman took her arm and grinned wickedly. "Escort me back up, sugar?"

"Love to."

As soon as the elevator door closed, Brit kissed Melanie on the cheek. "I know that old trick. You don't get to watch my ass until you tell me something good."

Melanie burst out laughing. "Damn."

They entered the room arm in arm. Caroline was propped up in the bed. She tried and failed to smile as they entered. "Brit, you bag, I'm at death's door and you're putting the moves on my girl."

"You snooze, you lose, Sis. Aw, my poor darling, you're still hurting, aren't you?"

"Yes, but the meds are holding it at bay for now. Sadly, they're fogging my brain a bit. Miss Rivers, you should have told me you were a deputy."

"Melanie, please. After all, if we're going steady, we should be on a first name basis." Caroline laughed then groaned and shook a finger at Melanie. "Actually, I wasn't a deputy when we first met. After the demise of the sheriff, the former sheriff was called back from retirement, but nobody would take the deputy's job. He came to me, and since I owed him a favor..."

"Oh sure, do a favor for a guy, but not your girl."

Melanie sighed and sank into the chair beside the bed. "I did try, Caroline. I did. I warned you to stay away from that place, but you wouldn't listen. I'm sorry this happened to you."

"So am I. Are you here for a statement?"

"Yeah, that and to see you. What can you tell me about that day? Do you remember?"

Caroline looked away and her body trembled as she fought to control her emotions. "I remember. The sheriff went into the basement. There were screams then he came running back up the stairs; that creature right behind him, slashing at his back. He was bleeding everywhere. I screamed and tried to run, but that thing hit me.

"The next thing I knew I was on the floor of the basement, tied down." she choked and fought for emotional control. "He beat me, he cut me, then he raped me and left me there. He came back and tied my legs tight together then he took out that big knife and started towards me. I managed to grab something and fought him.

I thought I was dead, but then you came crashing through the door and I passed out again.

"I know what I'm up against here. I may not get the use of my legs back, and I'll be covered in scars, including my face. Christ, I should have died in there; the world would be a better place."

"Carrie, no, don't you say that. You will walk again, and they can do wonders with reconstructive surgery, I..."

"Bullshit, Brit," sighed Caroline. "I've seen my face; I know how I look, and I don't believe for a minute they can fix this. Even if they can, who would want a woman with scars all over her body? A woman who was raped by a madman?"

"Oh stop the whining already. Good Christ." Both sisters turned on Melanie instantly. Brit started to speak, but Caroline grabbed her hand. "Listen lady, that scar on your face tells me one thing; you fought the devil himself and survived. You've proven your worth as a potential mate, that you're stronger than the rest. That's not a scar, it's a badge of honor, a testament to your courage and strength."

Caroline spoke softly, still holding Brit back. "You know, don't you? You know that wasn't a man. What was that thing, Melanie?"

"I don't know... No, listen, I truly don't know what that was, but I've fought them before."

"You knew it was there, didn't you?"

"I tried to warn you, Caroline, I did."

"No you didn't."

"Listen, first, if I'd told you what was there you wouldn't have believed me. Second, if I'd said anything, I could be made to disappear by the very people who trained me to fight them. I'm oath bound to silence. However, you saw it for what it was, on your own without any input from me. That opens up the discussion a bit."

"What was there, Carrie? Melanie?"

"Brit, if you breathe a word of this I will shoot you myself."

"Lips are sealed, Mel."

"Brit's a gambler, Melanie, she can keep her peace."

"All right. I don't know what that thing is. It could be a ghost, a demon, a scientist from another realm, or a thousand other possibilities. I do know that, by our standards, it is totally evil. I know that bright light hurts it, but doesn't do a lot more. I also know that one you fought is the biggest and baddest I have ever faced. Under normal circumstances I wouldn't go up against it without a full team of eight trained agents. Even then I wouldn't expect more than half to survive the encounter."

"There's more," said Brit. "I can see it in your eyes. Keep talking."

"It was important to capture him alive. The thing is hooked into him; it can't escape unless he dies suddenly. Shoot him and it's free to claim another. Starve him to death or give him slow poison and it will die with him."

"All of it, pretty girl."

"It threatened to claim me next. Somehow it plans to kill him and get loose then come for me."

"Oh, shit, Miss Rivers..."

"Mel. Please ladies. We're all co-conspirators now."

"Mel, what are you going to do?"

"Hope for the best and prepare for the worst. I'm hoping Billy Carter gets locked away and medicated into oblivion for a hundred years, but I'm not betting on it."

Stubborn And Beautiful

Deputy Melanie Rivers sat in the patrol car in the Brighton Hotel parking lot, waiting. As she waited she opened her notebook to gaze at the last entry she had made six days ago.

"Beauty times two
Willful, stubborn,
Unrelenting"

She sighed deeply as she put it away again. What was it about these two sisters? Yes, they flirted shamelessly with her and she loved that, the courage, the fearlessness of it. It would be easy to fall for either of these ladies, but it didn't look like either of them was truly interested, or were they? Worse, as badly as she wanted to protect them, she wasn't sure she could do it. Besides, that thing had made a clear threat against her. That had never happened before either.

Melanie had called her former boss and told him everything. Two days later he called back. Help was on the way. At least that much was comforting. Tires crunched on the gravel and she looked up to see Brit Majors smiling at her. All her troubles vanished with that vision of beauty. As she got out of the cruiser, Melanie wondered how many men had blown a poker hand to that smile.

Brit climbed out of her sports car wearing tight jeans, sneakers, and a tank top that set Melanie's imagination ablaze. "Mel, thanks so much for meeting me here."

"No problem, gorgeous. How's Carrie doing?"

"She's pining away to nothing because you won't come to visit her."

"Bullshit," grinned Melanie. "How is she, Brit?"

"Bad, Melanie. She's still freaked out about the scars."

"What else?"

"She has no feeling in her legs." Brit was startled at Melanie's response. The woman went from relaxed friendly to a dangerous warrior ready for battle. "Melanie, what is it?"

"Nothing."

"Bullshit, Melanie. Talk to me."

"Carrie wasn't so much raped as she was implanted. There's one of those things growing inside her right now and we have damn little time to put a stop to it."

"Oh my god..." Brit was reaching for her phone, but Melanie stopped her.

"It's too late for that now. You can't warn her or it will try to take control of her mind; she won't survive that. We have to sneak up on her and surprise it, kill it, before it has a chance to get full control of her body."

"When, how?"

"Tonight at visiting hours. I'll come over with you and we'll get it done. Once I start you will have to run interference for me."

"What do you mean?"

"It may kick up a fuss, make her scream. You can't let anyone interfere until I've managed to kill it."

Brit nodded her head slowly. "Will it hurt her, what you're planning to do?"

"Yes, but the alternative will be worse." Her phone buzzed then, and she answered it. "Melanie." Brit was close enough to hear both voices.

"Mel, it's Victor Perez. I'm in the line-up for a ferry to your island now."

"Negative, Vic. Abort. I'm coming over later. Emergency. Bayview Hospital, room 467 at 7:00 pm. It's a cleansing."

"Understood. Interference or control?"

"Interference."

"Roger that."

The phone clicked off and Melanie found Brit gazing at her with those piercing blue eyes. "You'll have help tonight, Brit. Vic is one of the best."

"Just who and what are you, Melanie Rivers?"

"Investigative agent Melanie Rivers, retired. Currently, Deputy Rivers of the Brighton Police Department. If I tell you any more I'll have to shoot you and you're way too pretty to shoot."

"So, mind my own damn business?"

"I'm sorry, Brit. I'd tell you if I could."

"Fair enough. So are we going in?"

"Can't change your mind?"

"Nope."

"All right then, follow me. I don't think there's anything there now, but I do want to make certain." Melanie led the way in, and Brit gasped as they stepped into the foyer. The chalk outline of a body was still there, and the place was a mess of blood stains.

"Is this where ...?"

"No, that was the former sheriff. The carpenter was killed upstairs and Carrie was held in the basement. Come on."

Brit had her hand over her mouth as with wide eyes she took in the scene Melanie showed her. "Oh my god."

"Now will you give up this idea and convince Carrie to buy another place, any other place."

Brit swallowed hard then squared her shoulders. "She can't, Mel. She's sunk most everything into this place. If you give the all-clear I'll hire a crew to come in and fix it up for her."

Melanie was getting lost in those liquid eyes. Finally she reached out to take the woman by the shoulders. "All right, but there are conditions here. I need you to play straight with me." Brit just nodded and stepped closer. "I check the place every day before anyone sets foot inside. You stay someplace else. You don't try to move in until I say so. Also, you help me convince Carrie to go slow with this. Is it a deal?"

"It's a deal. Melanie, I can see the sense in what you say. This place gives me the creeps. I want my sister to live a long and happy life. You're in charge here, I'll do whatever you say."

"Now that holds real promise."

Brit's mouth formed a perfect O as Melanie grinned. She stepped into Melanie's arms and kissed her soundly. She broke the kiss and turned away. "Now you can watch my ass," she said, as she headed for the stairs.

"With extreme pleasure." Melanie followed her back to the lobby, thoroughly enjoying the view along the way.

Brit continued on out the door and straight to the cars. "Is it safe now, Melanie?"

"Yeah, it's clear for now. Brit, why did you kiss me?"

"You liked it."

"Yes I did, and the view of that magnificent ass; I'm just curious as to why you did it."

"I don't really know; I just suddenly wanted to. I'm an impulsive girl after all."

"Thanks be for that. I'll meet you at the hospital tonight. Brit, don't breathe a word to anyone about what we're going to do, not even to Carrie."

"I won't. Mel, that thing growing inside her, would it make a black shadow around her? Like an aura?"

"It would."

"I thought I saw that this morning when I talked to her. Thank you for helping us."

"Can't have demons going around eating up all the pretty girls, now can I?" Brit blew her a kiss then got in her car and sped away, heading back towards the boat launch and a ride to the mainland. Melanie returned to the sheriff's office.

Hank looked up as she entered. "Those two crazy sisters still planning to fix up that hotel?"

"They are." Melanie sighed and sank into the chair at her desk. "I tried to talk her out of it, but no luck."

"Yeah, I can see that you gave it a real shot." He grinned at her puzzled look. "You've got lipstick all over your face."

Melanie wiped it off with a tissue then grinned. "The girl sure is tasty all right, but she won't change her mind. I'm going over to check on the sister tonight."

"Mel, is that place clear now?"

"It was today. Brit said she'll hire a crew from the mainland to fix it up for Caroline. I said I would check the place every morning before they start work. I guess I should have cleared that with you first."

"No, it's the right thing to do, Mel. I have no problems with it. You catching the six o'clock boat?"

"That's the plan."

"You'd better take off early then. I wouldn't want you to miss the boat and keep the girls waiting."

"Hank, don't make me shoot you," growled Melanie, as she rose and headed for the locker room, followed by Hank's deep chuckle.

MELANIE RETURNED TO the living room where her grandmother was knitting in her favorite chair. "So, do you have a hot date tonight or are you gearing up for war?"

Melanie grinned ruefully. "I'm not really sure, Nana. There's going to be war for certain."

"But?"

"Both sisters get to me, Nana."

"They're playing with you, Mel."

"I know, but I'm enjoying the game."

"Just be careful, honey, on both counts."

"I will, Nana."

"Are you going to kill one of those things?"

"I just hope I can. If it is too far along then the best I will be able to do is cut it loose from her."

"I thought you said it was better to leave them attached to a human."

"Not this human, Nana, not this time. I played by government rules for too many years. Too many innocent people have, and are still, suffering so those damn things can be studied. No more. This island is my home, and I won't have them around my home."

"So it's war then."

"Yeah, I guess it is."

The old woman sighed then levered herself from the chair. "All right then, you go do what you have to do and I'll get to work here."

"Nana?"

"Those things don't come near here, not to this house. There's a reason for that. I can't kill one, and I doubt I could do a lot of damage to one if it was determined, but I can sting 'em. I'll mix up a batch of the good stuff while you're gone."

"Nana, you're the best." Melanie kissed the old woman's cheek then fled the house. Ellen watched as the motorcycle roared away.

BRIT WAS WAITING AT the reception area as Melanie strode through the doors. Brit gave a soft whistle as the leather clad figure drew near. Melanie laughed and shook a threatening finger at her. "Brit, don't even go there."

"Made you blush."

"Okay, you did. Happy now?"

"Thrilled." She took Melanie's arm and steered her towards the elevators. As soon as the doors closed she released Melanie's arm. "Mel, I'm scared. Will this truly work?"

"There's no guarantees, Brit, but the odds are that she'll recover the use of her legs as well as speed up her overall recovery. That damn thing is dragging her back, waiting until it can take full control of her mind as well as her body. We're going to kill it so we get her back in one piece. Now, I need you to put on your game face, girl."

Melanie was startled at the shift in Brit. Suddenly the woman was cold as ice. "What do I do, Mel?"

"You keep everybody out of the room until I sound the all-clear. Carrie may cry out, but you can't let that affect you. You have to stay focused."

"All right. I'm trusting you will my sister's life here. Don't abuse that trust."

"We're here, be cool now."

They stepped into the room and Caroline looked up. Melanie was startled at how frail the woman seemed. The angry red scar that ran down her face to her jaw line was almost pulsing. Caroline tried to sit up. "Hey, Brit, you brought my girlfriend back. Thanks sweetie. Kids, this is Dr. Perez. He's new to my case."

"Hey Mel, long time, no see."

"Hi Vic, you ready?"

"Ready."

"Do it."

"We'll wait outside." Victor Perez took Brit by the arm and they stepped through the door and closed it behind them. Melanie dropped a wedge on the floor and kicked it under the door to keep it closed.

"Melanie, you're scaring me. What's going on."

"Nothing bad, pretty lady. I just have more stuff to tell you and don't want to take the chance anyone might overhear." She was pulling on a strange looking glove as she stretched out on the bed beside Caroline. "Come here and hug me while I whisper in your ear."

Reluctantly, Caroline put her arms around Melanie. "What are you doing?" She barely breathed it as their cheeks touched.

"I need you to trust me, Caroline. I want you to bite down on my jacket collar."

"What?"

"Just do it. Do it now." Melanie suddenly placed her hand at the small of the girl's back and pulled her tight. A searing pain lanced through Caroline and she screamed as she bit down hard on the leather of Melanie's jacket. She continued screaming as her body jerked and fought to escape.

Melanie held her tightly and kept up the pressure. Suddenly there was a sickly black mist rising above the bed and Caroline's pain was gone. She lay exhausted in Melanie's arms as Mel brought the gloved hand around to beam a strong green light at the mist. That mist howled and writhed in pain and rage, but Melanie kept the light going until the mist completely dissipated.

Letting her arm drop back protectively around Caroline's shoulders, Melanie softly kissed the woman's lips. A tingle ran through her as she felt the girl respond. Suddenly Caroline pushed out of her arms. "No, Melanie, no. Look at my face, you don't want a woman like that. Besides, I'm paralyzed from the waist down. You don't want..." She suddenly yelped as Melanie pinched her thigh. "What the hell did you do that for?"

"Do what?"

"Pinch me?"

"Where?"

"On my leg. You know damn well where you pinched me."

"Sure I do, but how do you know where I pinched you?"

Suddenly Caroline was hugging Melanie fiercely. "Oh my god, you fixed me. How did you manage to fix me?"

"You had one of the demons growing in you, Carrie. I killed it and that set you free. A couple of days and you'll be ready to go dancing again."

Caroline kissed Melanie hard, and then hugged her again. "Oh gods, Melanie, how can I ever thank you?"

"You just did, pretty lady. Put me down now, Brit must be going nuts out there."

"Okay, help me sit up."

Melanie fluffed the pillows and propped her up on the bed. She then went to the door and kicked away the wedge. Hearing the door, Victor turned away from the blustering security man and winked at Melanie. Mel nodded and smiled. "Carrie wants to see you, Brit." As Brit dashed into the hospital room, Melanie flashed her badge at the security man and he backed off.

They could hear the excited sisters inside the room and Melanie smiled. "We won this round, Vic. Let's go someplace and debrief." He nodded and they left the floor together.

Back in the hospital room Brit was tickling her sister's toes. Caroline was laughing and telling her to stop. "Brit, quit it. Go find Mel and bring her back here."

"Okay, if I have to." Brit returned a moment later. "They're gone."

"That guy wasn't a real doctor, was he?"

"Nope, he is part of Melanie's old team, or so she said, and I believe her. He sure jumped when she barked orders. Mel said he's the best. What did he do before we got here?"

"Nothing really. We just chatted and he studied my chart. It seemed like he was waiting for something. Now I know what. Did he do anything special in the hallway?"

"He's incredible, and I would have a hard time with him at poker. He double talked the nurses, doctors, and the security guard until Mel was finished. Honey, I heard you screaming in here. Can you tell me what happened?"

"You guys left then Mel put on some sort of glove. She laid down beside me and hugged me. She told me to bite down on her jacket then pulled me close. My god, the pain, Brit. It stabbed through my back like hellfire, but she wouldn't let me go and she wouldn't stop. Suddenly the pain was gone and one of those things was right over the bed. Melanie killed it with the light from her magic glove. Brit I'd do it again every day if it would free me from one of those things."

"Well, you won't have to. Melanie says you're free of it now so you can get better. What?"

Caroline had melted back into the bed, sinking into depression. "You know damn well what."

"Talk to me, Carrie."

"I'm all chopped up, Brit. Even if I got back to full strength, I'd still frighten small children. No man would ever want me for more than a drunken roll in the hay, no woman either. Christ, I look like Frankenstein's Monster."

"I guess I'd better find Melanie and bring her back here. That thing still has a hold on you because that's not my big sister talking. Aren't you the one who always said the bigger the obstacle the bigger the challenge, and the greater the reward?"

"So how the hell do you propose I overcome these?" Caroline angrily displayed some of the scars on her body. "This?" She pointed savagely to the scar on her face.

"Honey, we'll tackle this one together. Those will fade in time, and they can work wonders these days. I don't care what it costs; I'll pay it."

Caroline reached for her sister and Brit hugged her gently. "I love you, little sister."

"I love you too, Carrie. Oh gods, I came so close to losing you." Caroline was weak and Brit held her gently, crooning softly until the exhausted woman fell asleep. Once her sister was deep in sleep, Brit Majors left the hospital and called Melanie.

"Rivers."

"Hi sexy, it's Brit."

"Is Carrie okay?"

"She's sleeping now. Melanie, I don't know how I'll ever be able to thank you for what you did tonight."

"Oh, I'm sure you could think of something."

Brit laughed at the mischief in Melanie's voice. "Behave yourself, Deputy Rivers. You sound pretty pleased with yourself, Mel. You weren't completely certain about tonight's outcome, were you?"

"It's never a guaranteed success, Brit. We were lucky to catch this one before it had a chance to fully take her over. Yes, I'm pleased. We won this round; we don't always. Now tell me what's bothering you."

"What???"

"Hey, you're not the only one in the family who can read people, you know."

"Oh? So we're family now? Does that mean you and I are serious, or are you after my sister?"

"Can't I have both?"

Again Brit laughed and Melanie smiled with delight. "No, you can't have both, you greedy wench. Mel, it's her scars. I'll be the first to admit both of us have used our looks to our advantage. Beauty is like an ace in the hole and we both grew up learning how to use that."

"And now she thinks it's gone. She feel alone and defenseless, helpless."

"Right on the money, super woman. How can we help her?"

"You know her better than anyone, Brit. Use that knowledge and all your skills to motivate her. Get her fired up about something. The scars will fade and her life will go on. She wanted that damned hotel as a place to kick back and paint. Maybe that's the key."

"It's worth a shot. Are you saying it's safe to go in there now?"

"Let me know when you're coming; I'll check the place first."

"I will. Melanie Rivers, you rock. I'm glad I kissed you."

"I'm not, now I'm ruined for life. I'll never taste a kiss so perfect again."

"Play your cards right and you might, besides, I know you're full of it because Carrie told me you kissed her too. I think you're just fickle."

Brit smiled at Melanie's hearty laugh. "Good night, Mel. I'll call before I come over."

"Night, Brit." Melanie dropped the phone back into her pocket and pulled out her notebook. She gazed at the moonlit waters sliding by beneath the ferryboat for a moment.

"Victory

Rare and fleeting

Battle is eternal"

She gazed at what she had written for a moment then dropped the book back into a pocket and zipped it up. The boat was approaching the dock. Melanie fastened on her helmet and started the engine as the ramp touched down on the dock. There were only a few cars as this was the last trip of the day for the boat. They let her off first and she gunned the engine as she hit the road, racing up the steep hill and off towards home.

Ellen was waiting in the kitchen when Melanie arrived. She came through the door and set her helmet on the top of the fridge. "You waited up for me, Nana?"

"I did. Here, have some tea with me. It'll help you sleep."

"Nana, what's in this?"

"Just mint, girl. Now stop being so suspicious and tell me how it went."

Melanie sat and took a sip of the tea. It was delicious and definitely had more than mint in it. "Nana, you're a bad woman." Ellen just smiled lovingly at her granddaughter. "All right, it went better than I expected. We got the damned thing out of her and didn't kill her in the process. That woman is one tough cookie."

"I can see the teeth marks on your collar."

"Yeah. I told her to bite down hard and she did."

"Will she be okay?"

"Not sure, Nana. Carrie's a fighter, but she's messed up by what happened to her, and by the scars. I hope she can get past that and find a reason to enjoy life again."

"I have the same dream for you, sweetie."

"Nana?"

"You've got scars too, Mel. They don't show, but they're there."

"Yeah, you're right about that, Nana."

"So what else happened? Did your guy show up?"

"Yes, Vic was there and on top of his game. We talked afterwards and he told me the team is being revived. He is supposed to talk me into coming back to lead them."

"Oh?"

"It's not going to happen, Nana. I said I was home to stay, and I meant it. I'm not afraid, and I know we as humans have to fight these things, but I've done my share. It's time for somebody else to step up now."

"What happened, Mel? Why'd you quit?"

Melanie paused for a long moment before speaking. "I tried to pull one of those things out of a ten-year-old boy. He didn't survive it. I held him still while he died. I did kill the demon, but I can't escape that child's screams. He screamed for his mother, but Vic was holding her back. That one broke me, Nana. We'd have been better off to poison the kid and let him die slowly, peacefully, taking the demon with him."

"No you wouldn't, Mel. You forget, I've seen into their world. If you let them die slowly, the demon can take a piece of their essence with them. On the other side, the demons are fairly solid, but the remains of the humans are just ghosts, lost and terrified. I always thought that was just a bad acid trip until I saw one of those things here in this world."

"Talk to me, Nana. What are you holding back?"

"There's more of them now than ever before, the demons. At first there were only a few. Your uncle got into some bad prescription drugs, and one took him. The drugs lowered his natural defenses. Nobody would believe me, so I shut up before they had me committed. I tried to save him, but I couldn't. The stuff I gave him allowed him to see and that's what drove him off the edge. That hotel manager had a demon on his back and so did his wife. My son took the only way out he could think of.

"Ever since that time I've been working on a way to either kill those damned things or drive them back to their own world. I've also been working on a shield to protect against them, to keep them from being able to attach themselves to a human being."

"Is that what's in the tea?"

"Yes."

"Does it work?"

"Most of the time, yes. It's still a work in progress."

"Thanks, Nana. I'll gladly accept all the help I can get."

"That had power; what's going on?"

"According to Vic, this island has a hole, a passageway from that world to this. The gloves are off now. He's been sent here to enlist my help in closing the hole. I said I'd do that, but I won't go back to the team. He called the boss, and we made a deal. I work this operation and I'm still retired afterwards.

"It's war now, Nana. You're right, there's way too many of them getting through and our asylums are filling up with the victims. Honestly, I don't give a rat's ass about the rest of the world anymore, but I swear I will clear every damned one of them off this island."

"That sounds like a line in the sand."

"It is."

"Okay, then. War it is."

"Nana, Vic could help you with that tea. He's one hell of a com man, but he's a fair chemist as well a back yard inventor."

"We've got a spare room, Mel, but he has to pay room and board, I can't feed the nation..."

"Nana, the money for the family is now my problem. I'll have my paychecks dropped into the household account."

"All right, Deputy Mel, I'll put you on the account tomorrow, then that's all organized. Call your guy and tell him to get his butt over here first boat tomorrow. If we're going to war with demons, we have to get ready."

"Yes, ma'am." Melanie was smiling as she called Vic and gave him his marching orders.

The Road Back From the Brink Can be a Long One

C aroline awakened to the cheerful patter of the nurse who threw open the drapes to let the sunshine pour in. "It's such a beautiful day, Miss Majors. This sunshine should cheer you up." She was a bit startled at the woman who smiled back at her. If not for the angry red scar across her face she would have sworn the sister had changed places with her patient during the night. "Well, you do look a lot better this morning."

"Thank you, nurse. I slept like a baby for the first time in days." Caroline's smile broadened as she sat up and swung her legs over the side of the bed.

"Miss Majors, who disconnected the medication tubes for you? There's nothing on your chart about..."

"I did. The pain is gone, and I don't want the drugs fogging my brain. Now, look what else I can do." Caroline raised her leg and wiggled her toes.

"Oh my god, Miss Majors, what did he do?"

"What did who do?"

"That man who was here last night. I was told about him during report. He said he was a doctor, but he wasn't really and the security man..."

"Dr. Perez is a personal friend with a world of talents. He's dealt with cases like this before."

"I really should call in the doctor."

"Be my guest." As the nurse hurried away Caroline reached for her phone.

"Brit Majors."

"Out for a run, Sis?"

"How could you tell?"

"It was the heavy breathing, and since I know Melanie went back to the island last night..."

"Shut up," laughed Brit, as she coasted to a stop. "Besides, you wouldn't want me sleeping with your girlfriend, would you?"

"I will admit, I do like her Brit, but then, so do you. Admit it."

"Okay, I'll admit it. There's something about that girl. She's tough as nails, and a real take charge woman, ..."

"But there's a part of her that is deeply wounded."

"Exactly. Carrie honey, if you're truly serious about this woman, I'll back off and..."

"Forget that, Sis. Look, I do like the girl, a lot, but so do you. She in turn is playful with both of us, and I do believe she is starting to care, we have no right to make up her mind for her. Let's just let life evolve and see what happens."

"All right, big sister, on one condition."

"Condition?"

"On the condition that you're still going to try here and not back off because of your scars. Melanie doesn't see them and neither do I. So, as long as you be yourself, I will too, okay?"

"Okay honey, that's fair. Do you really think she could stand to look at this maimed face every day?"

"You'll have to ask her that, but yes, I do."

"I'm sorry I interrupted your run, honey. You go on. I have some explaining to do to the doctor here. Come visit when you can."

"I will, bye sweetie."

Caroline smiled as she dropped her phone back on the bedside table. "Good morning, Doctor."

"Good morning, Caroline. Can you tell me how it is that you are walking around your bed with no medications when yesterday you were paralyzed and in excruciating pain?"

"Well, an old friend of the family, Dr. Perez from Venezuela, arrived last evening. He was just passing through, but he stopped long enough to see me. He's had experience with cases like mine before. He gave me a quick treatment, then resumed his journey. I took the tubes out myself as 1 didn't want the drugs clouding my mind once the pain was gone."

"And just what sort of treatment did he give you?"

"Spiritual. He's a witch doctor."

"All right, Caroline, have your fun. I'm just happy to see you up and around. Let me check you over now." She obediently hopped onto the bed and remained silent while he inspected her wounds. "Well, everything seems to be responding nicely. We'll leave the bandages on for a couple more days then see how we're doing from there.

"I've contacted a friend of mine who specializes in reconstructive surgery. He says he'll see you as a favor to me. He owes me for a lost golf tournament." He chuckled at his own joke then straightened up. "I believe you're right about the meds. If you have no pain you don't need them. I'll keep them on order for you just in case though.

"Ah, here comes your breakfast. I'll just leave you to it."

Caroline picked at her breakfast, her mind mulling over her conversation with her sister. She had to admit to herself she did have an interest in Melanie Rivers. Their first meeting didn't go that well. Caroline had poured on the sex appeal to lure the girl into helping her, but it hadn't worked. This woman had real steel in her and had refused to help, even though it was easy to see she was interested.

The thing of it was, Melanie had been right. She'd warned Caroline to stay away from the hotel, but wouldn't say why. She couldn't say why. Obviously she was a government agent or had been and couldn't talk. However, once it became apparent that Caroline had seen the demon, she had become much more forthcoming.

Caroline shivered at the memory of that hideous thing clinging to the madman's back, urging him on to... she grabbed a basin and vomited into it. The memory of that violation seared her soul. Swallowing hard, she crawled back into bed, pulling the covers up to her chin. Unbidden came the memory of Melanie Rivers charging through the shattered door and fighting off that madman. It gave her comfort.

Fighting for control, Caroline pushed the covers back and sat up. The man was imprisoned and the beast with him. It had been Melanie who had captured him. It was also Melanie who had destroyed the creature invading her person, playing on her fears, weakening her mind. Melanie had held her tight and killed that thing. That was well beyond the call of duty.

The question was, had she done it for her or for her sister? There was no way to know, or was there? What had Melanie said about the scars? They were badges of honor, proof that she'd faced the devil and survived. Yes, that was what she had said. Maybe Melanie could see the real woman behind the scars.

Caroline searched her memory for what that woman had said at that relationship seminar she had taken two years before. It was all a decision, that's what the woman had said. People decide to fall in love, or out of love, and take no responsibility for it themselves, but it is always a decision, one made unconsciously. The woman had tried to teach that the same decisions could be made deliberately.

Caroline hadn't believed her, but the idea had stuck in her mind. Now she was beginning to wonder. She knew full well all of her past lovers would never be able to deal with the scars, beauty was too important to them. Could she fall in love with Melanie Rivers? Somehow that didn't seem like it would be a problem, the problem was, could Melanie fall in love with her?

Just as that thought ran through her mind the phone rang.

"Caroline Majors."

"Is a serious babe," came Melanie's voice.

"My heroine and savior. Melanie, how are you?"

"I'm just fine. The question is, how are you today?"

"Much better now that you've called."

"Okay, I can see you're on the mend." Melanie was laughing and Caroline smiled brightly to hear it. "So, no side effects of last night's exploits?"

"You mean besides being lonely for the hero that saved me, not once, but twice?"

"Yeah, besides that."

"Well, I was able to get up and walk around the room a bit, does that count?"

"Oh yeah, that counts big time. Carrie, that's great news. Oops, gotta get to work. Say hi to Brit for me."

"Hey, what about me, don't you love me too?"

"Now cut that out. You are not allowed to make me blush or embarrass me when I'm in uniform. Good bye, sexy lady."

Caroline smiled as she laid aside the phone. Yes indeed, she could fall in love with Melanie easily enough. All she needed was an indication that her feelings would be returned. She didn't want pity and she didn't want to stand in her sister's way. Having said all that, she did want to be in love, truly in love. Perhaps that woman was right, it could be done deliberately.

BRIT MAJORS TOWELED herself off after luxuriating in the shower until the hot water was all gone. She was still playing over in her mind the conversation she'd had with Carrie that morning. Brit was developing feelings for Melanie Rivers, that she could not deny. Melanie was truly an enigma, cold, deadly, and efficient on the one hand, and playful as a kitten on the other.

The big question here was, did Melanie return those feelings or was she just playing? Was she really hot for Carrie, or was she just being nice and doing her job? It was hard to say for certain, or was it? She'd been doing her job when she kicked in the door to rescue Carrie. She'd been doing her job when she caught the killer, but not last night. That had been well above the call of duty, or had it?

At first glance, it could look like she'd found a demon and called in a favor from another hunter. She'd killed the beast and saved the girl; job done. But was it? Melanie had been keeping tabs on Carrie and when she'd learned about Carrie's loss of mobility she'd gone into warrior mode. She has a thing for Carrie.

Does she? If she does why is she always so flirty with me? Melanie didn't seem like the type to play those kinds of games. Is she watching out for Carrie because she's my sister? Could be, but it's not clear. Alright, Brit, keep your game face on until something gives. This girl is awesome, and I won't fold this hand unless it becomes clear that she wants Carrie instead of me.

With that decision made, Brit dressed in a business suit and matching shoes. She had an appointment with a contractor about refurbishing the hotel. The meeting went well, and the man agreed to come to the island the next day to give her an estimate of the cost. If they could agree then he could start work in about three weeks. Smiling as she left the meeting, Brit took out her phone and called Melanie.

MELANIE STEPPED THROUGH the door of the sheriff's office and headed for the coffee pot. "Running a bit late this morning, aren't you, Mel?"

"I was out at the hotel, Hank. The crew starts work there today. The first thing I asked them to do was plug that bolt hole."

"Your girlfriend there too?"

"Which one?"

Hank just grinned and shook his head. "Either one."

"Yeah, Brit was with them. She and the contractor are working up the plans for the renovation now." Melanie sighed and sat to her desk. She took a long pull from her mug then faced Hank again. "What's on your mind, Hank?"

"Two things really, Mel. First, I hear Ellen has a new house guest. Should I know about that? Oh don't worry, Emily took the day off. We're alone here."

"His name is Victor Perez and he can show you any identification you want. Vic is a con man, an agent supreme, and a chemist by training. He's also the best demon hunter I had on my team, ever. He's here to help plug the hole."

"The hole?"

"There's a hole on this island between their world and ours. I've been recalled for one mission only, to lead the team in plugging that hole."

"Do I need a new deputy?"

"Nope, I'm actually enjoying this job. Oddly enough, it is giving me a chance to get over the past with the locals. It is also keeping them polite so we can talk like civilized humans. It's working for me."

"Good to know. That brings me to number two on the list. The mayor can't find anyone to take over this job so he's asked me to serve out a full term. I said I'd think about it."

"Go for it, Hank. Things are going to get crazy around here and all the locals know and trust you. If you are the sheriff it will go a long way to ease their minds."

"Thanks, Mel. There is one small problem."

"And that is?"

"I'm too damned old for all the physical stuff, for the most part. I can handle the public and political stuff."

"But?"

"I need you to stay on as deputy to do some of the harder stuff. You proved your steel on the Billy Carter case, Mel. You've got what it takes. The mayor says the town needs me and I need you."

"Hank, did you just offer me a full time job or did you propose?"

"I offered you a job; those two girlfriends of yours would shoot me if I proposed."

Melanie's grin matched his own. "All right, Hank. We do make a good team; I'll do it as long as you stay sheriff. You quit, I quit. Deal?"

"Deal. I'll call the mayor and let him know."

"And I'll finish my coffee then go out on patrol."

"To the hotel?" teased Hank, but Melanie wasn't smiling.

"Nope. I'm looking for a hole. Hank, three more people will be arriving on the island as soon as Brit gets that hotel ready."

"More demon hunters?"

"Ah-huh."

"Okay, I'll stay out of their way."

"Hank, I swear I'll keep you in the loop here, but..."

"Keep my trap shut? I got it, Mel." Melanie had reached the door before he spoke again. "Mel, when you find it, can you close it?"

"I don't know, Hank. Depends on a lot of things, especially on the size of it."

"Good hunting." She nodded and stepped through the door.

Melanie cruised slowly through town, her eyes searching everywhere. She was pleasantly surprised as a few people actually smiled and waved at her. She smiled and waved back. Yes, Melanie Rivers had come home. Nana always said things happen for a reason. Perhaps all that had happened to Melanie was preparing her for this war to save her home and its people.

As she drove out of town towards the far end of the island, she sighed. Most of the population lived in town. This end of the island had a few farms, a couple of fishermen and their families and a number of vacation homes. Everything was well spread out and peaceful. Melanie could feel the tension drain out of her as she slowed down to enjoy the scenery. She was actually standing by the car, leaning against the hood and watching the waves gently wash the sandy beach when her phone buzzed.

"Rivers."

"Hey there, deputy. How are all things policey going?"

"Better since you called, Brit. What's Up?"

"Flirt. I just called to ask you to lunch. How about it, Deputy Rivers; let a girl buy you lunch?"

"Sorry, can't. That would be seen as accepting a bribe, but I could buy you lunch, how about that?"

Brit's laugh was sweet and rich, bringing a bright smile to Melanie's face. "How about we go Dutch?"

"Works for me, pretty lady."

"Candi's Cafe in half an hour?"

"I can make that, providing nothing policey comes up to mess with me. See you then." The connection clicked off and Melanie pulled out her notebook.

"The heart sings
with Beauty's laughter
Divine distraction"

Melanie sighed as she gazed at the page, then closed the book and slipped it back into her pocket. As she drove back to town her thoughts were on Brit and Carrie. What the hell was going on here? Easy, she was falling for both of them. Get a grip, Melanie, you can't have both, Brit told you that herself. You're going to have to make a choice here.

So what happens if I make the wrong choice. I mean, what if I choose Brit, but she isn't really interested and Carrie is. What if I choose Carrie, but Brit is the one who's really serious? What if neither of them are seriously interested? What if they both are? No matter how this works out I'm going to get killed here. Why does life always have to be so damn complicated?

The sight of Brit's convertible in the cafe's parking lot ended that line of thought. There was a beautiful blonde woman standing by that car waving to her and brightening her world. She parked beside the convertible and got out. Brit took her arm and they walked inside together.

They sat easy, relaxed and waiting for the food. Melanie sipped at her coffee while Brit chatted about her plans for the renovation of the hotel. She had listened carefully when Carrie described her plans and hoped she was getting it right. As soon as their orders were on the table she leaned closer and spoke softly. "Mel, did you notice the guy in the corner booth? He has that same black aura."

"I saw." Melanie was bent over her soup and her voice was so soft Brit had to strain to hear it.

"Are you going to...?"

"No. It's too late for him." Melanie sighed and laid down her spoon. Picking up her coffee, she spoke into the cup. "There are three here. Can you pick them out?"

Brit sat back a bit and resumed her patter about her plans for the hotel. She wanted it all finished before Carrie returned. At length she leaned closer again. "Man in the corner, woman sitting across from him, and the older woman two tables to our left."

Melanie nodded, but made no response. She finished her meal then dabbed at her lips with her napkin. "I need you to take this news to my grandmother. Vic is with her."

Brit nodded and smiled like she'd just been asked out on a date. "I've got this one, you paid the last time," she sang, as she took the bill from the approaching waitress. Melanie shook a finger at Brit as she stepped to the counter to settle up. Mel dropped a ten on the table for a tip then went to the door. Brit joined her and they left together.

Melanie held the car door open for Brit. "Go down this road to Hemlock, take a right then go on to an empty house all boarded up. Nana's place is the next one to it as you pass. I'll let her know you're coming."

"Got it. Mel, what are you going to do?"

"Right now I'm going back to the hotel and check the place again."

Brit nodded and drove away, watching the road signs. She found the place easily enough and went to the door. An elderly woman who strongly resembled Melanie answered the door. "You just have to be Brit Majors. Come on in. Vic is making tea in the kitchen."

Smiling her thanks, Brit followed Ellen to the kitchen then sat where the old woman indicated. "Okay, now, would one of you explain why I'm here? Mel could easily have told you about the three dark ones at the cafe on the phone."

"She did, Brit. You're here because Mel wants you protected as much as possible. She believes you're as hard headed as your sister. Is she right?"

"She is." Brit had slipped into poker mode. She was keeping her cards close until she could see the lay of the land.

"I think she's wrong." Ellen was grinning and Brit smiled in spite of herself. "I think you're a lot tougher than your sister, and she's made of the right stuff. Brit, I've known about these demons for over fifty years. I can't fight them like these guys, but I can sting 'em, and I can protect myself from them. It took a lot of years and experimenting to get it close to right, but I did."

"Here, Brit, have some tea." Vic set a mug down for her and for Ellen then brought one to the table for himself.

"What's in it, Vic?"

"Something to make you taste bad to the bogey man. Ellen had the formula down, but it needed a few adjustments. We've been working on it for a while now and I believe we've got it right. Go on, taste it."

"You first."

Ellen's laugh was genuine delight. She winked at Vic as he reached over to grasp Brit's mug. He took a sip then smacked his lips making delight sounds. He grinned as he replaced it before Brit.

"That's all very fine, but I've seen the Princess Bride. I know how this works."

Vic laughed, but Ellen went serious. "You're right to be suspicious, girl, but we're the good guys. Look, Mel says you can see enough of those damn things to know what's going on. Your sister can see them, and she had one hooked into her. You saw it, you trusted Melanie to save her, and she did. Now trust that Melanie wouldn't send you into danger, but would try to protect you from it.

"This is coming down nasty and you can't afford to sit on the fence here. If you can't trust then take yourself and your sister far away from here before you get Melanie killed or worse."

Brit met the old woman's eyes for a long moment then raised her mug and took a long sip. "Mmm, that tastes pretty good. All right, people, what do I have to do?"

Ellen nodded her approval and patted her hand. "Vic, how's that new batch coming?"

"It's ready, Ellen. Brit, I'll give you enough for a few days. You should have at least two cups a day. I'll make sure you have enough for your sister too."

"How long do you see all this going on, Vic?" Brit was sipping her tea now and relaxing. These folks were on the up and up, she could tell.

"I have no idea, Brit. Keep this to yourself, but there's a hole on this island that lets them through, that's why there are so many here. Mel has sworn to close the hole and hunt down those who are here and eradicate them."

"Okay, so Mel's declared war. How can I help?"

"Keep yourself and your sister safe. Be careful, keep your eyes open, and stay in touch. Every time you see one of those things I want to know about it. Stay away from them, no matter what it takes."

"Vic, is there anything else we can do besides the tea? Is there no weapon against them? Ellen, you said you could sting them. How?"

Ellen sighed and shook her head. "Mel was right, you're every bit as tough as your sister. All right girl. Vic is trying to soup up my formula. We've got the tea right, or so we believe. Now we're working on the stinger. We'll get one to you as soon as we're sure they work. Now, there's something else you and your sister can do to help here."

"Of course, whatever it takes, Ellen. Tell me."

"Don't go twisting Mel's head around with stupid games. She needs to be focused here or we're all in the soup."

"We're not playing games with Melanie, Ellen. That's not our style. We both like Mel, and I believe she likes us. As far as Carrie and I are concerned, either one of us would be interested in taking a relationship with Mel to a higher level. However, that's her decision to make. If she wants one of us she has to declare so the other can back off and wish them well."

"Could you do that? Could you back away if she chose your sister?"

"I could. My sister's happiness would overrule everything else. I know she feels the same. Listen, everything between Melanie and us is just at the friendly flirting stage right now, and I would prefer it stay that way until this demon thing has been dealt with. I like to play one hand at a time and count the winnings when the game is over."

"I told you they were troopers, Ellen," grinned Vic.

"I can see that. Brit, thanks for laying the cards on the table for me. It's starting to get late and Mel should be home soon. Stay for dinner?"

"Another time, Ellen, I promise. Right now I have to catch a boat to the mainland. I want to be at the hospital as soon as visiting hours start."

"In that case you'd better scoot."

Brit tossed down the last of her tea, scooped up the bag Vic had put beside her on the table, and bolted for the door. "Scooting. Bye all!" With that she was out the door and the car roared to life.

Rocks In The Road

A few weeks went by and still Melanie was unsuccessful in finding the hole between worlds. Work on the hotel went on without incident and was drawing to a close. Caroline had been undergoing therapy to get her fully back to health and to let her wounds heal completely. Melanie continued to flirt with both sisters and they flirted back, waiting for her to make a choice. For the moment, all seemed well.

Brit came through the door of the hospital room and caught Carrie in her arms. "Brit, check this out." Caroline danced away from her sister and twirled around the room. "What do you think?"

"I think you're magic, my sister, and I'm thrilled to see you up and around so well."

"They're releasing me tomorrow, Brit. Can you bring me some clothes?"

"Of course, is everything at that apartment you rented?"

"Yes. Gods, I only took that for a month. I expected to be in the B&B long before now." She sat on the edge of the bed, sinking into despair. "I probably owe two months rent as well."

"No you don't. I've been staying there, and I've kept up the rent. Now, tell me what you'll need. Undies for sure. It's hot these days, shorts and a tank top?"

"No, for god's sake, Brit. I can't go out in shorts and a tank anymore, you know that."

"Why not?"

"The scars? Ugly as sin? Frighten small children? Bring me jeans and a long sleeved T-shirt, a pair of flip-flops, and a light scarf."

63

"Look, you are not ugly, you will not scare anybody, and what the hell do you want a scarf for?"

"To hide my face, of course. People are used to seeing Muslim women with a scarf covering their face. Nobody will say anything."

Brit sighed deeply and sat beside Caroline, putting an arm around her shoulders. "Honey, you don't have to hide your face. Please don't do this to yourself, Carrie."

Caroline burst into tears and tried to hide on her sister's shoulder. "Oh gods, Brit, I'm so scared, scared and scarred. I know what I look like. I can see the pity and revulsion in the faces of the people passing through the hospital. I don't want to live with that."

"Then don't." That voice came from the doorway and Caroline spun to see Melanie standing there. "People will only pity you if you act pitiful. I've told you before, the scars are a badge of honor. You fought a mass murderer to a standstill, and you survived. You're a hero and a warrior, not a pariah or a beggar."

Melanie slowly approached the bed. "Let me tell you what else you are. You're a beautiful, sexy woman who knows how to get she wants. You're tough, determined, incredibly beautiful, and utterly intoxicating."

Caroline stopped crying. She faced Melanie with wide eyes, searching the woman's face. "Intoxicating?" Her voice was soft, teary, yet wondering, hopeful.

"Yes, intoxicating. You both are..."

Brit reached out to take Melanie by the arm. "Melanie, what's going on in here?" She lightly poked Melanie over the heart. "Is it time for me to fold this hand and let my big sister take over?"

"Brit, I..."

"Ah-ah-ah. Nobody's going to get hurt here unless you can't make up your mind, Mel. I have a feeling that you're the type who can make a decision. Cards on the table now, is it Carrie you want to go out with?"

Melanie turned back to Caroline. "Yes, Brit, it is, if she's willing."

"So ask her out, you big chicken," laughed Brit, as she rose and headed for the door. "I'm going down to the cafeteria for a coffee. You two sort yourselves out."

"I don't want this, Melanie, not from pity."

Melanie reached for Caroline's hands. "You won't get it from me, girl. I've come to visit you several times a week for over a month and more. When have you ever had pity from me?"

"You *have* come to visit, and you've never given me pity. You've bullied me, nagged me, and made me laugh, but you've never shown me any pity at all. I don't understand you, Mel. I don't understand any of this at all."

"What don't you understand, Carrie?"

"What you want with me? Why are you attracted to me now? Are you some kind of pervert? Sorry, I didn't mean..."

"I'll tell you." Melanie pulled Carrie into a gentle hug. "It's lust, pure and simple. I had the hots for you the first time I saw you, and that has only gotten stronger. Yes, I'm a pervert, I am drawn to strong women with great asses."

Carrie pushed Melanie back to arm's length. "Hey."

"What? You wanted honesty..."

"You know damn well what I meant. Do the scars turn you on or do the repulse you? Tell me the truth."

"I don't see the scars, sweetie. I only see you. I see Caroline Majors who put the moves on me to bring me onside. I see fierce Carrie who realized I wasn't caving in and just walked away. I see warrior princess Caroline who fought the demon and survived. I see the woman who haunts my thoughts every day and night.

"Yes, I enjoy flirting with Brit, and had I never met you I surely would try for her, but I did meet you. I saw your strength, your courage, your stubbornness, and that cute..."

"Oh shut up." Caroline grabbed Melanie's collar and pulled her into a kiss.

Melanie gave a soft moan as she melted under the fire of that kiss. Her body suddenly came alive with desire, and she crushed the woman to her, her hands starting to explore. Caroline broke the kiss and pushed Melanie back slightly to look into her eyes. What she saw there wasn't pity, wasn't just lust, it was desire, desire for her. She started to speak, but Melanie put a finger lightly against her lips. "No. You're not allowed to speak of scars ever again and you're not allowed to doubt my feelings for you. Carrie, I want you in my life, you and me, together against the hordes of hell forever."

Caroline was still gazing into Melanie's eyes, getting lost in them. "I believe you, Mel." She flung herself into Melanie's arms and hugged her fiercely, tears filling her eyes once again. "Oh gods, Melanie, can you really...?"

"Ah-ah-ah. No doubts, remember? Carrie, the first time we met you knew your worth, your value to the world. That has not changed, nothing about you has been diminished. Not your worth. Not your beauty. Not your intelligence or value as a person. A person I want to spend a lot of time with from now until I'm a hundred years old."

"Only that long? What will you do with me then?"

"Oh, then I'll start courting your sister."

"What? You beast. Put me down. You're awful." She pushed Melanie away and gave her a stern look, but couldn't hold it. She pulled Mel back into the hug. "You're a nut, Melanie Rivers, among other things."

"Oh, what other things?"

"My girlfriend."

"Carrie, does this mean that title is official now?"

"If you want it to be."

"You know I do."

"Then it's official. Now kiss me to seal the deal."

Melanie pulled her close and kissed her gently, softly, lovingly. This time Caroline was the one to moan with pleasure. She was starting to explore inside Melanie's leather jacket when Brit returned. "All right you two, break it up. Don't make me get a bucket of water."

"Go away, Brit."

"Why, Carrie, I'm hurt."

"You're not; you're a brat."

"So, are you guys official now?"

Caroline looked at Melanie who smiled and nodded. "Yes we are, Sis. I'm sorry, but..."

"Ah-ah-ah, none of that. I'm thrilled for both of you. Now, time's nearly up. Mel, Carrie is getting out tomorrow. Any chance you could be here to pick her up? I have to be at the hotel to supervise the work crew."

"I'll take tomorrow off. Carrie, want to have a picnic on the island tomorrow?"

"You're going to make me look at that house on the other side of the island, aren't you?"

"Busted."

"All right, sweetheart, but I won't change my mind."

"I know."

"Mel honey, is my car still over there?"

"Yeah, Brit's got the keys, but it's still at the hotel."

"Brit, sweetie, give Mel the keys to the car. I'm not riding on the back of that motorcycle until I have a proper leather outfit."

Brit winked at Melanie as she handed over the keys. Melanie dropped the keys into her pocket then kissed Brit on the cheek. She kissed Carrie full on the lips then disappeared through the door. "I'll be back in the morning," she called, as she vanished from sight.

Caroline turned to her sister with a serious look. "All right, Brit. What did you do?"

"Me? I didn't do anything? I have no idea what you're talking about."

"The hell you don't. Now talk or I'll call Mel and rat on you."

Brit sighed as she relaxed into the chair beside the bed. "All right, I'll talk. I had lunch with Mel a few days ago. We spotted three possessed people in the cafe, so Mel sent me to her grandmother for that tea I've been bringing to you. It's to make you taste bad to the demons so they won't want to inhabit you ever again.

"Anyway, the old gal is pretty sharp. She warned me to quit the games with Melanie. This demon thing is going to go down ugly, and soon. Melanie needs to be on top of her game. I told Ellen we weren't playing games, but if Melanie wanted one of us she had to say so and the other would back off.

"Obviously she told Melanie. Mel took a few days to sort out her feelings then came her tonight to present her case. Congratulations, big sister. You win this hand, and I'm thrilled for you. You're strong, Carrie, and Mel will need your support in the coming weeks."

"You're not fooling anyone here, Brit. I can see you're pleased as punch the way this worked out. You think that by having to be a support to Melanie I'll forget all about feeling sorry for myself, right?"

"Busted. Will it work?"

"Yes it will and you know it. What I'm wondering is how much of that thinking was involved with Melanie's decision."

"Oh, I don't think that entered her mind at all, Sis."

"What do you mean?"

"Melanie has scars too, sweetie. You can't see them, but they're deep and they've been there a lot longer than yours. I think Mel hopes that you'll be better able to understand her pain, and that you can be a support to each other."

"You knew you'd pushed her into making a decision, but you didn't know which way it would go, did you?"

"No, I didn't."

"Honey..."

"Yes, I'm disappointed, Carrie. Why wouldn't I be? But this wasn't my pot to win. The warrior chose her princess and I get to love them both. Not such a bad deal after all."

"Brit..."

"I'll be fine, Carrie, honest."

"Promise?"

"Cross my heart. Now stop this and start planning how you're going to lead Melanie Rivers astray. She wants you for her girlfriend. You want that too. So what's the next move?"

"Keep it light and easy until the demon thing has been dealt with then see where we are with it all."

"Now that's my big sister. Welcome back."

THERE WAS A SMALL TEA party going on in the kitchen of Ellen's house when Melanie arrived home. Mel stopped as she came through the door. "Hank, Vic, Nana, what's up?"

"I'll pour you a cup of tea, Mel. Pull up a chair."

"Thanks, Vic. Hank?"

"The shit hit the fan while you were gone tonight, Mel."

"Oh?" Melanie sank into a chair and took a sip of the proffered tea.

"Billy Carter committed suicide."

"What? How the hell did that happen. We told those people to watch him carefully."

"I know." Hank sighed deeply and shifted in his chair. "Apparently he was showing improvement so they started giving him more freedoms and cut his meds."

"Ah, for Christ's sake." Melanie slumped in her chair. "Goddammit anyway. That shoves a brick into the mixer. That big bugger will be on the island already, looking for a way to take my scalp."

"I've got your glove all charged up, Mel. The rest of the team will be here in a couple of days. How do you want to handle this?"

"I'll drink lots of tea, keep the glove handy, and wait for the team to show up; then we go on the warpath."

"What about the big one?" asked Hank.

"There's not a lot I can do about that one until someone makes a move on me. I'll stay sharp, Hank. Once the team gets here we'll go on the hunt.

"Now, on another note, I need to take tomorrow off."

"Gearing up for war?"

"Picking up my girlfriend from the hospital and taking her for a picnic down by the farm sites."

"Girlfriend? Anyone I know?"

"Caroline Majors."

Ellen smiled and patted her hand. "I thought you'd choose her. Can I ask what made the difference? I know you like Brit a lot too."

"I couldn't choose between them, Nana, but what Brit said to you told me it was time to step up or lose both of them. Since I couldn't choose between them I went for Carrie because she has committed herself to this island. I came home to stay, and she means to stay as well. On the other hand, Brit will be all over the world much of the time. That made the decision easier."

"Any regrets?"

"Not a one."

"Good. That was her car you drove home?"

"It was. I left the bike at the hotel."

"So, we're in a holding pattern for now?"

"Yeah, we are, Hank. Hank, when it hits the fan you're going to have a lot of folks beating down your door wanting me lynched. When the team gets here they'll have a story all ready for you about an infection that makes people violent. You can say it was what was wrong with Billy Carter. They'll set up a field hospital where we can hopefully kill those things off and set some of the victims free."

"But not all?"

"Hank, I'd sell my soul for a hundred per cent win here, but you have to know we've always counted ourselves lucky if we can go fifty-fifty."

"How bad is this thing, Mel?"

"I've seen at least ten wandering around the island. So far I haven't managed to find the damned hole between worlds. I'm starting to think it might be in that cave near the hotel where Billy Carter hid out. I plan to check it out soon, but I want one more chance to talk Carrie into staying away until we've cleared the place completely."

Hank heaved himself from the chair and reached for his hat. "All right, Mel. You go play for a day and I'll start working on my story. Thanks for the tea, Ellen."

"I'll walk you out, Hank." Ellen rose and walked out to the police car with him. As he closed the car door she leaned close and dropped a bag into his hand through the open window. "More tea, Hank. Make sure to have at least three cups a day. Oh, and don't ask what's in it."

He nodded and chuckled then drove away. She watched until he was out of sight then returned to the kitchen. "Are you sure you're okay, Mel?"

"I'm sure, Nana. What's wrong? What did I miss?"

"Janet Carter has been raising hell since her brother-in-law checked out. She says it's all your fault, that you had it in for her family all along."

"That woman is such a pain in the ass."

"And always has been," sighed Ellen as she resumed her seat at the table. "The fact that you arrested her husband for abetting his brother doesn't help. That fool woman has a lot of influence in the church and she's using every bit of it to stir up trouble. Her brother is in politics and she's leaning on him too."

"Same shit, different town," sighed Vic. "Ellen, this happens everywhere we go."

"Fair enough,Vic, but Melanie has to live here. She can't just shoot the bad guys then ride off into the sunset."

Vic just chuckled and winked at Mel. "Ellen, my darling, you don't need to worry about our Melanie. The good people of Brighton have no idea what they're playing with, but I do. Trust me, Mel can take care of herself. We'll sort out this demon thing, then disappear into the sunset. We've got a few connections and will see what we can do to put a lid on things before we go, but if there's trouble you can count on it not being Mel who's in it."

"It's getting late, let's go to bed and forget all about this."

"Forget that, Victor Perez. I'm not sleeping with you. I know damn well you'll just use sex to try to get the location of my secret herb garden." Vic nearly fell off his chair with laughter as she tossed her hair back and marched off to her bedroom.

Melanie just grinned and shook her head as she too headed for her bedroom. Once she closed the door she put the pillows under the covers to make it look like someone was sleeping in the bed. Melanie then curled up on the closet floor with a clear view of the bedroom door and the bed. She was wearing the glove and holding a nine millimeter pistol.

A Moment of Sweet Peace

C aroline Majors fussed as she waited for Melanie to arrive. The paperwork was finished and the nurse was holding her hostage in the wheelchair. "I can walk, for pity's sake. I don't see why I have to stay in this stupid chair."

"Miss Majors, I've told you already,..."

"It's hospital policy. Foolishness, I..."

"Actually, I wanted to push the chair out. Want to go for a ride, pretty lady?"

Caroline spun in the chair. Her first look at Melanie caused her to suck in her breath. Melanie was in a short sundress, her dark hair pulled back in a ponytail, bra-less. The girl was gorgeous, her well muscled athlete's body being hugged by the dress. She smiled brightly as with liquid grace she approached, her soft sandals making no sound on the hard floor.

Caroline let out a long wolf whistle. "Oh my dear girl, you clean up right pretty, you do. I've only ever seen you in leathers or the deputy's uniform. Melanie, you're gorgeous."

"Thank you, sweet woman," blushed Melanie. She'd spent far too much of her life in combats or in leathers. Melanie wasn't accustomed to hearing compliments on her appearance. She was a bit startled at how much she liked it. "Here, let me take that chair."

"Forget that," grinned Caroline. "You lead the way so I can watch your legs."

"You just want to ogle my ass."

"Oh yeah."

"As you wish." Still blushing, Melanie led the way to the waiting car near the door. The nurse who pushed the wheelchair was blushing too. Once outside Melanie opened the car door then offered Carrie her hand. Caroline accepted the hand and was guided from the wheelchair and into the car seat. Melanie thanked the nurse then made a great show of getting into the driver's seat, showing off her legs as she did. She drove slowly away.

"Is there anything special you'd like to do before we head for the boat line?"

"Can we stop for an ice cream cone?"

"Perfect. I know just the place." Within moments they were seated on the hood of the car enjoying the shade of a spreading maple tree while feasting on ice cream.

"Oh dear gods, this is decadent," sighed Caroline. "I've been force fed that sludge they call food at the hospital for over two months."

"I sure hope you're not a vegetarian."

"Oh, I'm not. Why?"

"Because Nana is planning a barbecue tonight. Vic is making up his special barbecue sauce and Sheriff Hank is bringing the steaks."

"Sounds like heaven to me. What are we bringing?"

"Watermelon and ice cream. It's already there."

"Perfect," laughed Caroline, "but first I want our private picnic, just you and me."

"And you shall have it. Finish your cone, sweetie, and we'll get on the go."

They had a few minutes to wait in line then boarded the boat. Once on they left the car and climbed to the observation deck above. It was a bright sunny day with a soft breeze. Caroline leaned against the rail and sighed with contentment. It was so wonderful to be out of the hospital and in the open air.

The wounds on her legs had healed and the scars were well hidden by the jeans she wore. However, her tank top failed to conceal the angry red scars on her arms and chest. She noticed that people were giving them lots of space and she began to withdraw into herself.

Melanie noticed instantly and put her arm around Caroline's shoulders protectively. "Easy, sweetie, easy. These folks aren't looking at you."

"You think not?"

"No dear, they're not. It's me they're trying to stay away from."

"Mel, what aren't you telling me?"

"About fifteen years ago my uncle went postal all over the manager of that hotel you bought. Killed him and his family then turned the gun on himself. The good people of Brighton made life damned hard for my family for a couple of years after that. Mom and Dad cracked and ran, leaving me with Nana.

"Things got worse and Nana talked Hank into helping me escape before things went down too ugly. Now that I'm back they still seem to be afraid of me, but not as bold about it as they were when I was a kid."

"Tell me about it, Mel. All of it. I know all too well that sharing helps take the power away from old wounds."

"I will, Carrie honey; I will. That's what today is all about, the picnic. It is to give us a chance to share some old stuff. You know, fill in a bit of background. Give you a chance to reconsider if you don't like what..."

"Stop it, Melanie, my sweetie. There will be none of that kind of talk. If I can't whine about my scars then you can't..."

"Yes ma'am, got it. Look, we're getting close to docking. Let's get back to the car."

Once they departed from the boat Melanie drove slowly to the far end of the island, pointing out things of interest for Carrie. As the passed one farm, the cows near the road, Melanie grinned and spoke. "You know the first time I ever saw a cow up close it was a mooooving experience."

Caroline laughed then got into the game. "Really? Wow, that is udderly fascinating, sweetheart." Melanie cracked up and nearly lost control of the car.

The game went on as they passed the only beach area on the island and headed up into the rest of the farms. Past the farms she parked by an overgrown field, a farm abandoned long ago. Gathering the picnic basket and blanket from the back seat, she led Carrie up the hill until they were near the cliff edge. Melanie spread out the blanket, then sat facing the view.

Caroline sat beside her. "My god, Mel, what a magnificent view. This is a perfect spot; I'd love to set up here to paint."

"There's no reason you can't. Look over that way, you can just see the hotel roof through the trees. There's the town of Brighton, and over this way is the house I wanted to show you before the world went all to hell. Sadly, it's been sold to a retired writer or something."

Caroline gazed at the old, but refurbished house that looked across the beach and towards the mainland across the water. "Wow, that would have some view. Probably cost as much as the hotel did, but would have been worth it. It wasn't on the market when I first came here, but I'd have gone for the hotel anyway."

"Why?"

"I'm not that rich, sweetie. I still have to earn a living, and I'm not naive enough to think my painting will support me. Maybe someday but..." She waved her hands in the air and shook her head. "I did well in real estate, but it's a high pressure job if you want to succeed, twenty four hours a day. I guess I just burned out and wanted a slower pace of life. I thought I could run the B&B through the tourist season and have the off season to paint and recharge my batteries."

"Sounds perfect." Melanie smiled then kissed Caroline's cheek. "Under normal circumstances there should have been no problem."

"Yes, but you've solved the problem, haven't you? For the hotel at least?"

"I don't know, honey. I can't make that promise right now, but I will solve it or die trying."

"Hey now, none of that negative stuff, okay?"

"Okay. Sorry. Is there any chance of you staying in the apartment on the mainland until this has been put to rest?"

"You're staying on the island aren't you?"

"I have to."

"It's more than that, Mel. You could leave if you wanted to. From what you've told me you have no real reason to stay."

"I have my reasons."

Caroline laid back and shaded her eyes as she looked at the clouds scudding slowly by. "Care to share with your girlfriend?"

Melanie smiled at her then wrote in her small book.

"Beautiful day

Beautiful woman

A moment to live for."

Melanie stretched out beside Carrie and closed her eyes. "All right, I'll talk. I have memories of being happy, completely at peace with, and a living part of, my world. That was on this island before it all went nuts. As a child I knew in my soul I belonged here, was a part of this place, and it a part of me.

"When I left, I managed to survive living in a shelter and flipping burgers. I wanted more out of life. I was nineteen when I signed on with the military. I loved the harsh training as it made me forget. I excelled. A master sergeant introduced me to European Martial Arts. Tough training, hand to hand combat, weapons, etc. I loved that too, for the same reasons.

"It didn't take long before I was sent into combat for real. Turns out I seem to be a natural leader and was promoted. After one tour I volunteered for another, but was recruited for a special team instead."

"Demon hunters?"

"Yep, demon hunters. Somebody had figured out I could see them and always went after them first. I was given more training and a team of my own. After a few years the team was removed from the military and placed under a special branch of the government, highly classified. Things were getting uglier and we were forced to do things nobody would ever willingly do.

"About six months ago we were trying to take one out of a young boy. The team stood guard, Vic held the terrified mother back while I did the nasty. The boy didn't survive. He died in my arms, screaming for his mother. It fucked me up royally, Carrie. I quit and decided to come home. I wanted to recapture some of those good memories, to find peace again."

Caroline gathered Melanie into her arms and held her gently until she felt the tension seep away and the girl relax in her arms. "You came home to the anger and the demons instead of the sweetness of the child's innocence."

"Right on the money."

"So why stay? Why didn't you move on?"

"Where would I go, lover? Those damned things are everywhere now. Besides, my grandmother is here and won't leave. To top it off some blonde bombshell bought the old hotel then started putting the moves on me. How can I leave now?"

"Oh, you can't. Not now." Caroline's eyes were dancing with mischief.

"Of course I can't. Now enough of my sad story; I want yours now."

"My story? All right, let's see. I was five when my father was locked away suffering with PTSD. He managed to kill himself the next year. Mom did her best to raise us and teach us how to survive. Brit and I grew up learning to use our wits and looks to get ahead. We got good marks in school, were both popular, then Mom got breast cancer and died.

"I was nineteen and Brit was sixteen when we were thrown out of our house. It was sold along with mom's old car to pay the medical bills. We moved into a rundown apartment while she finished school. I worked three jobs to keep us alive until I could send her to college.

"Brit was there less than a month when she got into her first poker game. Within six months she was a full time gambler and supporting us while I took real estate courses. We're both hard bitten survivors, Mel. We haven't faced anything like you have, but we've had to make our own way. Are you sure you want to get mixed up with us?"

Melanie laughed and gave Caroline a squeeze. "I love both of the savage sisters. I'm completely lost."

"Can I ask you something, Mel?"

"Ask away."

"Why did you choose me over Brit? Be honest now, it wasn't because of what happened to me, was it?"

"Nope. That had nothing to do with it, Carrie. All right, you want honesty, here it is. I can say with complete honesty that the both of you were driving me crazy in a sweet wonderful way. I would have given anything to have a real chance with either of you. The problem was I had never really dated much before, not really. This was my first real experience with women actually showing interest in me and not being ashamed of it.

"That's heady stuff. That's why I said you're intoxicating because you are. I was loving every minute of the whole thing, my brain completely fogged with lust and infatuation. Then Brit talked to Nana and Nana talked to me.

"Suddenly I didn't know what the heck to do next. Brit actually said you both were interested in me for real, but I had to choose. Me. I had to choose and make the first real move. I didn't sleep for days, trying to decide between you, but I couldn't.

"Finally Nana told me to stop thinking with my heart and think with my head. Considering what we're facing here I need to stay focused, so I took her advice. For the first time in my life I really asked what I wanted for myself. The answer was easy then. I want a loving relationship with a woman. I want a woman who will know and love me in spite of all the things I've done and what I've become.

"I was pretty sure either of you would fill the bill beyond all expectations, but you've gone head to head with the worst of the demons and survived. I thought we'd be a better fit in the long run. Besides that, you've committed yourself to this place I want to call home. Brit will be all over the world, but you'll be here with me."

"And if you chose Brit you would have me around all the time while she was away. That would be hard on both of us. Wow. I'm going to have to be careful about asking you for honesty."

"Too much?" Melanie started to untangle her arms from Caroline, but Carrie pulled her closer again.

"No, Mel, not too much. Thank you for being so up front with me. I'm just not accustomed to it. I'm more used to people trying to get round me with guile, running games on me to get what they wanted.

"If there were no Brit you would still have wanted me. If nothing had happened to me you'd still want me. Even with Brit and her magic charm here, you still chose me. The best part for me is that you didn't mention scars at all."

"Wasn't part of the equation, honey. Never will be."

"I promise you, Melanie Rivers, I will do everything in my power to make this work between us."

"So will I, love. So will I."

The sweet interlude was broken by Carrie's phone playing Mozart. "Caroline Majors."

"Hey sis, how's the picnic going?"

"Perfect. How are things at the hotel?"

"All finished. There's a group of people here looking for a room. They mentioned Mel's name." Caroline hit the button to put the call on speaker.

"Mel's right here, Brit."

"Hi sexy."

"Hi gorgeous. What's up?"

"The hotel is all ready. The contractor and his men are packing up to go. There's a group of people here looking for a room. They say they're friends of yours. What do you want to do?"

"Give them rooms and tell them I'll check in later this evening or early tomorrow."

"Can do, girl. I'm guessing I can leave the keys with them for now?"

"You bet."

"Where are you going, Brit?" asked Carrie.

"Back to the apartment to change into something sexy. I've been invited to a barbecue tonight."

Melanie laughed with delight. "I see you didn't waste any time."

"What was I supposed to do? Everybody was going to the party without me."

"Aw, Brit, you know we'd never leave you behind."

"Sure. You already ran off with my sexy sister."

"Oops, busted. Brit, when you come over, pick up the gang at the hotel. I'll hit the store for more supplies."

"Got it, Mel. See you guys later." With that she was gone.

"You're sneaky," said Caroline, as she tossed the phone back into her bag.

"What?"

"You're sneaky. Moving your team of demon hunters into the hotel. Honey, I don't need protection as much as I need paying customers. I've lost a big chunk of this year's tourist season."

"These are paying customers, love. They'll pay up and get reimbursed, no problem. They're also deadly on demons, so if I'm not there to..."

"You're going to protect me no matter what I say, aren't you?"

"Yep. Better get used to it. You may be as self sufficient as all get out, but I will still try to protect you. It's my nature; it's what I do best."

"Thank you, Melanie. I will feel a lot better with them there the first few days. How long will they stay?"

"Until we clear the island and plug the hole between the worlds. They're not going anywhere until this place is safe once again. After that I'll be on watch all the time."

"Me too. Train me."

"What?"

"Teach me what I have to know, what I have to do to help you. Don't try to put me on a shelf, Mel. Let me stand with you against these things."

"Are you in such a hurry to face them again?"

"Oh hell, no. However, I have no illusions here. They're here. We have to fight them to survive. Surviving is what I do best. Here is where I've chosen to live. This is where my woman is, where I want to make my life. Let me help."

For an answer Melanie kissed her softly, sweetly, savoring the taste of her mouth, the closeness of her body. "All right, sweetheart. Side by side then," she whispered as she slowly let her lips part from Carries. "We'll take a stand together against all comers."

"Melanie, sweetheart?"

"Mmm?"

"Kiss me like that again?" Melanie was more than happy to oblige.

THE PLACE WAS BUSTLING when they arrived at Ellen's house. Everyone was already there. Melanie exchanged greetings with the three newcomers then introduced Caroline. The food was delicious, and Ellen's special blend of tea was a hit also. Once the meal was finished and the clean up accomplished, they settled down to a council of war. Melanie brought the team up to speed then they began making plans.

Of the three newcomers, Luke, the tallest, was now the official team leader, but he deferred to Melanie as this was her home turf. Bjorn was the muscle of the team and Lizzie was its eyes.

As they finished washing up, Lizzie took a stroll around the property. "All clear, Luke, sorry, Mel."

"Of course it's clear." Ellen was trying to appear indignant, but failed. Her delighted grin gave her away. "You've been there, haven't you, girl?"

"Been where?"

"To the other side, the demon world or whatever the hell it is."

"How did you know?"

"I was there before you were born, child. I can read the signs. Since you've been there, you're the eyes for the team, right?"

"Right on the money," laughed Melanie. "Everybody on the team can see them, but Liz can spot them a mile away. See any since you arrived, Lizzie?"

"Six so far, but there's more. There's something else too."

"Oh, what?"

Ellen smiled and nodded her head. "Go ahead, girl, tell them."

"You've all got something new in your aura, something bright, shiny, and dangerous maybe. What's up with that? I can see it starting in Luke and Bjorn too, me as well. What did you do to us?"

"It's in the tea," replied Ellen. "I invented it to keep the buggers off me. Vic helped me beef up the formula and now it's a sure thing."

"Vic?"

"True words," smiled Vic. "Ellen and I tested it just the other day."

"Tested it? How the hell did you test it?" That was Hank and he was all attention now.

"We went hunting and found one wandering alone. Vic dropped his guard and got in its path. It tried several times, but just slid off him. I saw the whole thing."

"Nana, Vic, are you two crazy? What the hell were you thinking?"

"We were thinking we'd finally got it right. Now Vic's working on condensing the formula so you can take it in pill form, just like your morning vitamins."

Hank grunted and shook his head. "There's nothing illegal in it is there?"

"Of course not, Hank. Perish the thought."

"Ellen Rivers, you're a bad woman," sighed Hank. Everyone laughed at that.

Luke spun a chair and straddled it, folding his arms across the back. "This one is your show, Boss. What's our next move?"

Melanie sighed and turned to Lizzie. "First things first. Nana has told me that if we kill one slowly it takes a piece of the human host back with it to the other side. You knew that all along, didn't you, Liz?"

"I wasn't sure, Mel. I never said anything because I wasn't sure. There was nothing we could do about it anyway."

"There may be now," said Vic. "I'm working on a way to strip them off people and send them back alone. Ellen's formula is the basis of that research. I've got a couple of possibilities I'd like to test out."

"Test them out? How the hell do you propose to do that?"

"Easy, Sheriff. That's Melanie's job, to figure out how we go about it."

All eyes turned to Melanie, but she was lost in thought. Finally she nodded then spoke. "Okay, I've got it, but it needs a bit of work. Nana, have you got anything up your sleeve that will help people to see the demons?"

"I could make up something, but it would be highly illegal."

"Crap, okay, we'll have to do it the hard way. Hank, what do you think, can we trust Emily with all this, or do we need to get her out of town for a while?"

"It'll take some convincing, but I think we can trust Em. If we try to get her out of town for a while she'll smell a rat. She already suspects us of some sort of skulduggery. I'd be surprised if she hasn't already contacted the FBI."

"Okay then we bring her into the loop. Then we go hunting. Bjorn can start a fight at the cafe where they seem to hang out then we drag him and his victim off to jail. Once we get our test subject locked up, Vic can try out his magic formula."

"What can we do to help?"

"Brit, what do you mean, we?"

"Melanie Rivers, you don't think you're going to be able to keep us on the sidelines, do you?"

"Perish the thought." Melanie grinned and shook her head. "I need you and Carrie to be extra careful, but we can use your help. Once we have a test subject in custody somebody will have to stand interference. Usually that is Vic and Bjorn, but they can't on this one. Do you think you two could distract anyone trying to enter the sheriff's office?"

"I think we can manage," purred Caroline. She had completely forgotten her scars. These people took no notice of them and so she momentarily forgot all about them. Brit smiled as her sexy sister took command of that assignment. She had told the team of Carrie's ordeal and they understood completely.

"I'll just bet you can," grinned Melanie. "All right folks, first thing tomorrow we go hunting for a lab rat. Hank, Carrie, and I have the unenviable task of convincing our skeptic co-worker. Once we're sure it's a go we'll contact Luke so he and Bjorn can bring us a test case."

Melanie finally convinced Carrie and Brit to go back to the mainland for the night. They left in Caroline's car, hurrying to catch the last boat. The rest of the team returned to the hotel, checked it out, then retired for the night.

Ellen took Melanie aside for a moment as Vic headed off to bed. "What's up, Nana?"

"You are, honey. I can see that you and your sweetie are getting along just fine."

"So?"

"So, are you planning to tell her you sleep on the floor in a different spot every night, or are you going to get back in the habit of sleeping in a bed. She will expect to wake up with you beside her, Melanie."

"How did you know?"

"I can hear you tossing around in the night, sweetie. Mel, trust me, nothing is going to get into this house, nothing. You're safe here."

"Sorry Nana, old habits are hard to break."

"Think of it this way, I'm old and haven't had a decent night's sleep since you came home and started rolling around on the floor over my head every night. Do it for your old granny if you won't do it for your lover."

"Nana, you're a bad woman," chuckled Melanie. "All right, since you and Vic have perfected the tea that takes away one of my worst fears, but there's another one."

"Oh, what's that?"

"Humans. If a demon controlled human sneaks in I don't want to be an easy target. That extra few seconds it takes for them to find me can give me a strong edge. It has kept me alive in the past."

"That makes sense. All right, but remember what I said. Caroline may be tough as nails, but I doubt you'll be able to talk her into sleeping on the floor. Good night, honey."

Melanie kissed the old woman's cheek then climbed the stairs to her room. With a deep sigh of resignation, Melanie surveyed the room. The bed was back from the window. Good. She dropped a floor wedge by the door then kicked it under to brace the door closed. She then took some fine wire from her saddle bags off her motorcycle and strung a trap just below the window so anyone trying to break in would have a nasty surprise. When that was done she turned and faced the bed.

For the first time in years Melanie Rivers stripped off and climbed into bed with full intentions of sleeping there. She tossed and turned for a few minutes then sighed deeply. "Oh for Christ's sake, Melanie; what the hell is the matter with you? You can do this; you're safe here. Look, you've got a chance at the whole dream here.

"You survived the war, you survived the black ops, the killings, the demon battles, and you've come home to look for some peace and a woman to share life with. You've got a shot at the dream here. You can clear out the demons, and you have a good woman who wants to build a relationship with you. All you have to do is learn to sleep in a bed. What the hell are you, six months old? Stop this foolishness, go to sleep."

The self talk didn't work. She tried counting sheep but gave that up as just plain silly. Finally she called up a picture of Carrie in her mind. With thoughts of Carrie's sweet kiss and delicious curves, Melanie allowed her agile fingers to relieve her tension. Sadly the orgasm left her more awake than sleepy. She continued to toss around a lot, but did manage to get a few hours of rest before morning.

A Convincing Story

Next morning Melanie was baggy eyed and grumpy. Silently she drank her tall glass of the magic tea then went for a super sized mug of strong coffee. "The bed was too damned soft," she growled as Ellen raised a questioning eyebrow. Ellen's broad grin did nothing to improve her mood.

The parking lot at the sheriff's office was busy as the motorcycle roared in. The Majors sisters were just climbing out of their car and the team stood by, waiting for them. Hank was in the doorway as Melanie slammed on her brakes and a shot rang out. Melanie pitched forward off the bike and rolled behind a car.

Hank bellowed for everyone to take cover, but the team was already in action. They laid down cover fire as they hustled the sisters into the building. "Melanie! I have to go to her..."

"We'll get her, Carrie. You stay put." With that Vic was back outside with his team. A few moments later they heard Luke's shout. "Clear!" Everyone hurried outside.

Caroline rushed to Melanie who was leaning on the police cruiser and swearing profusely. "Goddamn son of a bitch. When I get my hands on this guy I'm gonna rip his lungs out through his backside. I'll..."

"Melanie Rivers. Wherever did you learn language like that?" Carrie's giggle made her pause then she too grinned sheepishly. Carrie took Melanie into her arms and held her tightly. "That scared the life out of me, Mel; seeing you fall like that."

"Sorry sweetie, old habit. Something hit my helmet and nearly took my head off. I went for cover. Look at this, the bastard ruined my helmet."

"Let me see that, Boss." Melanie tossed the helmet to Luke. He looked at it then turned and stepped forward. "Okay, you came in this way, but slammed on the breaks. The bullet came from above and behind. That roof there most likely. If you'd been slower to stop it would have been a clear lung shot through the back."

"Dammit, we need to get up there," growled Hank. "We need to get that shooter..."

"Our team will handle this one, Hank," sighed Melanie. "Let's get inside; I need more coffee."

"That's our boss," grinned Luke. "Always add a caffeine buzz to an adrenalin rush."

Emily had witnessed the whole thing through the window. She was shaking as they all trooped back inside. She swallowed hard before she spoke. "What just happened out there?"

"Somebody just took a shot at Mel," growled Hank. "It was meant to kill. Emily, these folks are government agents. We need to bring you into the loop, and we need you to believe what we have to say."

"Why?" she asked softly.

"Because, Em, some things are going to happen here that are probably not legal or even moral, but they have to happen if we're going to save the people of this island."

"You're starting to scare me, Hank."

"Sadly, it's only going to get worse. Go ahead, Mel. Tell her what you need to."

Melanie came to sit at Emily's desk. "Em, this all started back when we were kids, maybe even before. Something happened to make a crack, a hole, between our world and a dark one, a world of demons."

"There's a gateway to hell on this island? Really? This is your story?"

"Just shut up and listen, will you? Demons started to get through. Think back now, to when we were in high school. Remember the man who was manager of the old hotel?"

"Mr. Janes, his son Tommy was a year behind us in school."

"Okay, remember how Mr. Janes seemed to get mad really easy and for no reason, his wife too?"

"I remember them fighting a lot, with everybody. What has this got to do with..."

"I'm getting there. Stay with me now. Some people can see the demons, most can't. The medicine my uncle was on made him see them. Mr. Janes and his wife both had a demon attached to their backs. To his horror, my uncle realized he had one attached to himself as well. He didn't know what to do, but rather than let the demons take him over, he killed the Janes family and then himself."

"He was trying to get rid of them, Em, but it didn't work. Over the years more and more of them have managed to get through. The past number of years that's what I've been doing, fighting them all across the globe. I got sick of it all and came home only to find it is worse here than anywhere else.

"Emily, the biggest demon I've ever seen was hooked into your cousin Billy. I took him alive and tried to keep him that way. Once a demon is hooked into a person they can't escape until that person dies."

"So that's why you were so adamant he be kept alive but sedated."

"That's why, Em. Girl, you've got to believe us here."

Emily's eyes were wide and she didn't speak for a moment. She swallowed hard then asked, "What does it look like when you see them?"

Carrie approached the desk and sat near Melanie. "It looks like a black aura at first. If you look just past the person you can see it easier."

"Is there any way to get it off without killing the person?" Emily was trembling now. She gripped her coffee cup tightly to steady her hands.

"It's an iffy sort of deal." Melanie was studying her own hands as she spoke. "Sometimes you win, sometimes you don't. Mostly you don't. If the demon is a new attachment, or a small one growing, your chances are way better."

"And if it's been there for a long time?"

"Folks don't often survive it. Vic has a new theory he wants to try out. He thinks it will up our odds big time. However, the removal process is very painful."

"I can attest to that," said Carrie, "but it's worth it." She had laced her fingers through Melanie's.

Once again Emily was silent, this time studying her own hands on the desk. "Em?" She sighed then looked up with tears in her eyes. "My mom has one of those black auras. She's all achy, complaining of the pain constantly, and she talks mean like she never did before. Do you think you can help her?"

"We can try, Em, but no guarantees."

"And if it is left alone?"

"She gets like Billy was, or worse."

"I remember him as such a gentle guy, Mel. He started to get mean and nasty then vanished. I just thought he ran away. So did everybody else, but it was really him killing all those people at the hotel.

"You said that man thinks he can help folks, but needs to test it. If it works will you help my mom?"

"I swear it, Em."

Emily swallowed hard. "All right, what do you need me to do?"

"We need you to ignore whatever goes on here," said Luke. "We also need you to fudge the paperwork on any arrests we might make."

"You want me to break the law and look the other way while you experiment on people."

"Yes."

Emily's face registered the torment the decision caused her. Her father and been a man who preached the gospel of honesty. He believed it was the only way to live a good life and he impressed that on his family every day of his life. Emily had worshipped her father and tried to live up to his ideals. Now she was faced with deliberately turning her back on his life's code in order to save the woman he had loved so deeply. She swallowed hard then made her decision. "All right, but you have to help my mom. If anything happens to her I'll blow the whistle..."

She got no further as the door burst open and Bjorn shoved a disheveled man into the room. The man was in restraints. Lizzie followed, carrying a hunting rifle. "Here's the shooter's weapon and the shooter. Vic will be right here with his supplies. Looks like we have our first volunteer." Vic arrived right at that point.

Emily looked past the man on the floor. She could see the black aura. After a moment she could see it moving, struggling and she could see a vague shape. She nearly fainted as the man glared at Melanie and spoke in a voice that could not have come from a human throat. "We will have you yet." Emily grabbed her wastebasket and threw up her breakfast.

"Not today you won't," snarled Melanie, as she rose from the chair and grabbed the man by the collar. She dragged him into a cell then pulled out her magic glove and put it on. "Glove up, people." They already had. "All right, Vic, this one is your baby now, what do you need us to do?"

"Well, I'd prefer he didn't flop around a lot while I give him the injection." At sight of the needle the man began to struggle wildly.

Melanie's arms slid around his neck and his struggles soon stopped. She lowered him to the floor again. Bjorn picked him up easily and laid him on the bunk where Vic gave him an injection.

Vic massaged the man's arm to help the medicine move more quickly. A moment later he came to and began to struggle, screaming in pain and rage. It took all of them to hold him still. It was only after the man lay exhausted that Emily was able to see the darkness rise from him. It struggled and fought to keep its tentacled hooks attached to the man's back, but something was causing it to slip away. Finally it was clear and the man's struggles ceased as did his cries.

The entire team turned their gloves towards the rising, struggling, mist. As the greenish glow from the gloves enveloped it the demon screamed in pain and frustration then dissipated into thin air. Emily heard the collective sigh of relief from the team members as well as herself and the sisters who had watched with held breath.

"Is it really gone?"

"Yeah, Em, it's really gone." Melanie slowly pulled off the glove and stuffed it back in her pocket.

The man on the floor groaned and tried to sit up. He failed. Bjorn lifted him back onto the bunk then everybody filed out of the cell, locking him inside. He tried to stand, but was too weak and he sank back onto the bunk, gazing all around. "Hey, Hank, why the hell have you got me locked up in here?"

"You took a shot at Deputy Rivers. A few inches lower and she'd have been killed. You're in there for illegally discharging a firearm within town limits, for assault with a deadly weapon, and for attempted murder. Now sit there and shut the hell up until we get this sorted out."

"Murder? I didn't try to murder anybody. What the hell are you talking about?"

"Is this your rifle?"

"Yeah, so?"

"It's been fired recently." Hank easily caught the shell casing Lizzy tossed to him. "This shell matches your rifle. It was found on the roof top where you hid and fired at Melanie. Do you want me to keep going or will you shut up?"

"Look, I didn't fire that rifle. I have sheep on Cooley Island and somebody said there were coyotes headed this way. I was going over there to protect my flock. I have no idea how I ended up here. Deputy Rivers, I don't remember shooting at you, but you're still alive. If I'd shot at you, you wouldn't be."

Melanie strode over to face him through the cell door. "Stop yapping and start remembering. Think over the past few days. Let this morning seep back into that pea sized brain of yours." She spun on her heel and headed for the coffee machine.

Melanie took a long sip from her mug then sighed. "Looks like you've got a winner, Vic."

"Thanks, Mel, but it could be a fluke. I'd like to test a few more before I call it a win."

"How much of that stuff have you got with you?"

"Three more doses then I'll have to brew up another batch."

"All right, let's go hunting." Melanie reached for Carrie and gazed earnestly into her eyes. "Things have changed a bit, sweetheart. I don't want you getting shot. I really wish you and Brit would focus on moving you into the hotel and getting settled in."

"Nope, not after what I've just seen. We want to help."

"I think Mel is trying to tell us we can help by staying out of the way and letting the professionals handle this, Sis. Am I right, Mel?"

"Pretty much, Brit. Look, you guys keep your eyes open and call me the instant you spot one of these buggers, but keep yourselves safe. This thing is getting out of hand, and I don't want you to get hurt. Please, Carrie, for me."

"Okay, under one condition. You keep yourself in one piece and you come to me as soon as you've free to do so. Deal?"

"Deal, pretty lady."

The sisters left the sheriff's office and drove away. Melanie watched them go. When they were out of sight she turned back to the room and found Emily looking at her intently. "Mom is on her way down here," she said. "I told her I was sick and asked her to come for me. She's pretty mad, but she's coming. Please, Mel, please help her."

"We'll do our best, Em. You saw that one, didn't you?"

"Yeah, I did. Mel, that story of yours; it's true isn't it? All of it? That's what made your uncle do what he did, isn't it?" Melanie just nodded her head. "Mel, I'm sorry, sorry for all of it. The way I acted, the..."

"Easy, girl, easy. We were just kids and you closed ranks with your family, exactly what you were supposed to do. All water under the bridge now. Here comes your mom, brace yourself."

BRIT MAJORS DROVE STRAIGHT to the hotel, a smile playing on her lips. She was excited to show Caroline what she had done. She hoped she'd got it right. Carrie smiled at her sister. Brit had always been easy for her to read whenever there was a secret to be shared. She had no idea how Brit managed to turn it off when she played cards.

They pulled into the parking lot and Brit grinned with delight as Carrie sucked in her breath. The grounds had all been landscaped and the hotel freshly painted in the colors Carrie had chosen before the attack. The old sign was gone and in its place was stylish new one declaring Majors B&B. Welcome. "Wait until you see the rest of it."

"Oh, Brit, it's beautiful. What did you do to the inside?"

"Come in and see." She led the way up the steps to the large door with the stained glass.

Caroline swallowed hard as she stepped through that door, but inside there was no body, no blood, or chalk outline of a body on the floor. The new hardwood floor gleamed in the morning sunlight. Carrie gazed around in wonder. The old front desk was still there, completely restored. The lobby had been somewhat extended and turned into her new living room.

The large dining room had also been restored to resemble its former glory. Attached was a new professional kitchen. Beyond that was Carrie's personal room, huge, with walk-in closet and luxury bath. "Oh my god, Brit. This must have cost you a fortune."

"Ah, ah, ah, none of that now. Let's go upstairs." The second floor held eight rooms, completely modernized with a full bath each. There were three occupied by the demon hunter team. They went on up to the third floor. There were two suites there, one obviously for living, the other was an open studio with a tiny kitchen and powder room attached. There were windows everywhere and the huge room was filled with light.

"What do you think, Sis, will this do for a studio?"

"Brit, you crazy woman, what have you done? I expected it would take me years to get the place to this point. I'll never be able to pay you back what you've spent here."

"Oh yes you will. You see, this suite next to your studio is mine."

"Brit?"

"Look, if my sister is going to insist on living near the hell mouth, I plan to be there to watch her back. At least whenever I can. I expect your new woman will do a much better job of it actually, but..."

"Brit, do you mean it? You'll make this place your home base?"

"Yeah, I will. I'll help you run the B&B in the summer then I'll travel for work in winter while you paint. Is that okay with you, honey? I mean, if you'd rather I..."

"Forget it, little sister," laughed Caroline, as she hugged Brit tightly. "You're not getting out of it now." She stepped back and turned to gaze out the window. The view looked out over the harbor and across the water. She could see the ferry boat making its way towards the island and she smiled. It was perfect, just like she'd dreamed it could be. "Show me the rest of it, Brit."

"There's just the basement left, honey."

"I know. I can face it, honey. I have to. I can't spend the rest of my life cowering in the attic, afraid to go down to wash my clothes. Mel would tell me to strap on the old armor and get on with it."

"She's a tough cookie all right."

"I think she's had to be, Brit. I got some of her story and I am amazed she's come through it all as intact as she has. She's amazing and I want to be worthy of her."

"Wow, Sis, you've got it bad. I think you've had a real case for her all along."

"Okay, I'll admit it. There is just something about her. I knew it the first time I saw her. I'll admit I was disappointed, and a bit pissed that I couldn't sway her to help me here, but I couldn't get her out of my mind either."

"Oops, then I came along and started flirting."

"Yes you did, you bag. Gods, Brit, you're so gorgeous, sexy, and nobody can resist you."

"And that broke you. Oh sweetie. You should have said something."

"I was all sliced to ribbons and sewn back together like a rag doll. I knew that with the scars and the rape she would never want me. I kept quiet so you two could be happy."

"Yeah, well, Mel wasn't having any of that, was she? Carrie, she chose you and I'm thrilled that she did. Are you going to be alright with me living here, I mean with Melanie and all... It's not going to complicate things, is it?"

"Stop that. I love you, Brit, and Melanie does too. She will be happier with you nearby and so will I. Look, I'll admit that I'm a bit desperate to make this work with Melanie. She's made her choice and we both know that for her, that's all there is to it. I'll need you to help me figure out how to make it work. I mean, what can I do for her? You know, to make her...?"

"Hey, hey, now, none of that. Sweetie, talk to the girl. Let her guide you. Watch to see what she likes and doesn't. Make sure she knows she's your number one priority."

"Yeah, you're right. Too many bad breakups in the past, I guess. I'm just stalling now. Come on, show me what you've done with the basement."

Brit led the way down the stairs. There was a brightly lit open area with professional laundry machines and large folding tables. All the plumbing and wiring were new and easily accessible. This wasn't a standard finished basement, this was an industrial basement with easy access to all the hotel's vital systems, heat, water supply, air conditioning, etc. One wall was fresh new concrete. Carrie pointed at it; her face unreadable.

"Mel said that was where the guy had his bolt hole to the cave beyond. The tunnel to the cave has been filled with concrete and this wall has sealed it off. That wall is two feet thick, honey. Nothing's coming through that way."

"My god, Brit. It is all so different. This must have cost a fortune. How did you get it all done so fast?"

"I had a contractor who knew his stuff. Once he knew what I wanted and when I needed it, he brought in extra crews. Yes it cost, but I don't care. I wanted this for you, for me, for us. The home we always talked about making for ourselves. A place safe from the world, all fixed up and completely paid off. Once I knew how much you'd sunk into this island and what you were facing here, I knew what I had to do.

"So, no BS now; do you like it?" Can you be happy here?"

"Brit, honey, I love it, I truly do. Yes, I can be happy here. Can you?"

"I can. Carrie, I promise I won't get in the way. You know, with Melanie and all."

"Oh stop. There will be no holding back from us. Besides, like I told you, she loves you too, and I need your help. I need you to help me keep her."

"Carrie, come on, let's go up and grab some lunch at the cafe. I want to know what going on in that head of yours."

Caroline followed Brit up to the lobby. "What do you mean? What's going on in my head?"

"Honey, you almost seem desperate. Tell me you're not afraid Melanie is your only chance to be happy."

"Brit, you know damn well with these scars I'm ruined, at least in the eyes of the rest of the world. Melanie doesn't see them. I know that. Yes, I'm desperate to keep her. The woman makes me tingle all over when she kisses me, she makes me feel like a girl again. Brit, she makes me feel whole again. Do not let me screw this up."

"You won't screw it up, honey. You won't. Just be yourself; that's what she wants. She wants Carrie Majors, force of nature. I know it is. You're getting all depressed on me. Let's go eat something; you need carbohydrates."

"You're right, Sis. After we eat can we go across to the mainland and pack a few bags? I'd love to get moved in here today. We can have a moving company bring the rest another time..."

"But you want to get in here today. Trying to stay close to your new girlfriend?"

"Busted," laughed Carrie.

"All right, we have a plan. Let's go."

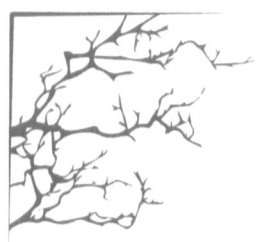

Closer

Melanie sighed as she dropped into her chair in the sheriff's office. The others weren't doing any better as they collapsed into whatever chairs were available. There were three people in the cells, sitting quietly on the bunks. Finally Emily spoke. "So, what happens now? What about Mom?"

Hank sighed and shifted in his chair. "Now we fudge the arrest reports so we can hold these folks for a while. I have no idea what happens after that. What is the standard procedure, Mel? What do you normally do with these people?"

"That one's Luke's call, he's the team leader now."

"I have no idea, Mel. This one's is all new to me. Just look what happened. We made three kills and every victim survived relatively in one piece. We had three successes in a row, no losses. Better yet, these folks seem to be in pretty good shape. Usually people have to be sedated for a while, and then face a long road of therapy to help them reintegrate into their old lives, if they ever can.

"I could be completely wrong here, but these folks look pretty good. Maybe we can just hold them until we clear the island then let them go. I'll check in with the people upstairs and see what they say."

"Sounds good to me."

Just as Melanie spoke the phone rang. "Sheriff's office, Deputy Rivers speaking. What? Okay, sounds great. See you later.

"It was Carrie saying they were on the mainland, waiting for a boat back to the island. Looks like I have a dinner date for tonight."

Vic heaved himself from his chair and sighed. "You can ride with me, Mel. I'm headed back to the house."

"Hank?"

"Go on, Melanie. You folks have done your duty for the day. I'll see to feeding our prisoners then I'm heading home as well. I'll route all calls through my cell. I'll call Freddy in to keep an eye on them."

VIC AND ELLEN WERE in the kitchen discussing a new batch of the formula. Melanie was in the shower trying to shake off the day. This was the part she hated, the aftermath. Today had been a win. An unprecedented win, but she still had the shakes. It was always the same. She could be all business when the action was going on, but afterwards, she fell apart.

She sat on the shower floor, crying. The water was cooling before the shakes settled down. When she felt herself coming back Melanie climbed to her feet, quickly washed her hair, and then got out of the water. She dried her hair then gazed at her reflection in the mirror. She looked okay, she guessed, nothing special, but not too bad either. She wondered what a powerhouse woman like Caroline Majors could see in her.

"It's probably desperation," she sighed as she continued to gaze into the mirror. "Carrie thinks that the scars will make her unlovable or desirable. She probably thinks this is her only chance for a relationship. She doesn't know, can't know, that I have more scars than she does. The difference is mine aren't on my skin, they're on my soul. How could she know I'm even more desperate than she is."

Gods, how Melanie did hate the fits of self-loathing and depression that took her after a mission. She had to shake the mood. She had a date, and the mission wasn't over, not by half. Worse yet, once it was over she wouldn't be able to just ride away. She'd have to stay and face these people every day of her life.

"Shake it off, Rivers, find something pretty to put on. You have a woman to impress." Angrily shoving her fear and depression aside, Melanie poked through her limited wardrobe. "Yep, I guess it has to be the dress." Melanie pulled on a black thong then dropped the little black dress over her head and settled it on her body.

A smile slowly touched her lips. She loved the way the dress clung to her athletic body and made her feel like a woman again. She added silver earrings, chain and amber pendant, rings, and bangles for her wrists. Strappy sandals with heels completed the outfit. She finger-combed her hair one last time then descended the stairs. Ellen gave a soft whistle when she saw her granddaughter, but Vic's face dropped into concern. "Aw, Mel..."

"Relax, Vic, I'm fine. I have a date tonight, and this is all I have to wear."

"Honest?"

"Honest."

"Liar."

"It'll be okay, Vic. I promise."

Ellen gave Vic a questioning look, but he shook his head slightly so Ellen let it go. "Honey, you look beautiful. You're the image of your mom at that age."

"Thanks, Nana."

"Have you got your purse ready?"

"What do you mean?"

"Oh for pity sake. Your overnight purse. In my day, when a girl went out for the night it was often for the night. We carried a bag with spare undies, tooth brush, shorts and T-shirt, and a small bag of weed. It can all fit in a small bag."

"Nana, I'm shocked at you."

"Oh don't be such a prude, Melanie. Go pack a purse before Carrie gets here, just in case you get lucky." At that point there was the sound of tires on the driveway. Ellen pointed fiercely at the stairs.

Melanie sighed then went back up. When she returned carrying a purse, Caroline was waiting for her.

Carrie whistled and licked her lips. Melanie blushed and looked away for a moment. The sudden rise of her heartbeat and the sight of Caroline in that long clingy dress made the depression vanish. Carrie kissed Melanie's cheek then winked at Ellen before taking Mel's hand and leading her out to the car. She settled her in the passenger's seat then drove to the cafe/restaurant where they drew a lot of attention.

Both women ignored the stares and focused on each other. Caroline could tell Melanie was out of sorts and tried her best to cheer her up. Melanie glanced up to see Caroline smiling at her. As their eyes met, Carrie let her gaze drop slowly to Melanie's cleavage then she licked her lips. Melanie blushed.

"Stop it, Carrie."

"What?"

"Making me blush in public. It's bad for my fierce reputation."

"I'm sorry, sweet pea." She was still looking at Melanie's cleavage and grinning.

"Quit it, woman, or I'll..."

"What? What will you do to me?"

"Patience, dear," purred Melanie. "The night is young. I'll think of something." Melanie's gaze was now firmly fixed on Caroline's breasts, bringing a blush to her cheeks as well.

"Stop it, Melanie."

"Got you back."

"You're bad."

"So are you. We're made for each other." They both giggled softly then fell silent for a few moments.

At length, Carrie spoke again. "Mel honey, you okay?"

"Sure. Why do you ask?"

"You've been out of sorts for a few days."

"I know. Sorry."

"Anything I can do to make it better?"

"Lots, but let's save that for a more private setting."

Carrie's mouth made a perfect O and Melanie grinned. "Stop it, you bag. That's it, you just wait until I get you alone."

There was a snort from the next table. Caroline looked over to see two men leering at them. They both had black auras. "Can we watch?"

"Not without eyes." They both turned to see the blazing eyes of Melanie on them. She'd shifted to warrior mode. Even in that little black dress, her energy screamed of danger, and they backed off, turning away to inspect their food.

"Let's get out of here, Mel. Suddenly the place smells bad."

"Must be the vermin." She rose and picked up her handbag. Carrie handed the waitress a wad of cash and walked towards the door. As Melanie joined her, Carrie took her arm and escorted her to the car and settled her inside.

Carrie spoke softly as she guided the car out of the parking lot. "Mel, honey? You saw, didn't you?"

"Both those jerks were carrying demons? Yeah, I saw."

"I was afraid you were going to go all warrior on them."

"Not this time." Melanie sighed. "I just want a quiet evening with you. I want to forget all about demons and get lost in the magic of Caroline Majors."

"Oooh, I like the sound of that, and I know just the place to make it happen."

"Oh, where might that be?"

"My suite at the hotel. I plan to make it your safe place, Melanie my darling. No demons or talk of demons will be allowed there, only happy loving stuff to make the stress slip away."

"Oh gods, that sounds good to me. Take me home, girl."

"With extreme pleasure." Caroline smiled as she stepped on the gas.

"WHAT DO YOU THINK? Brit had it all set up for me."

"I think it's gorgeous." Melanie was awestruck as she gazed around at the luxurious apartment.

"Brit had a studio made on the top floor where I can paint. I'll show you that another time." Carrie stepped close and gently pulled Melanie tight to her. "Right now I really want a kiss." Melanie moaned with delight and melted under the fire of that kiss.

Caroline held the kiss until she felt Melanie fully relax in her arms. "Now, my darling warrior woman, tell me what's going on."

"Huh?"

"Honey, either I've completely lost my touch or you've got something eating away at you."

"I'm sorry, Carrie. I..." She tried to turn away but Caroline held her tighter. "Oh no you don't, my darling girl. You stay right here in my arms and talk to me." She gently kissed Melanie's earlobe then worked her way along her jaw line with soft kisses. Melanie moaned softly. "Talk to me, lover," she whispered softly.

"I can't..."

"Talk to me, Melanie." More soft kisses on Mel's throat started her knees shaking. She melted deeper into Carrie's embrace.

"I can't..."

"Yes you can. Talk to me." The kisses were now working their way along Melanie's bare shoulder.

"I'm scared and embarrassed."

"That's better. Tell Carrie what you're afraid of."

Melanie was in a fog. Usually she was the one taking charge in a liaison, bringing the woman gently under her control. Having this woman take charge was sending her into a fog of sweet delight. "I'm afraid of losing you."

"Never happen."

The kisses had reached her elbow and she was near to falling. Caroline led her to the sofa and pulled her down where she could continue the kisses. She started with Melanie's throat once again. "Whatever makes you think you would lose me?"

"You don't know that much about me..."

"I know all I need to know."

"No you don't."

"Oh yes I do. You taste delightful, I don't need to know any more than that." The kisses were now tracing the path of the spaghetti strap across Melanie's shoulder and down toward her breast.

Melanie moaned with pleasure then suddenly started to cry. Caroline pulled her close and held her as she sobbed. "I'm a murderer, Carrie. I'm a cold blooded killer, and everyone knows it."

"Stop it, sweetheart. That was the war. You were a soldier. You had no choice and you know it."

"No, I mean after that."

"When you hunted demons?"

"Yes." She'd stopped crying and just held on to Carrie as though she was afraid Carrie would run away. "I tried to help those people, but I ended up killing most of them."

"Honey, I'm living proof that you did the right thing. Frankly, I'd rather be dead than completely controlled by one of those things like that man who attacked me was. You're not a murderer, sweetie. You're a hero."

"Most of them died, Carrie. They died screaming in my arms."

"And how many more would they have tortured and killed if you'd let them go?"

"Yeah, I guess."

"You guess what?"

"I guess you're right."

"Of course I'm right. Look into my eyes now and tell me the truth. Did you take any pleasure or satisfaction from the deaths?"

"No. Of course not."

"Then you're not a murderer. You're a hero. You managed to save some of those victims, including me. Melanie, you could have walked away, and I know you wanted to, but you didn't and I'm alive because you didn't. I will love you forever for that. That and the way this tastes right here..." The kisses at the top of Melanie's breast had resumed. Melanie moaned and shuddered both with delight and relief. "Now tell me the rest of it."

Melanie's voice was dreamy as she surrendered to Carrie's exploring lips. She shuddered again as she felt the strap slip off her shoulder allowing Carrie greater access to her breast. The soft kisses continued to explore. "What rest?"

"That was the scary stuff. Now tell me the embarrassing stuff."

"No...I can't...It's too dumb..." Suddenly she gasped as those exploring lips clamped down on her nipple and sucked hard.

Melanie's nipple was suddenly hard as a bullet and Carrie lightly grazed her teeth across it, making it harder still. "Talk to me, Melanie my lover."

"No, not even if you torture me."

Carrie giggled with delight as she slid down the sofa and ran her fingers lightly up Melanie's leg. "Your challenge is accepted."

Melanie groaned with lust and delight. Those soft kisses were on her thighs now and she was completely lost. Melanie had enjoyed a few short relationships with other women, but she had always been the one in control. This was completely new, and she was somehow paralyzed, just lying there, lost in the fog of emotion and aching for Carrie's touch. She groaned again and parted her thighs.

Carrie moved between Melanie's legs, lifting them onto her shoulders as she continued kissing her way up towards the treasure she knew was waiting for her. The sweet rich aroma of aroused woman filled her nostrils, driving her lust. She fought to keep her progress slow, teasing, when all she really wanted was to bury herself in Melanie's warm welcoming body. "Talk to me, sweet girl."

"No," moaned Melanie. "I won't talk. Do your worst, but I'll never talk."

That brought a warm lusty chuckle from under her skirt. "Oh yeah? We'll see about that." Gentle exploring fingers found their way into the waistband of her panties and pulled. The flimsy material slid over her hips and down her legs, leaving her fully exposed to Carrie's touch. "Talk to me."

"No. Never."

Melanie's legs were gently lifted up and parted further as Carrie squirmed up on the sofa. Warm soft kisses reached the silky softness of Melanie's inner thighs and then she felt the warm breath on her soaking pussy. "Talk to me." A groan was the only answer she got.

"All right, Missy, you asked for it." Melanie cried out as lips met warm wet lips. She groaned again as Carrie's tongue slipped into her and began to explore. The exploring tongue found the magic love button and Melanie exploded, her world dissolving into stardust then slowly returning as wave after wave of ecstasy washed over her.

She lay limply on the sofa, her fingers tangled in Carrie's hair. Her lover's mouth was still on her, the exploring tongue slowly, gently, moving inside her. She felt the lust begin to rise up again and she gently squeezed Carrie with her thighs. "All right, you beast, I'll talk, but if you laugh you'll be in trouble."

"I am the very soul of seriousness," purred a lusty voice from between her thighs.

Melanie groaned and spread her legs wider. "I can't get used to sleeping in a bed."

Caroline suddenly popped up with a wide grin. "What? You can't sleep in a bed?"

"Get back to what you were doing," panted Melanie. "If you stop I won't tell you the rest of it."

Dutifully, Carrie began kissing her way down Melanie's abdomen until she was back licking and sucking gently on Melanie's clit. "Tell me," she purred, giving that delicious love button a flick with her tongue.

Melanie gasped and raised her hips, begging for more. "If you sleep in a bed someone can kick in the door and know right where you are. For the past several years I've been sleeping on the floor where no one would expect to find me. It gives me a few more precious seconds of advantage when someone is after me. Hey, you stopped. Get back to what you were doing."

"Yes ma'am." The sweet tongue returned to its explorations and Melanie moaned with pleasure.

"Nana gave me stress about sleeping on the floor. She said now that I have a girlfriend I need to be sleeping in a bed, so I've been trying."

"Aw, poor Mel. That's why you're all messed up. You've not been sleeping. Well, my delicious, you will tonight. Once I'm finished with you we'll grab a few blankets and curl up together on the floor."

"Carrie, you don't have to do that."

"What? You want me to stop?"

Melanie laughed and gently grabbed Carrie's hair again. "That's not what I meant, and you know it. That's it, lady, no more torture games. Get back to business."

"I hear and obey," chuckled Caroline, as she lowered her mouth to Melanie's pleasure core once again. A few moments later Melanie was racked with the most intense orgasm she had ever experienced.

Caroline wriggled her way back up the couch to hold the limp and satiated Melanie in her arms. Mel purred with contentment as she rested her head on Carrie's shoulder. Carrie kissed her hair and cuddled her close. After a moment to recover Melanie was able to feel the tension in her lover. She raised her mouth for a kiss and moaned with pleasure as she tasted herself on Carrie's lips.

"Mel, honey, relax. Just let me hold you and go to sleep."

"Oh no, woman, there will be none of that."

"None of what?" Caroline gasped with delight as Melanie's lips began to kiss their way down her throat while agile fingers moved up under her dress, tracing the shape of her thighs.

"Hiding your beautiful body from me. Now it's my turn to go exploring."

"Mel..."

"I know you're scared, honey, scared I won't like you with those scars. But you're wrong." Her lips had found a nipple, and her fingers were tracing their way up those long delicious thighs.

Suddenly she stood up and whipped the rumpled dress over her head, standing naked in the moonlight. This brought another gasp of delight from Caroline. "Your turn."

"No, Mel..."

"Yes, Carrie. Yes. Come to me now." She took Caroline's hands and gently pulled her to her feet. The frightened woman trembled in fear while Melanie slowly undressed her. She puled Carrie tightly to her and kissed her deeply, her tongue exploring Carrie's mouth, tasting her own juices.

Caroline moaned with pleasure as she returned the kiss. Melanie savored it for a moment then stepped back. She licked her lips as she slowly turned Carrie around in the moonlight, drinking in the sight of this magnificent woman. As Carrie finished her turn she fearfully raised her eyes to Melanie.

Melanie licked her lips as she gazed lustily at the tall figure in the moonlight. "My god, Carrie, you're incredible. I was in love before, but now I'm in lust. Come here to me." With tears in her eyes, Caroline melted into Melanie's arms.

SUNSHINE FILLED THE room and pulled Melanie from a deep restful sleep. She fought it for a moment, the sleep was just too delicious. Memory began to seep into her awareness, and she smiled with delight. Her head was resting on a soft pillow and the sheets beneath her were satin. She had slept in a bed.

Better yet, she had slept like a baby. She felt rested, fully rested. A soft moan of delight sounded beside her, and she turned. She was greeted by Caroline's dazzling smile. "Good morning, my warrior princess."

"Good morning, Lady Caroline. Tell me, what magic is this? I slept in a bed, and I slept well. What did you do to me?"

"Oh honey, if you can't remember that then I must have lost my touch."

"My lover, your touch is just fine," laughed Melanie. She pulled Carrie close and kissed her. "In fact, I can honestly say, I want a lot more of that magic touch."

"Then I guess we should move you in here with me."

"Carrie..."

"Oh all right, I'll slow down, but I won't like it. Do you think that someday..."

Melanie stopped her with a kiss. "I was trying to say I don't get another day off until Saturday."

"Oh gods, Mel, I do love you. I want you here with me. Can you love me..?"

"I can and do love you, silly woman." Melanie kissed her gently. "I was hot for you from the beginning, but when I saw you battling that demon, I was sunk. I love you and want to spend the rest of forever with you. My question is, can you truly want to be with me.

You know what I am now, and you know what I've done, what I'm capable of."

"Yes, I do know what you're capable of and I have to say, after last night I know I can't live without you."

Melanie's rich laughter made Caroline's heart soar. "You're a nut, Caroline Majors, and I love you."

A soft tap on the door interrupted the sweet interlude. Brit's voice came through the door. "Rise and shine, my sisters. Breakfast is ready."

"You cooked breakfast?" Caroline rose and wrapped herself in a soft robe.

"This is a B&B, Carrie, and we do have guests," said Brit. "Hop to it girls, the gang's all here."

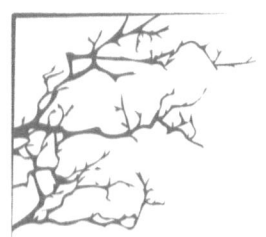

A New Plan

"The gang's all here?" Carrie tossed a tracksuit to Melanie and pulled on her jeans. "What the heck does that mean?"

Melanie grinned as she set aside the tracksuit and pulled on the shorts and top she'd brought with her. Carrie was grinning at her. "Oh yeah, you were expecting to get lucky, eh?"

"Nana made me do it. She's an old hippie; you know, free love and all that?"

"Ah-huh. Right."

Melanie blushed to her roots and then laughed, throwing a pillow at Caroline. "Stop it. You're not allowed to tease me until after I've had coffee."

"Of course not. What the hell was I thinking?"

"I know what I'm thinking. I'm thinking you're a thoroughly bad egg. Now kiss me quick and let's get out there before Brit sends in the troops."

Caroline pulled Melanie close and kissed her softly. As their lips parted Melanie hugged her tightly. Returning the hug, Caroline realized for the first time just how much Melanie needed this relationship too. "Come on, lover, you have to feed me." Smiling, Melanie took her hand and led her out to the dining room.

The whole gang was indeed there. Brit, Luke, Bjorn, and Lizzie were there, as well as Vic and Ellen. Melanie seated Carrie then took the chair beside her. "Forgive me, people, but this looks like a council of war."

Luke looked up from his eggs and nodded his agreement. "It is, Mel. Vic and Ellen have some new stuff for us. Also, Lizzie has been scouting. The news isn't great."

"Okay, this is your team now, Luke. Take over."

Luke chuckled and shook his head. "Forget that, Mel. I'm more than happy to hand this one over to you."

"All right then, we'll wait until after I've had coffee and a chance to finish this delicious breakfast." The conversation shifted to more pleasant things as they enjoyed their meal. Brit and Ellen teased the lovers until both were blushing and making threats of revenge.

Once Melanie set her empty coffee cup down the team shifted into warrior mode. The change was startling. Ellen, Brit, and Caroline exchanged glances then Brit rose to refill everyone's coffee cup.

Melanie was quiet, thoughtful, for a moment then she started the meeting. "Vic, report."

"Downside first, Mel. There was a bit of a ruckus in town last night. Hank called for you, but your phone was turned off. I went instead. We locked up another three people, all possessed. It looks like there are more of those things here now.

"Upside. We let the other folks go home as they seemed to be all right and we needed the cell space. On the tech side, yesterday's tests seem fairly conclusive. The serum I developed, using Ellen's basic formula, does loosen the demon from a human and we have been able to make a clean kill without damaging the human host. I've already forwarded the formula on to the big boss. Ellen's magic tea is also completely effective in preventing a demonic possession.

"Also, the boys in the labs have managed to finally start mass producing the glove weapons. The new ones are on the way and are stronger than what we're using now."

"Luke?"

"We have new weapons. Not just the souped up gloves, but new tranquilizer pistols as well. With these we can drop a victim, loosen the demon, then blast it with the gloves. Instead of days maneuvering a victim someplace where we can jump them, now we can just take them down and exorcise the demon. There's a backup team on the way here right now bringing a full shipment of new weapons and ammo for us."

"Lizzie?"

"I've scouted this whole island, Mel. There's a lot of demon activity here, but most of them seem to be lying low. I have no idea why you don't have a bloodbath going on right now. I still can't locate the hole, either. I'm thinking your idea about that cave must be the right one."

"Bjorn, analysis."

The big man set down his coffee mug and leaned his elbows on the table, carefully inspecting his hands. He was quiet for a long moment before he spoke. "This could go either way. As I see it now, we can hit them hard with new tech. We should be able to clear this island within a matter of days, provided we can locate that damned hole. Best case scenario, we send them packing, never to return again."

"What's the worst case scenario, Bjorn?"

"We drive them out with new tech. They lick their wounds, then come back in force, looking for blood. Either way this goes down, we most likely aren't going to be able to keep the secret of their existence from the public. Too many people on this island can already see them. The word will spread, the general public will panic and start killing each other in fear of demons."

For the first time, Melanie noticed the full coffee mug at her right hand. With a nod of thanks and a shy smile to Brit, she took a long slow sip then set the mug back down, studying it thoughtfully. Finally she looked up and began.

"Opinions? Options?"

Bjorn sighed then sat up straight. "We have no options, Mel. We have to clear this island and plug the hole if we can. Somebody higher up than me will have to figure out what to tell the public. The old *new disease released* ploy will probably be the best bet."

"Anybody else?" No one responded. "All right, here we go. I'll go to work and fill Hank in on what we have on the go. You guys wait until the new gear and back up crew show up. Nana, you're on tea production. Vic, you're on serum. Luke, you connect with the reinforcements. As soon as they arrive I want everybody, including Carrie, Brit, and Hank all packing gloves and tranq guns.

"Bjorn, you, me, and Lizzy will check out the cave as soon as I get into uniform and bring the sheriff up to speed. If that damned hole is in there I don't want anybody going in there alone."

"What about us, Mel?"

"Nana, I want you to take Carrie and Brit home with you. You'll need the help and if this thing explodes in our faces they'll be safer with you."

"There must be something we can do."

"Yes, Brit, there is. You guys work on some sort of bullshit story we can dish out to the locals and the media that will keep this under wraps. We'll have to bring a few folks on side, but we can't risk full scale panic if we can prevent it."

"This is all well and good, my love, but I'm going with you."

"Carrie, you can't. Please let me keep you safe."

Caroline took Melanie's hand and squeezed it gently. "Honey, I will compromise this far. I will wait until I have those weapons, but as soon as I am equipped for the battle I will stand at your side. Those things hurt me, implanted something vile in me, and tried to take control of me. They've left me scarred and broken. Now they have threatened you personally. I want revenge and I want to be watching your back."

Melanie met her steady gaze for a long moment then nodded her head slowly. "All right, I'll ask Hank to deputize you. That way you won't cause a panic for carrying weapons openly on the street.

"Okay folks, let's get to it. The sooner we can put this all to rest the happier I'll be."

"SO NOW I'VE GOT A NEW deputy?" They were relaxed back in the sheriff's office. Melanie had brought Hank fully up to speed. He sat gazing thoughtfully out into space for a moment. "All right, Caroline. This is only temporary until this situation is under control."

"I'm not some giggly female, Sheriff. I can handle myself and I can..."

"Whoa, I wasn't arguing that in any way. I just..."

"Sorry, Hank. Didn't mean to get all defensive on you. I agree, once the situation is under control I will happily go back to my B&B and let you guys do the police stuff. I just want to help Melanie with this, and I want some payback on these damn things."

"Can't say I blame you for that. All right, you're a temporary deputy. You are permanently assigned to Deputy Rivers as partner. That work for you?"

"Oh yeah, it sure does."

Melanie sighed and rolled her eyes. "Woman, I swear, if you make me blush..."

"What? What will you do to me?"

Melanie grinned and licked her lips. "Patience, my darling, patience."

"All right you two, knock it off. There will be no lascivious behavior while in uniform."

"Uniform? I get a uniform?"

"Mel, you go on and join your team. I'll get Caroline set up and then let you know when she's armed and dangerous."

Melanie headed for the door. "Thanks, Hank. See you guys later." With that she was out the door and gone.

Melanie raced away towards the hotel. She flicked on the flashing lights, but not the siren. She was there in short order to find Bjorn and Lizzie waiting for her. They hopped in the car then Melanie drove away. Another short ride and they were parked at the beginning of the footpath Melanie had found when stalking Billy Carter.

"It's up this way, guys. Lizzie, here's the tranq rifle I borrowed from the vet. I doubt we'll find any humans in there, but it won't hurt to be ready. Okay, gloves on, here we go."

Melanie led the way along the path. It was a short walk through a forest of spruce and fir trees, filling the air with sweet scent. On any other day she would have taken it slow to enjoy the experience, but not this day. They stepped around a huge stump to see the mouth of the cave. A soft click was enough to trigger Melanie's instincts, and she crouched slightly as Lizzie fired over her shoulder.

A woman's scream came from the cave, followed by an ill aimed shot that clipped a branch near Melanie's head. The team was already moving through well practiced evasion techniques by the time Melanie's near-instant order was heard "Shit! Take cover!"

They dove behind the stump then separated. Melanie lay prone behind a boulder, peering out towards the cave mouth. "Lizzie?"

"Here and whole."

"Bjorn?"

"Same, same. All good. Looks like this is the place all right. I wonder how many are in there."

"I don't know, but we're not charging in when they're armed with rifles. Lizzie, tranq anyone who tries to get out. If they get past the tranquilizer, then Bjorn and I will take them down. The plan is to hold them here until our reinforcements arrive."

Melanie pulled out her walkie-talkie. "Mel to Sheriff, come in, Sheriff."

"Hank here. What's up, Mel?"

"We've got somebody cornered in the cave. I think there's more than one. One of them took a shot at us and I can hear voices."

Caroline surged towards the radio, but Hank put out a hand to stop her. "These folks are pros, Carrie. Relax." He turned back to the radio. "What's the plan, Mel? What do you need?"

"Contact Luke and bring him up to speed. We'll keep them bottled up until everybody gets here. Oh, bring a canister or two of tear gas with you just in case. Mel out."

As Melanie put her radio back on her belt she heard another shot from the tranquilizer rifle. There was another howl from the cave then a hail of gunfire. "Touchy bunch of buggers, aren't they?" grinned Lizzy.

Melanie chuckled at that. "How many more loads have you got, Lizzie?"

"There were six in the car and one up the pipe, so I've got five left. With any luck I will be able to get them all before Luke gets here."

"Trying to show up the new boss?"

"Sadly, no. Just trying to impress a guy." Melanie chuckled and Bjorn laughed. "What's so damn funny, Bjorn?"

"Impress the guy? Girl, he drools all over the place whenever you walk by."

"Yeah? Well he never gives a hint or says anything."

"Maybe you should just tranq him and drag him off somewhere," grinned Bjorn.

"Hey, do you think that would work?"

Before anything else could be said Melanie's radio came alive. "Sheriff to Deputy Rivers."

"Mel here."

"Just heard from Luke. Your people are on the water. The boat will land in fifteen minutes. Caroline and I will meet them then lead everybody to your position. Over."

"Roger that, Hank. We'll hold. Melanie, out. That's it, guys. The reinforcements will be here in about a half hour. We just have to keep them pinned down."

Lizzy grinned. "No problem."

"Don't get too cocky."

"Bjorn?"

"Look, if we're careful and can keep them bottled up there's a chance we could clear this up without any casualties. However, if there's a lot of them and they rush us, it could get ugly. Mel?"

"That had crossed my mind, Bjorn, old buddy. So here's the deal. If they rush us we tranq as many as possible and try to take the rest of them the hard way. No shooting if we can avoid it. Shooting them just lets the demon escape and kills the victim."

"And if they come out shooting?"

"Knee caps and shoulders, no center mass shots."

Lizzie was sighting carefully along the rifle barrel, her steely gaze fixed on the cave entrance. "Keep the demon locked to the victim?"

"At all costs. That's our bottom line, guys. The demons must not be allowed to escape."

Two voices responded in unison. "Understood."

All seemed quiet as the time ticked down. The reinforcements were expected any minute when the screaming started. Sudden screams of pain and maniacal rage erupted from the cave. It took Melanie's barked orders to restrain Lizzie and Bjorn from charging into the madness.

"Stand fast. Stand fast, that's an order. Lizzie, stay sharp and keep that rifle trained on the entrance. Bjorn. Glove up and be ready."

Melanie was wearing her glove as she leaped to her feet and charged the cave mouth in a zig-zag pattern.

A shot rang out as she ran, but it missed completely. Melanie plastered herself against the stone beside the cave entrance. A man, bleeding profusely ran from the cave, but Lizzie brought him down with the tranquilizer gun. The woman who chased him was flailing wildly with a huge knife and Lizzie's shot was deflected. The woman screamed again as Melanie hit her with the light beam from the glove. She vanished back into the cave.

The reinforcements made a timely arrival and Caroline raced to Melanie's side. "Carrie, stay back, for Christ's sake." Two more shots came from inside the cavern.

"You're here, I'm here. What's our next move? How do we get at them?"

"Carrie."

" Give it up, Mel. I love you, and I'm not going anywhere. What's our next move?"

Melanie gazed into Caroline's eyes for a long moment. "Follow my lead and stay sharp." Carrie grinned and nodded. "Luke!"

"Here, Mel."

"Knockout gas?"

"Got it."

"Launch one in." A moment later a small canister hurtled past them and into the cave, exploding inside. There was coughing, more frantic screams, two more shots from a rifle, then everything went quiet. Carrie started to move, but Melanie put out an arm to stop her. "Give it a few more minutes to let the gas dissipate." She nodded and settled back against the stone.

Several minutes later Luke called out. "Should be clear, Mel. Tossing up a mask just in case." A breathing mask floated high into the air and Melanie caught it as it fell back to Earth, another followed for Carrie.

Melanie held her mask ready, but didn't put it on. "Let's go, lover. I have the glove ready, you keep your tranq pistol ready. Shoot anything that moves. You do know how to shoot don't you?"

"Just watch me."

"We're going in," called Melanie. She led the way inside, her glove at the ready. She didn't need the flashlight, there was a sickly glow emanating from the walls. It was enough to see by.

Melanie fought to keep her stomach down as she took in the scene of carnage in the cave. Something leaped out at her but Carrie's gun popped and the knife wielding woman stopped in her tracks, staring down at the dart in her breast. The hideous creature clinging to her back snarled and writhed in an attempt to get at Melanie, but Mel hit it with the light from the glove.

A croaking voice, filled with pain and rage escaped the woman's lips as she melted towards the floor. "You again. I will have you yet. Tell me where you got that glove?"

"Hey, asshole, mine's even better," snarled Caroline as she turned the light from her glove on the creature, causing it to howl in pain. "Remember me? No? Well I remember you. It's payback time, dipshit."

At that point the others appeared and turned the light of their gloves on it as well. Howling in frustrated rage and pain the creature managed to tear itself from the unconscious woman. It leaped through a glowing circle on the roof of the cave. The glow from the walls died and the circle on the ceiling faded to a dull pulse of sickly light.

A generator fired up outside and the cave was suddenly full of light. Five weapons swung around to see three of the new team helping a fourth stabilize a large floodlight as Hank crept in behind it. The sheriff swallowed hard and fought to keep his breakfast down. The floor was littered with brutally murdered people. He knew them all. The pain and horror of their deaths was clear to read on their unmoving faces.

"I've got a pulse," said Carrie as she stood back from the last woman to fall. "She's going to make it."

Melanie nodded. "Hank, call the medics. I hope they have strong stomachs. All right, people, let's pull back until the medics can clean this place up. We've found the hole; now we just have to figure out how to close it, permanently."

"I can help with that," said a small man, as he stepped forward. "My team found one last month and managed to figure out how to plug it."

"It's all yours. We'll all stand back and watch. We need to learn how to do this for ourselves." Melanie sighed and sank to a cross legged position on the ground. Carrie sat beside her.

"Hey sweetie, you okay?"

"I'm fine, Carrie. I have to say, you're a lot tougher than I expected. Now I know how you survived. Thanks for having my back."

"So, no more trying to keep Carrie out of the action?"

"Nope. All you need now is some martial arts."

"Would a black belt in Brazilian Jiu-Jitsu count?"

"Carrie?"

"I told you I can handle myself. I'll admit I got caught off guard when I was attacked in the hotel. He was a big guy and he caught me with a sucker punch. It won't happen again."

"Oh my god, you are so sexy when you get all fierce." Carrie blushed and looked away, slapping Melanie lightly on the shoulder. Hank was returning with the medics.

"I've warned the boys what to expect," he said, as he approached Melanie and slowly sank down beside her and Carrie. "The coroner is on the way. Janet wake up yet?"

"Nope. Once the boys have her cleaned up a bit we'll put her in the back of the cruiser."

"Sounds good, Mel. What did I miss?"

"We've found the hole from that world to this one. Our back up team has done this before so they're going to close it. I want us all to watch so we know what to do next time, if there is a next time."

"I sure as hell hope there isn't. Does this mean we're clear now?"

"Soon. We'll comb the island and free everyone we find with a demon attached. We've got the means now to do this hard and fast. Once we've got the island clear it will be up to us to make sure it stays that way."

"That's for sure. How did your new partner work out?"

"Hank, Carrie's got what it takes and more. I just wish she had been with me the past six years. She's a lot tougher than she looks."

"That's good to know. Congratulations, Deputy Majors. I don't suppose you two would consider making this a full time job?"

"What's going on, Hank?"

"The next election is October, two months away. Nobody has expressed any interest. The mayor wants me to sign on for another four years. I'll need a couple of tough deputies."

Caroline laughed and shook her head. "Oh no, I plan to run my B&B and paint."

"Well, I did promise Hank I'd stay if he did. I'm in, Hank."

Carrie sighed and leaned against Melanie's shoulder. "Can I be auxiliary? You know, on call, but not active otherwise."

Hank grinned. "I don't know, Mel. What do you think?"

"I think that is a fine compromise, Hank. Trust me, Carrie can handle herself in a situation."

"Then it's a deal. Look, they're bringing Janet out now." Hank heaved himself to his feet. "Is she awake now, fellas?"

"Barely, but she's not hurt bad. You can take her in if you have to."

"Oh yes, I do have to. Help me get her into the back of the cruiser. Melanie, you and Carrie stay here and finish up. You can get everybody's statements and bring them in to me in the morning."

Luke joined them as Janet Carter was led away. "Statements? We're giving statements now?"

"Nope."

"Thought not. Toss you for who has to lean on him."

"It's okay, Luke. I got this. I'll fill Hank in tomorrow. We still have to clean up here once the paramedics are finished. You talked to them already?"

"Yeah. They figured it would be the same drill as last time at Carrie's hotel. So, what's your best guess at what went down here?"

"Ask Bjorn. I'll bet he has it all figured out."

"I did. I just want to get your perspective on it."

"Okay. I think they were planning something big here on the island. We stumbled on them before they could get it going. Once they realized we had them cornered they started killing the humans so they could escape. I expect Janet was supposed to commit suicide after she finished the others. What did Bjorn say?"

"Same thing."

"So now we have something new in our bag of tricks. Now we know they come here through portals, holes. Better yet, we know what those portals look like and apparently we know how to plug the holes."

"Yeah, the big trick from now on will be to find the holes. If they drill 'em from the other side they'll be totally random, a bitch to find. On the other hand, maybe there's some kind of a pattern. That's for the math guys to figure out."

"Amen to that."

"So, can't talk you into coming back?"

"Nope. I've got a girl, a home, and a good job. I'm staying put."

"Mel, I honestly hope it works out for you. I do."

"But?"

"If Bjorn is right, this could break out in a full scale war."

"Zombie Apocalypse?"

"Or something like it."

"That would really suck," sighed Carrie. "If that happens, Mel..."

"We will re-evaluate the situation together, if and only if, that comes to pass. Agreed?"

"Agreed, my love."

"All right, ladies. I gave it a shot so I can tell the big boss in all good conscience. Looks like we're up again."

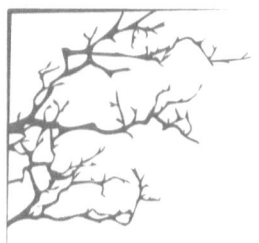

Betrayed

D arkness grows
       In the garden
Of death

"Just what do you write in that book of yours?" Melanie tossed the book to Carrie then sat in the shade of a tall tree.

Caroline sat beside her and flipped the book open. She read a few poems, but stopped at the places that referred to her. At length she passed it back. "Some of those are quite beautiful."

"And some are dark and scary?"

"Yes they are. They're more than just poems, aren't they Mel?"

"They are. They're a code that shows where I am in my head with any situation. After my first real up close fire fight I went to the military shrink. The woman was actually very good. She'd seen combat herself and she recommended this to help me cope. To understand what's going on inside.

"Once I started hunting demons the boss wanted me to use this to secretly document the events. Look here.

"Bliss dissolves
In waves of
Darkness."

"That tells them I was feeling good, but concerned about a battle."

"Waves of darkness. That means battle?"

"That's right. If I'd just said Darkness, it would mean I was feeling depressed, usually after a battle."

"Okay, let me see if I can decode some of this." Carrie was smiling now, and Melanie was lost in that smile. The world of despair and murder faded into the background, hidden behind the light of her lover's delight. "Hmm, let me see.

"Beauty recovered
Breaths new life,
Welcome changes."

"Hmm, this is new. You must have written it last night after I fell asleep. Aw, Mel, you old softie. You enjoyed yourself, didn't you?"

"Beyond all measure, my darling. You took me to a new and brighter world. As long as I know I can go back there with you I can face anything."

"You're so sweet. I want to find where we first met." She hungrily leafed through the book. "Ah, here we are.

"Beauty arrived
Passionate, bewitching,
Misguided"

"Bewitching? So I did make an impression after all?"

"Yes you did." Melanie smiled lovingly at Caroline who bent forward to kiss her cheek.

"Misguided? No, girl, unguided would be a better word. Now let's see about... here's where I got attacked and you saved me. Oh, Brit sure made an impression. Aw, you sweet thing, you were worried about me. Here's where you made your choice between us. Wow, that decision was tough on you."

"Yeah, I'll admit it. It was. Please don't be angry, Carrie. You are both such amazing women."

Carrie giggled. "Gods you suck up nice. Now let's see...here's where..."

Her voice trailed off, but Melanie was suddenly on full alert. The leader of the back up team had walked aside and was speaking into his phone in hushed tones, his eyes darting from Melanie to Luke and back again.

Caroline had sensed Melanie's energy shift. She stopped reading and looked up. Following the direction of Melanie's gaze she watched as the man finished his conversation and put his phone away. He rejoined the other, but wasn't making eye contact with anyone. "Oh crap. Something just went south in a hurry."

Melanie sighed and turned away from the man to closely study the tree she was sitting under. "Yeah, it did. How could you tell?"

"I was in real estate for years, remember? I can tell when a deal falls apart at the seams. Any idea what's going on?"

"By the looks of his face I'd say he was reporting in to the boss and was ordered to double cross us somehow. Looks like the paramedics are about finished. We should know how the government is going to screw us over any minute now."

The paramedics exited the cavern and took a deep breath of fresh air. "This is the last of it. The place is all yours, Deputy Rivers."

"Thanks, guys." Melanie retrieved her book as the paramedics carried the last of the human remains away in a bag atop a stretcher.

"Eyes averted

Intuition screams

Betrayal."

She dropped the book back into her pocket then rose to her feet. "All right, guys, let's get that hole plugged then head for the coffee shop."

"Ah, there's a bit of a problem there," said the man who'd been on the phone. "We're not closing the hole just yet."

"Oh?" Melanie's voice was low and dangerous. The man actually flinched and took a step back.

"Yes, this is now my case. I've been ordered to hold until some of the scientists and top brass can arrive to observe the closing of the gateway. This is the first big one we've found, and they want to see first hand how well the system works."

"I thought you said you've done this before." Melanie had taken another step forward and he involuntarily stepped back again. It was obvious he knew her reputation.

"I have," he replied, "in the simulator. And one really small one." He still wasn't making eye contact.

"In the simulator?" She took another step, but Luke suddenly stepped between them.

"As senior agent here, I'm still officially in command and will remain so until ordered to step down by my own commander. Bjorn, analysis."

Bjorn's deep voice sounded troubled. "This is going sour. We've stung the enemy badly and they're in full retreat for the moment. However, there are still far too many of them among us. Worse yet, we have no idea if they're in contact with those we recently defeated.

"The determination in the voice that threatened Melanie told me they will not give up and leave us alone. The stupidity of our superiors will give the enemy time to regroup and plan ahead. If we act now we could block them and strengthen our position. If we wait we could face a renewed attack.

"The evidence we found in the cave says they were planning something big, and soon. Waiting could allow that to happen."

"Suggestions?"

"Here's my badge. I suggest you accept my resignation. I'm looking for employment on the local police force."

"Are you crazy?"

"No, Luke, I'm not. I'm a survivor; you know that. I can see this evolving into a full scale war, and I believe staying here to fight beside Melanie is my best chance for survival in the long term."

Lizzie stepped up beside Bjorn. "I'm sorry, Luke, but I'm with Bjorn this time. I..."

"Knock it off, both of you. Keep your badges for now. If this fucks up like you think it will I'll stay here with you. For now, let's just see if we can contain the situation. All right?" Both Lizzie and Bjorn nodded and stepped away.

Luke turned back to face the other man. "All right, mister. Just exactly are your orders?"

"I'm to assume command of the scene and contain the area. We go into lock down until the brass arrives."

"Exactly what brass?"

"General Paxton, two aides, and three scientists. I'm to book six more rooms in the local hotel and wait."

"What's their ETA?"

"Three days."

Luke thew out an arm to hold Melanie back. "All right, buddy, here's the deal. You're a five man team, you get the night shift. My team gets the days. We keep this cave sealed up, no humans go in, and no demons come out. Clear?"

"Yes, sir." The man was beaten and clearly relieved to see a solution that didn't include getting killed by Melanie Rivers.

Luke turned to Melanie. "That's the best I've got, Mel. If you've got something better I'm wide open to suggestions."

"I have an option." All eyes turned to Carrie. "This is a crime scene. Several local people were murdered by other local people. Therefore, this is local jurisdiction. You make a fuss and we go public. Try telling the media and the general public that it was demons from hell and that's why you won't let the police do their jobs.

"Our crime scene. We confiscate all your equipment and close the damned hole ourselves."

"Do you actually think you could use this equipment, Deputy?"

Once again the man stepped back from an angry woman. "Perhaps not, but I bet you'd do it for me if I offered to shoot your balls off, smart ass."

"I like that," grinned Melanie. "Sadly, honey, Luke has the best solution. It's bad enough we have to fight these demons, but if our own government turns against us we're screwed. They'll march in, lock everybody up, then the soldiers guarding us will be taken over by demons they don't even know exist. For now, we should play along.

"Listen, mister, I'll personally be making random checks through the night. If I find any of you people asleep on the job, they don't wake up." She turned on her heel and stalked away towards the police cruiser. Carrie was right by her side. "Seal it up, Luke."

They reached the car and Melanie tossed the keys to Carrie. She sighed deeply and took out her small book.

"STUPIDITY REIGNS SUPREME
Evil wins
Darkness falls.
"You can say that again." Carrie had glanced over her shoulder as Melanie wrote. "Where to?"
"Sheriff's office. We have to bring Hank up to speed."

HANK DOYLE TOOK A LONG sip of cold coffee. His face betrayed none of the anger coursing through his body right at that moment. "Are you telling me we can't close the gates of hell until some asshat with more brass medals than brains shows up to hog the glory?"

"That sums it up nicely," grinned Carrie.

"Well now, ain't that just dandy. Mel, this demon thing is your case. What do you suggest we do?"

"We have to play along, Hank. You know that. If we start fighting the government then we're screwed. However, we do have some advantages and assets."

"I'd love to hear them."

"First, we have Nana. She has already brought us a long way in the battle with the demons. She's working on more magic as we speak. We also have the advantage of Luke's team. If it all goes down ugly, I know they'll side with us. I'm hoping that doesn't happen; we need their access to weapons and materials.

"We can add to that some of the local folk that we've freed from the demons. It's been enough time now for all their memories to have returned. Some of them might want some payback. We could secretly form them into a militia and train them to fight the demons.

"Vic tells me he's figured out the magic of the gloves. It's not just the wavelength of the light, but the glove also emits a high frequency sound that we can't hear. It's the two factors combined that rip the demons apart. He's working on a way to improve the weapon. If Vic can improve our weapons we stand a much better chance when it goes down ugly."

"So you don't think we've beaten them?"

"No, I don't. We stopped whatever big mojo they were cooking up in the cave, but that's all. There's still a number of them on the island and, thanks to the government, more could arrive at any moment. It'll take three days for those idiots to get here. If we'd just closed the hole we could have the whole island clear in that time."

"So what do you want to do?"

"Everybody will be taken up with guarding that cave, leaving us on our own. I want to commandeer Vic and go hunting. We can spend those three days clearing as many of those things out as possible. That's all I've got, Hank."

"It works for me, Mel. Now, from my end. While you two were out at the cave site I had a call from the feds. We've been ordered to co-operate completely with them."

"Like we weren't already," growled Melanie. Carrie reached out to pat her hand gently.

Hank heaved himself from his chair. "All right, Mel. You and Carrie go pay a visit to Ellen, then go home. It's been a long day."

As Melanie and Caroline headed for the door, Emily spoke softly. "Mel, about that militia you spoke of. Count me in."

"Em?"

"Those damn things have destroyed much of my family, Mel. I can see them, and I can shoot. If you need me..."

"I won't hesitate, Em. I promise." They left and headed for her grandmother's house at the edge of town.

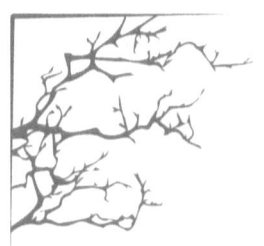

Real Magic

Caroline was driving as they headed for Ellen's sanctuary. "Everybody seems to have already moved you in with me. Isn't that sweet?"

"What?"

"Hank told us to visit Ellen then to go home. He's..."

"Assumed that we're already living together. No, love, that didn't slip by me."

"So?"

"So...what?"

"Are you going to move in with me? We're certainly compatible sexually."

"Carrie!"

"Gods you're delicious when you blush."

"Stop laughing at me, woman." Melanie was blushing and grinning. "Was I being that much of a sad sack?"

"You were carrying the load all by yourself, Mel. We're a team now. Let me help."

"All right. Sorry. Yeah I guess I was carrying it all. So what are we going to do about this habit of mine?"

"Move you in with me."

"And how is that supposed to change things?"

"I love you and want you with me. You say you love and want me too; therefore you should move in with me so the tension of the separation is removed. I also know you're very protective of me. It will be easier to keep an eye on me if we're living together. And..."

137

Melanie laughed and squeezed Caroline's arm. "Okay, okay, I get it. Thanks for cheering me up."

"All my pleasure, love. Now, here we are. Let's go see what Ellen and Vic have brewed up."

Ellen was waiting for them at the door. She looked past them for a moment as they entered the house. "Vic brought you up to speed, I see."

Ellen turned and led them to the kitchen. "You know, Mel, it's a sad thing, but in all my years I have just watched the government get dumber, not smarter."

"Can't argue that," sighed Carrie, as she and Melanie sank into chairs at the table.

Tea was soon forthcoming. As Ellen poured, Vic came in through the back door, a wide grin on his face. Carrie saw as he winked at Melanie and the girl visibly relaxed. She took a sip of her tea and smiled. At last, something good was going to come out of the day.

Ellen shook her finger at Vic, then poured a cup of tea for him. "Sit. Now, mister, you've been hiding in my workshop for days. What have you got up your sleeve?"

"Why, Ellen, I have no idea what you mean." Vic sat and sipped his tea. "All right, I'll talk. After Bjorn called and explained that display of pure lunacy at the cave today, I knew I had to finish what I was working on. Mel, you're going to love this. That guy actually brought me the specs for the new gloves."

"And you've already figured out how to improve them."

"Of course. Once I knew exactly what the gloves were doing I remembered the original research that brought them into being. It was an easy matter to improve things from there.

"Sorry, Ellen, I ruined your flashlight."

"So I see. So, what did you build, Obi-Wan? A light sabre?"

"Pretty darn close. The demons are susceptible to both infrared light and high frequency sound. The glove was developed to be easy to carry and focus on a single demon at a time. Up until now they were so scattered we had to hunt them down and then it was only one at a time. The glove was perfect. It allowed the use of both hands while using the weapon and it is easy to disguise.

"However, we seem to have the bastards on this island in large numbers. This little gadget will broadcast to a whole warehouse full of them at once. I've used some of our technology and some of Ellen's defense system."

He tossed the light to Melanie who turned it over and over in her hands, getting the feel of it, inspecting it closely. "Are the batteries included?"

Vic's grin widened. "Solar powered. Just leave it in the sun for an hour or two once a week. I had to take the batteries out 'cause I needed the room inside for secret science stuff."

Melanie passed the object to Caroline who fitted it into her palm and smiled. "What activates it?"

"Just like a flashlight," replied Vic. He leaned forward and touched the slide switch. "Just push this forward and watch the fur fly."

"Awesome," replied Carrie. She rose and headed for the door.

Perplexed, the others followed her out. Caroline Marched across the field towards the boarded up house next door. Reaching the unused driveway, Carrie pointed the weapon at the house and turned it on. A moment later there was a scream from inside. She held the light on and a teenage boy came stumbling out of the house, swatting frantically at his back.

It was easy to see why. Attached to him was a large demon. Its form writhed and fought desperately to dislodge itself from the boy who was suddenly fully aware of it and fighting for his life. Caroline was relentless as she held the weapon on the struggling pair until the demon was completely dissolved. The boy lay face down in the long grass, sobbing.

Caroline tossed the weapon back to Melanie and grinned at Vic. "Works great, Vic. We'll take a few dozen. When can we expect delivery?"

"As soon as the hardware store opens tomorrow I'll get started. Are we arming the locals?"

"Oh yeah," said Melanie. "We sure as hell are."

"Then I guess I should turn in my badge tonight."

"Vic?"

"I'm fifty-five years old, Mel. I could have retired three years ago. I'm fed up with all the government bullshit. I have no family and damned few friends. I'll make my stand with them."

"You sure you're not just trying to get round Nana?" Vic blushed to his roots and Ellen laughed. "Oh my god, you already did. You bastard, you slept with my grandmother."

"Oh for god's sake, Melanie," said Ellen. "We didn't sleep together. But we did have sex. I'm old, Mel, not dead. Besides, I'm only sixty-two. I've got a few good years left in me."

"Nana, you're a thoroughly bad woman. Did you seduce my young colleague?"

"So what if I did? I'm getting on. Gotta grab the brass ring while I still can." None of this conversation was helping Vic's embarrassment. "Better suck it up and get used to it, sweetie. Mel can be relentless when she gets going."

At that point the boy on the ground stopped sobbing and pushed himself up to a sitting position. "What the hell was that thing on my back?"

Ellen looked at him and sighed. "You wouldn't believe me if I told you."

"Try me."

"Okay, it was a demon."

"No shit. What was that she used to kill it?"

"Special weapon, kid. Now that you've been bitten, you will always be able to see those things. You see one, you come straight to me or the sheriff."

"I swear it."

"What's your name?" asked Vic.

"Edgar. Everybody calls me Egg."

"Well, Egg. How would you like to have one of these?"

"The weapon? Hell yeah."

"All right then, meet me at the hardware store tomorrow when it opens. I have to build a bunch of these, and I'll need help. What do you say? You up for it?"

"Absolutely. Can I ask something?"

"Sure. What's on your mind?"

"What did it do to me? I mean how did I get here? What was I doing?"

"That's what they do, they take you over. You've probably had that thing on you for days. As to what you were doing here, I have no idea. However, the memory will come back to you by tomorrow. You can tell me all about it while we work. You go on home now, and don't tell a single soul about any of this, okay?"

"Deal." He surged to his feet and left at a run.

Melanie raised an eyebrow at Vic. "A helper? Since when do you allow anyone near your work space?"

"Teenagers know more about electronics that the lot of us rolled together," grinned Vic. "Besides, I'm about to retire."

"You need a sorcerer's apprentice."

"Exactly. That kid has a world of fight in him, and even as crazy as it sounded, he was willing to accept the explanation of what happened. He's motivated to learn and willing to fight, the rest I can teach him. If you're building a militia you'll need tech guys and weapons builders."

"So, Bjorn thinks this is going to go down ugly?"

"He does. Mel, when it hits, the team is with you. To hell with the consequences."

"Thanks, Vic. I still have hopes of heading it off. I hope we can, but we'll start building the militia just in case."

They started walking back to Ellen's house. Suddenly, Vic got a huge grin on his face. "Mel, you need any help moving out?"

"What? What the hell makes you think I'm moving out?"

"Come on, admit it, you're moving in with Carrie."

"So, why are you in such a hurry to move me in with Carrie? I think you're just trying to get my grandmother alone."

"Busted," laughed Vic.

"You're awful, you know that. You're as bad as she is. You two are made for each other."

"So, was that a yes? You need help moving?"

"I arrived on a motorcycle, Vic. How much do you think I was carrying? I can handle it."

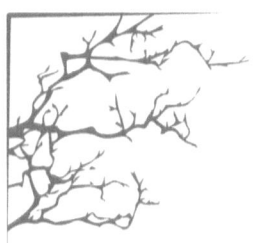

Powder Keg

Caroline awakened with a start. It was still dark. She was alone in the bed and she could hear the water running in the shower. It made her bladder want to join in. Softly she padded to the bathroom and sat on the throne. The shower was definitely running, but she couldn't see Melanie's silhouette. She rose and approached. "Mel?"

There was no response, but she could now hear sobbing over the sound of the falling water. She opened the stall door and peered inside. At first she saw nothing, then spotted Melanie crumpled on the floor, wedged tightly in the corner, her face buried in her arms and shoulders shaking with the power of the sobs. "Mel? Oh my god, Mel."

Caroline sank swiftly to her knees and swept the distraught woman into her arms. "I've got you, Mel. I've got you. Hush now, Carrie's got you." She rocked Melanie in her arms until the storm of emotion faded and the girl lay still in her arms.

"You're nightie is all wet," sniffed Melanie, as she clung to Carrie.

"I know. Doesn't matter."

"What are you doing here?"

"Holding you as long as you need me to."

"I'm okay."

"Fibber."

"Yes I am, but the worst is over and the water's getting cold. We can get out now."

"Okay. I'll towel you off then you crawl back in bed while I dry myself off." Melanie just nodded then allowed Caroline to pull her to her feet. She stood quietly as Carrie shut off the water and reached for a towel. She dried Melanie off then shooed her towards the bed. By the time she returned to the bed, Melanie was already dressed.

"Hold your horses. Where are you going? Melanie, are you leaving me?" The pain and fear were clear in her voice and that broke Melanie. She pulled Caroline tightly to her and began to sob into her shoulder. "No, never. You will never be rid of me, beautiful woman. Not ever."

"Hush now, Carrie's got you, Mel. Honey, where were you going?"

"To check on those morons guarding the cave. That's all. I'll come right back. I promise."

"You'll wait right here while I get dressed. I'm coming with you." Melanie waited while Caroline pulled on a sweat suit and stepped into a pair of running shoes. She swept up her new weapons and strapped them on. With a nod she stepped through the door.

They slipped through the kitchen and dining room, but met Luke returning as they reached the reception area. "Relax, girls. I was just at the cave and they're all wide awake. Go back to bed and get some rest."

As Luke headed for the stairs Caroline took Melanie's hand and led her back to the suite. She removed her weapons and laid them beside Melanie's then tugged Mel back to the bedroom. They stripped off and crawled back in. Caroline cuddled Melanie into her arms and kissed her gently. "Go back to sleep, my love. I'll hold you close while you rest."

"Aren't you going to give me a hard time about earlier?"

"Nope. Mel, you make tough decisions that affect lives. You're cool and logical when you do, but I know it weighs on you. I'd be worried if you didn't have some way to release it."

Melanie started to sob again. "Gods, Carrie, six more people are dead, and I could have saved them. If we had charged their position we could have saved some or all of them, but I held back. Now they're dead and it's my fault. I killed them."

"No you didn't, sweetie. You didn't kill anyone. You contained the situation and protected your people from an unknown danger. Those people had guns and were shooting at you. You had no idea how many there were or how many guns you faced. If you'd charged in you could have gotten your team killed. You might have died as well, and those people would still have been murdered.

"You're not a murderer, Melanie; you're a warrior. A reluctant warrior, but a warrior none the less."

"I see their faces, Carrie. All of them, and I hear their screams. All I ever wanted to do was help them, save them from the demons, but so many..."

"Yes, there were deaths, Mel honey, but there are lives saved as well. Look at me. Without you I'd be dead, locked up in an institution, or worse. You saved me. You saved me from the possessed killer, from the demon implanted in me, and from my own fears.

"Now, Melanie my darling, tell me about your grieving process."

"My what?"

"Grieving process. That's what this is, isn't it? Tell me how it works so I can help you."

"You're so amazing."

"Thank you, but you're stalling, sweet woman."

"Okay. It hits me hard when it comes. Usually I can hold it off until the mission is completed, but not always. Mostly what I do is cry my eyes out in the shower until I have nothing left inside at all. Until I'm completely empty. Then I put on that little black dress and go out on the town looking for someone to make me feel something, anything at all."

"So that explains it. Vic had this sick stricken look on his face when I picked you up for our date. He knows and he saw the dress, so he thought you'd cracked before the mission was over."

"Yeah, Vic tends to worry about me a lot. I tried to convince him I had a hot date and that was my only dress. He didn't buy it, not completely."

"All right, I've got it, but the next time you wake me up. There will be no hiding from me, sweetie. We'll go into that damned shower together and I'll hold you until the storm passes. Then I'll bring you back to this bed and make doubly certain you feel something before I let you sleep again. Okay?"

"Yes, Ma'am. Carrie, I'm so sorry to come all unglued on you like this. If you don't want to hook yourself to a crazy person, I'll understand." Melanie tried to gently withdraw from Caroline's arms, but that wasn't happening.

"Oh no, you're not getting away from me now, woman. You said you love me, so that means I get to keep you. Crazy person? Girl, you ain't seen nothin' yet. Wait until I crack, then you'll see a whole new level of crazy." Caroline smiled as she felt the tiny giggle escape Melanie's control. "Honey, we're a team now, together against the world. I will never willingly part with you."

Melanie finally relaxed. Caroline felt it when it happened. Melanie just sighed and melted against her, snuggling down onto her shoulder and lightly kissing the jagged scar there. "You won't have to, Carrie my love. I will stay in your arms forever." She sighed again and her breathing deepened. Carrie smiled with delight as Melanie allowed sleep to claim her and erase the fatigue from her heart.

Caroline awakened alone in the bed once again. This time the morning sun was flooding the room with hope and a promise of wonder. She smiled and arose. Melanie's little book was lying by the bedside. She opened it to find a new entry.

Beauty shines
Loving light
Into dark places

Carrie smiled and replaced the book. Sweeping on a light robe she headed for the kitchen where she could hear laughter. She found Brit and Melanie making breakfast together. She had a momentary flash of jealousy, then Melanie spotted her and smiled. The loving light in that gaze dispelled all fears and brought a blush of delight to her cheeks. "So, what mischief are you two up to?"

"Come out to the table and we'll confess all," laughed Brit. She, Melanie, and Caroline gathered up the laden plates and headed to the dining room. Once everyone was served Brit spoke again.

"Well, guys, it seems I made a big boo-boo yesterday. I booked our five empty rooms for the enemy, aka the fools that want a show in the cave. The general and his people will arrive late tomorrow. Had I known who they were, and what they'd done, I would never have done it. I was going to cancel the bookings, but Mel talked me out of it."

"Talked you out of it?" asked Carrie. "Why?"

"We've got a better plan. Tell them, Brit."

"I works like this, guys," smiled Brit. "They messed with us; they have to pay a price for that. We can't do anything about what they did, but we can sting 'em, as Ellen would say. Once they're here and settled into their rooms, Mel is going to start a poker game then ask me to take her seat at the table."

"So the plan is to take them financially?" asked Luke.

"Yep," replied Brit, going cold. "I plan to bankrupt the lot of them if I can."

"Whoa," said Bjorn as she sat back in his chair. "Remind me never to piss you off. So, can I sit in for a few hands?"

"Sure you want to, big fella?"

"Go easy on me, Brit," he sighed. "It's just that it'll look better if one of us sits in."

"I'll sit in for a few hands too," grinned Luke. "Man, this is just too good. So, me, Lizzie, and Bjorn will be on watch today, what are you guys going to be doing?"

Melanie thought for a moment then spoke. "First we'll check in with Hank then we'll go on the hunt. We'll take out as many demons as we can find hiding around the island. Vic has developed a new and more powerful weapon. It can broadcast the signal, hitting several demons at one time. He's going to be working on mass producing them today."

Lizzie sighed and shook her head. "There's dozens of them now, Mel. I took a fast cruise earlier. I can feel the damned things everywhere. We need Vic to work fast."

"Bjorn?"

"Mel, this is all going to go to hell in a hand basket, and soon. My guess is as soon as we make a move on that portal they'll come at us. The general and his crew will be caught right in the middle of it. Brit, after the poker game, would you consider taking in a tournament on the mainland for a few days?"

"No bloody way, big fella. However, once I have this place tidied up I will go visit Ellen and scrounge as much as I can to make this place a secure haven like her house. The demons won't go near it, and I want to make this hotel the same way. Will that work for you?"

Bjorn met her eyes for a long moment then slowly nodded. "Damn fine idea. I'll sleep better at night."

Melanie looked from Brit to Bjorn then back to Brit. Brit had her poker face on, but she could read Bjorn pretty well. "Bjorn old buddy, is there anything you want to tell me?"

"No, Melanie, there isn't. Not a damn thing."

"At least not yet," said Lizzie, causing him to blush deeply.

"Brit?"

"Yes, Mel?"

"Thanks for cooking breakfast." A bright smile spread over Brit's face as Melanie winked at her. Bjorn was still studying his fingers. "All right, folks, go relieve those guys at the cave. They still have to catch a boat back to the mainland and their hotel. I wonder why they didn't book in with us."

"We weren't ready yet," replied Carrie. "I told them to use the hotel near the hospital."

"I asked them last night," grinned Luke. "The team leader confessed he was afraid of being that close to the demons. He wanted a safe place to sleep."

"Smart man. All right folks, let's roll. Brit, sorry to leave you with the mess."

"Sure you are, Mel. Sure you are. Go on now." There was something in her voice as she spoke that caught Bjorn's attention. He smiled sadly as they left the dining room.

THE FIRST THING MELANIE noticed as they entered the sheriff's office was the glove sticking out of Emily's pocket. A tranquilizer pistol was on the desk beside her. Melanie gave her a nod of approval and Emily responded with a weak smile. "Em?"

"Mom is having nightmares, Mel. Just like your folks did back when we were kids."

"That should pass, Em. It might take a while, but it should pass."

"She wants weapons, Mel. My gentle loving mother wants a gun and glove for protection. Those damn things are everywhere, and she can see them. She's really freaked out and so am I."

"We all are," sighed Carrie. "We all are, Emily. On the bright side, Vic has invented a new weapon. It looks like an ordinary flashlight and it works great. I tested one yesterday. It pulled the demon out and destroyed it. The victim took only a few minutes to recover and today he's helping Vic build more. We'll get you one as soon as we can."

"Now that's the best news I've had all day," rumbled a deep voice. They turned to see Hank, coffee mug in hand, come out of the inner office. "The mayor wasn't happy with my morning report about the state of the union. I've been ordered to do something before the entire tourist season has been ruined."

"The tourist season? That's what he worried about?"

"Apparently so, Deputy Rivers. Since this is your case, I now pass the mayor's commands along to you. Do something." Hank was grinning as Melanie just shook her head and sighed. "What are you planning to do, Mel?"

"We have to wait for the brass before we can close the portal, but we can go hunting. You guys get ready, Carrie and I are going to fill up the cells. Come on, Deputy Majors. Let's go hunting for demons."

"Gods, lover, you say the sweetest things, take me to all the exciting places..." Melanie blushed as she led the way out to the parking lot and the waiting cruiser.

It was still early, but the coffee shop parking lot had a number of cars. Melanie pulled in and parked the cruiser. "Carrie, you start looking over the cars. That should make a few folks nervous and draw their attention. I'll go inside and see if we have any volunteers." Carrie smiled and got out of the car. She began slowly inspecting license plates.

Melanie stepped through the door and glanced around. All eyes turned to her, but quickly returned to the window where they could see Caroline checking the cars. There were nine people in the room, three sharing a table were possessed. The waitress approached and asked if Melanie needed anything.

"Do you know any of these folks?"

"Sure."

"The three at that table. Know what car is theirs?"

"Blue Chevy sedan and black Ford pick-up, why?"

"Thanks." Mel smiled and walked back outside. As Caroline looked up she pointed to the pick-up truck. Carrie nodded and approached the vehicle.

"Hey, what the hell is going on? Get away from my truck; I haven't done anything wrong." Two men and a woman came rushing out of the coffee shop.

Melanie was impressed as Caroline moved to place the man between herself and the window. "Is this your truck, Sir?" she asked with a nod to Melanie.

The man was angry and letting it show as he reached them. "You're damned right it..." he got no further as his world suddenly went to hell in a hurry. Caroline fell to the pavement and Melanie grabbed him from the side throwing him against the truck and twisting his arm behind his back. Caroline already had the other two on the ground.

Melanie's gun was out and covering all three. Nothing more was said as the three were placed in restraints and stuffed into the back of the cruiser. "What the hell was that?" asked Melanie as they headed back to the sheriff's office with their prisoners.

"From the windows it would look like he'd hit me. Brazilian Jiu jitsu, remember? I'm a grappler. I do my best work on the ground."

"So you made it look like an attack. That gave us a reason to take them in. Woman, you're amazing."

The woman in the back squirmed in her restraints. "That was illegal."

"I really don't care," replied Caroline. "I know what you are. Just sit there and shut the hell up."

"Well, that didn't take long," grinned Hank as they hustled their three prisoners into the cells. "Now what?"

"Now we do what we do." Melanie turned to the nearest cell and shot the man inside. He let out a yelp and plucked the tranquilizer dart from his chest. "What the hell was that?"

"The beginning of the end," replied Caroline as she pulled out her glove and put it on.

"Noooo," screamed an inhuman voice as the man slowly succumbed to the effects of the drug and sank towards the floor. The demon was now clearly visible, struggling to free itself from the unconscious victim. It howled and screamed as the light from three gloves was trained on it.

"Keep the light on him a bit longer. We have to make sure we got all of it or it can grow back," said Melanie as she held her light on the man long after the demon had dissipated. Finally a sickly gray mist rose into the air then vanished. "Okay, that's one down. Next."

Hank sighed and leaned against Emily's desk. It was close to quitting time. The door opened and Caroline entered, followed closely by Melanie. They had no prisoners. Hank raised an eyebrow. "You two all alone this time?"

Melanie sighed and tossed her hat onto her desk. "Yeah. Looks like they've all gone to ground. Once we started hauling them in they wised up and disappeared. We did get eight of them though."

One of the prisoners leaned against the cell door. "Hey, when are you going to let us out of here?"

Hank sighed and faced the man. "Just as soon as your memory comes back."

"What the hell was that thing attached to everybody?"

"It was a demon. You had one too. That's why you're here. By tomorrow your memory of what went on while the demon had control of you will come back. You and I will have a long talk about that, and then I'll decide if I should charge you or let you go."

"A demon? Really?"

Caroline had approached the man. "Yes, a demon. Have you got a better idea of what it was? I sure don't. Let's wait until tomorrow then see how skeptical you are." She turned and went to her own desk and sat. "Moron."

"Wrap it up, girls," said Hank. "You've had a long day. I can handle things from here. Go home and get some rest."

As they left, Emily stopped them at the door. "Mel, I've got five volunteers for the militia. All former victims. All we need are weapons. Two wanted to go hunting with rifles, but I talked them down. That would be murder. We have to kill the demon to save the human. That's how we'll build our ranks. Right?"

"Jesus, Em, you're the woman. Yes, you're one hundred percent right. The idea is to kill the demon and free the human. Tell them to be patient a bit longer; we'll get the weapons. Do you want me to meet with them?"

"Would you?"

"Can you set it up for tonight?"

"Sure. I'll call you. Thanks Mel." Melanie smiled and nodded as she and Caroline left the building.

LUKE SAT WITH HIS BACK against a tree, his eyes fixed on the mouth of the cave. He'd been there all day, Lizzie right beside him, her tranquilizer rifle at the ready. It had been deathly quiet all day and he was thankful for that.

On the other side of the tree, Bjorn sat watching the back trail, making sure nobody sneaked up on them. Brit sat beside him. She had brought them lunch then stayed to keep them company. Few words had passed between them, and Bjorn was content with that. There was something about this woman that drew him. Especially her sharp mind and her ability to be content with her own thoughts. Sadly, he also knew Brit was in love with Melanie. There was no way in hell he was getting involved in that.

Luke finally broke the silence. "You know, guys, this isn't the worst assignment I've ever had."

"Second that," chuckled Bjorn. "How about you, Lizzie? Bored yet?"

"Cuddled up to Luke all day? How could I be bored?"

"Shut up, Lizzie," sighed Luke, blushing. She giggled and elbowed him in the ribs. "Bjorn, what's your gut saying?"

"It's too quiet, Luke. In truth, I don't like it. It's making me nervous."

Brit laughed and gently poked his ribs. "Oh thank god, I thought it was me."

Bjorn shook his head and grinned. "No, girl, not you, but the thoughts of facing you in a poker game sure does."

"Just don't bet more than you can afford to lose, Handsome."

The sound of Luke's phone interrupted. "Luke. What? Okay. Thanks, Mel. All right guys, sharpen up. Mel and Carrie hauled in eight and fixed them up, but the rest have gone to ground. She's not liking that and neither am I. We both think it could mean they're likely to hit this place. Bjorn, take Brit to her car then come back. Lizzie and I will hold the fort."

Bjorn stood and offered Brit his hand. She took it and allowed him to help her to her feet, but she noticed his eyes stayed on the trail. "Stay behind me, Brit. Just in case. If anything happens, beat feet back here as fast as you can." He released her hand and started off towards the parking area, Brit close behind him. She smiled as she followed him through the trees. She liked him, his thoughtfulness and soft spoken ways. She also liked his strength. It was like Melanie's, rock solid. Brit felt safe with him. Maybe she could learn to love him in time.

They reached the car without any trouble. The area was quiet and empty. He watched until she drove away then returned to his post. "What?" he asked, as Lizzie looked him over with a grin.

"Nothing. Just checking for lipstick, that's all."

"Shut up, Lizzie. Besides, I can see that yours is all smeared."

Her hand flew to her mouth then she blushed. "You jerk, I'm not wearing lipstick."

"Doesn't matter. Now 1 know all I need to know. Luke's been fraternizing with the crew. That won't look good on your resume, old buddy."

"Shut up, Bjorn. Look, we all know that this is going to go down ugly. We also know we're not going to have any choice but to fight and fight hard."

"Yeah," replied Bjorn, "and we also know we're not going to be able to do that if we're bound by government rules. So, when do we officially quit? Today? Tomorrow?"

"Let's let it play out as long as we can then toss in our shields. We might get lucky."

"By the look on Lizzie's face your chances look pretty good."

"Shut up, Bjorn. I swear I'll shoot you in the ass with this tranq gun if you don't shut up." He just chuckled and went back to watching the trail. Darkness was falling when the relief shift arrived.

The Game's Afoot

Melanie drove to her grandmother's house when they left the sheriff's office. Both women were tired and content with their own thoughts. When they arrived, Ellen was waiting at the door. She'd seen the car coming from her chair by the window. "Come in, girls. I'll make some tea." They followed her inside and gratefully sank into chairs by the kitchen table. "How was your day?"

"Busy," replied Melanie.

"Thought as much."

"Oh? Nana, what aren't you telling me?"

"I was in town today. Grocery day, you know. At first I saw a lot of demon activity, but when I went back for a few things I'd forgotten, there wasn't a one to be found. I thought it was you guys on the warpath.

"Vic had to go to the mainland for parts. There wasn't enough at the local store. He and Egg just got back and are in the workshop. I expect he'll work late trying to get those flashlights ready."

"He will, Nana. Vic knows how tight things are getting. He'll probably work through the night."

"He'd better not," sighed the old woman. "As badly as we need the weapons, overtired people make mistakes. We can't afford mistakes on this one."

"We heard that," said Vic, as he and the boy entered from the back door. "We've laid out enough parts to make six more DKs and then we'll quit for the day. Egg will take one home with him just in case."

"You take some of this tea home with you too, Egg." Ellen passed the boy a small bag. Make sure your mom drinks some too."

"What is it?"

"It makes you taste bad so they can't lock onto you again."

"Oh yeah, I want lots of that."

"What's wrong, Egg?" asked Caroline.

"Nothing."

"Liar."

"Vic says it doesn't matter. I couldn't help it." Suddenly the boy sank into a chair and covered his face with his hands. "Mostly I tortured some animals. I also beat up a girl. Mrs. Rivers, I'm so sorry. I was here with a knife to kill you yesterday, but I couldn't bring myself to get any closer to your house. I..."

"Hush now, Edgar," soothed Ellen as she put her arms around the boy and held him against her hip, lightly stroking his hair. "That wasn't you, Egg. That was the demon. He made you do it. Carrie killed him for it and now you're going to help us drive the rest of them off this island. You'll get your payback, Vic and I will see to that."

He got control of the emotions and gave her a tentative hug then she released him. "Thanks, Mrs. Rivers."

"Drink your tea, dear." She smiled and patted his hand then turned her attention to Vic who winked at her.

"Sorry we were gone so long. Egg and I had to go to several stores to get enough components for what we need."

Melanie set down her cup and leaned forward. "Vic, talk to me."

"We bought enough to make a hundred of those DKs. Sorry, demon killers. Bjorn thinks this will get ugly and so do I. We'll arm every human on this island if we have to. We also got some other stuff. Egg has a few ideas. We thought you'd approve."

"I do, Vic, old friend. I surely do. Nana, did Brit come for a visit today?"

"Ah-huh. I gave her what I had, and she went back to get it set out. I'll make up more for her this evening while the boys are in the workshop."

"Just exactly what is this thing you make to keep the demons away, Ellen?"

"I can't tell you that, Caroline. You're an officer of the law, for god's sake."

"Aw, Nana."

"All right, Mel, all right. It's a tincture I make from a certain variety of mushroom. I add a few secret herbs and spices to it then dilute it in lots of water. I spray that around the house once a week and they don't come near me. For some reason it irritates the hell out of them. I gave Brit all I had and told her to use every bit of it. The hotel should be safe enough for a few days. Plenty of time to make more."

"Nana, you're a bad woman and I love you for it."

"Ellen, I didn't hear a thing," laughed Caroline. "Come on, Mel honey, let's go home and get out of uniform. We have guests arriving tonight."

"Tell Brit I'm sorry I'll miss her shearing the sheep," grinned Vic as they rose to leave.

The general and his people were just arriving as Melanie and Caroline reached the hotel. Brit put on her best smile and signed them in while the girls changed into civvies. Since the hotel was actually a B&B, Brit directed the newcomers to the cafe for a meal. When they returned, it was growing dark and Luke's team had returned. They'd picked up take out food and were finishing up in the dining room.

The general made a show of introducing himself then sat to the table with them, indicating the rest of his followers should as well. "Report."

Lizzie flinched at that, but Luke squeezed her hand under the table and she was still. "This island is a hot bed of activity, General. We managed to stop something big going on in the cave, but there were civilian casualties. The portal was discovered inside and the area was sealed off."

"Where's Grant and his crew?"

"Standing guard at the cave. We needed to keep it sealed up so his crew took the night shift and we took the days."

"Did Grant submit to that to keep Rivers from killing him?"

"Does it matter?" asked Melanie, as she and Caroline joined them at the table.

"I suppose not. First thing tomorrow you will guide us to the site of the portal where these gentlemen will close and seal it."

"What about her?" asked Caroline, as she indicated the silent woman who was studying her hands.

"That's Alicia. She'll be documenting the procedure."

"You mean filming the whole thing with you on camera the entire time," thought Melanie, but she remained silent.

"Well, since there's nothing to do until morning and the night is young," grinned Luke, "how about a friendly game of poker. Carrie, have you got any cards and chips here?"

"Sure do, Luke. Just to keep you honest I'll open a fresh pack of cards."

Luke laughed as she rose to fetch the tools of Brit's trade. "Carrie, I'm shocked that you don't trust me. Okay, who's in? General?"

"Sure, why not?"

"Brit? How about you?"

"No, Luke, I..."

"Oh come on, girl. It's just a friendly game."

"Well, all right. I guess I could play for a few hands."

"This'll be fun," grinned the general as he reached for the deck and began to shuffle the cards. Brit winked at Bjorn and the general's fate was sealed. Everyone sat in for a few hands, but one by one, slowly dropped out. By midnight only Brit and the general were left. Luke remained as dealer to keep everything honest, so he said.

The general sat staring at the table. He had tried raising the stakes several times to scare this woman off, but she went with him every time. He won a few hands, but she won more and he found himself several thousand dollars poorer. He could try to bluff her, but if she called him on it he would lose his house and probably his wife in the bargain. How the hell had it come to this? He slowly pushed in all his chips. "All in."

Brit gave him her brightest smile. "Does that mean I have to put in all my chips too?"

"That or you can fold the hand," said Luke.

"But I have a good hand. I'll put all mine in too." Brit shoved her massive pile of chips into the middle of the table.

With shaking hand, the general flipped his cards over. A pair of jacks. Brit smiled again as she turned over her cards. Three eights. The general had lost again. "It will take me a few days to raise the money to pay off the marker." His hand was still shaking as he wrote out the IOU. He shoved it across the table and rose, leaving the room without another word.

The woman, Alicia, had sat quietly watching the game. "I know who you are. You're Brit Majors, professional gambler, currently ranked number three in the world."

"So?"

"Well done." She quietly rose and went up to her room.

"Mel, you okay?" They had just crawled into bed. Carrie reached for Melanie, but she seemed distracted.

"Huh? Oh, yeah, I'm fine, honest, sweetheart."

"But?"

"I've got a bad feeling about tonight. I think we should sleep with one eye open from now on."

"I know, I feel it too. It was fun to watch Brit in action, but it was only a distraction. When suddenly all the demon possessed people vanished today I got a bad feeling. I think tomorrow will be an interesting day."

"Yeah, me too. Come over here and let me cuddle you."

"Is that all you want to do?"

"No, lover, it isn't."

"But?"

"For some reason I don't want to sleep too soundly. I'm sorry, sweetie. I could..."

"No, lover, I agree. We should sleep lightly tonight." Caroline snuggled closer and laid her head on Melanie's shoulder. Mel kissed her hair then closed her eyes. They both slowly drifted off to sleep.

That sweet slumber was broken about four a.m. by the sound of distant gun shots. Melanie was instantly out of bed, dragging on her clothes. "Mel? What is... Oh shit, that's gun fire." Carrie leaped up and pulled on her uniform and weapons. She and Melanie reached the front door barely ahead of Luke and the rest of his team.

"What the hell is going on here?" bellowed the general as he hurried down the stairs.

"Gunfire, General," replied Melanie as she jerked open the door. "Coming from the vicinity of the cave with the portal. Let's go, team."

"Hold on, I'm in charge here."

"Not until you get your pants on," snarled Melanie. "Wait here, you'll get a full report when we get back."

"I'm coming with you."

"The hell you are. Let's go people."

Melanie charged through the door with her team close behind. They piled into their cars and raced away. Cursing wildly, the general turned back into the hotel and ran for the stairs. A moment later he returned, fully dressed and armed.

"Going somewhere, General?" asked Brit.

"I have to get there right now." They could still hear the gunfire.

"Know the way?" That stopped him in his tracks. By now all his people were gathered by the door as well. "Now, if this goes ugly we'd better be ready to defend ourselves here. Since you seem to have the only gun. I suggest you remain with us for protection. Come back to the table. I'll make us some coffee, then I want to talk to you."

"There's a lot going on here that you're hiding, woman."

"Yes there is, now go sit down and I'll bring you up to speed."

The general bristled at her tone, but he sat. A few minutes later she emerged from the kitchen with coffee makings for everybody. "All right, pour a cup and gather round, folks." Brit waited until everybody was settled before she continued. Her eyes were hard and her voice so cold even the general shivered and was quiet.

"So, here's what's happening. This island seems to be a hotbed of demon activity. For whatever reason, they're using this place as a major entry point to this world. Using your people and resources plus a lot of locally grown talent and ammunition, we managed to stop that flow.

"That, General, is when you decided to hog the spotlight and fucked everything up."

"Now look..."

"Shut up and listen. We had them stopped. If you had allowed those people to close that portal when they found it, this island could have been completely cleared of demons by now. However, that's not what happened. You made us wait and gave them time to regroup. Now there's a gunfight at the cave.

"I promise you, General, if my sister or her partner get killed out there I will take the money I won from you and hire a hit man. You will pay with your life. If they return unscathed, I'll tear up that IOU.

"You see, what you don't understand here is these things aren't other humans. You can't play the same games and hope to survive. A demon will invade your person, take over your mind and control you utterly. If you had let these people do their jobs..."

"All right, all right. I get it." He sighed deeply. "I get it. I fucked up. However, in my own defense, I'm trying to keep this program from being scrapped. I was hoping that we could get something real on film to use as leverage."

"Drink your coffee, General."

"It tastes funny. Aw shit. You drugged me."

"Nope. Well, yes, but in a good way. Actually it tastes a lot better as a tea. What it does is helps you see the demons, and it makes it a lot harder for them to get a hold on you. Ellen says it makes you taste bad, but Vic says it makes you really slippery. Harder to get a grip on. I personally drink three cups a day."

Tentatively the general took another sip. "Not so bad at that. Ms. Majors, do you know where they've gone? I just want to help in any way I can."

Just then the house phone rang. Brit answered. "Yes, Sheriff. It's at the cave. Mel and team are already there. Swing by here and pick up the general. He has a gun and is combat trained." She set down the receiver and turned back to the table. "The sheriff will be here in a minute, General. Go with him and do exactly as he says."

The general nodded as he rose to his feet and headed for the door. "Thank you."

"Don't thank me yet. Your life is still on the line." She was talking to empty air. The general was already climbing into the sheriff's cruiser.

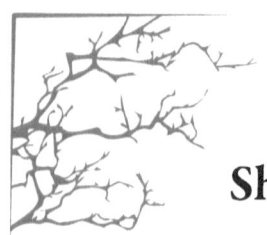

Shots in the Dark

The five men sat around a tree, facing the cave mouth. They had a flashlight beaming into it, but it was flickering. Unfortunately, it was just a flashlight, not one of Vic's new DKs. They were bemoaning their lack of sleep.

"I still say, we're supposed to be in charge, Bill. We should have the day shift and those out of date second stringers should be out here in the bugs and the dark."

"Doesn't matter. You saw the look in her eyes. I didn't see you volunteering to face down Melanie Rivers when she's pissed. She'd kill you in a heartbeat and say you were demon possessed.

"I heard that she took out three of her own people for sleeping on night watch. That was her excuse. They were possessed and came at her. Three trained agents came at her, and she took them out. That old fart on her crew back up her story. I'll bet she..."

Blood suddenly spurted from his shoulder, his scream of pain nearly drowning out the sound of the gunshot. More shots rang out. The men scattered for cover. Two didn't make it and one had presence of mind enough to lay still where he'd fallen. Those were rifle shots and all they had for weapons were sidearms and tranq guns.

There was silence for a moment then several people carrying hunting rifles came into the small clearing. They were barely visible in the fading moonlight as they weren't carrying lights. They didn't seem to need them. They approached the cave and put out the flashlight there. All was in darkness.

From their hiding places in the trees, the remaining agents could see the people sniffing the air, scanning the area, searching for survivors. Sounds started coming from the cave, low then rising to a maniacal howl for several minutes. When the howling stopped shadows began to flow from the mouth of the cave.

Realizing what was happening, the men in hiding opened fire with their pistols. Three humans dropped instantly and several more were wounded. The rifles started again, the bullets piercing the trees, seeking the source of the gunfire. When the men ran out of bullets the used what they had in the tranquilizer pistols.

In the confusion, the man who'd played dead managed to find cover and join in the gunfight. By the time their ammunition was gone, help had arrived.

The sounds of running feet were followed by the sudden pop of a flare over the clearing. Several humans with rifles were exposed as well as the steady stream of writhing figures pouring from the cave. The humans began to fall to the steady pop pop pop of the tranquilizer guns as Melanie and team swiftly captured the clearing.

More gunfire came from the cave and Bjorn fell to the ground as did Luke. Everybody took cover and returned fire. As the light from the flare died, Melanie popped another. Her radio crackled to life.

"Sheriff to Deputy Rivers, come in Mel."

"Hank, we've got a war zone at the cave. They're using rifles so come in heavy, over."

"Roger that. I'll be right there."

"We've cleared the way. Come up to the clearing, but stay out of sight of the cave mouth. Oh, Hank, bring anything you have that will shine light."

"Roger that. We're at the parking area now. Hank out."

Melanie dropped her radio back into its clip then took roll call. "Carrie!"

"Here and clear, Mel."

"Luke!"

"He's down and out, Mel," came Lizzie's distraught voice. "He's alive, but he needs help badly."

"Lizzie, are you hit?"

"I'm good. I've got Luke to a safe spot for now."

"Do what you can to help him. Bjorn!"

"Here. I'm down. I took one in the leg. Hurts like hell, but I'll survive."

"Can you fight?"

"Negative. Can't bear weight on the leg."

"Vic!" No answer. She called again, but still no answer.

Caroline's voice sounded right by her ear. "Ellen's house is a lot further away, Mel. He may not be here yet. He may not have heard the shots."

"Agreed," smiled Melanie, as she lightly kissed Carrie's cheek.

"Mel, do you see what I see?"

"You mean that steady stream of demons pouring out of that cave? Yeah, I see them. Bjorn was right as usual. I should have let you make that moron talk then close the hole ourselves and be damned to the consequences."

"Mel, we have to stop them from getting out."

"Yep. Glove up, girl. We'll rush the cave mouth. You go right; I'll go left. Stay back so they can't target you, but get that light focused on the opening. Bjorn, can you shoot?"

"I can."

"Give us some cover fire for a minute." Her answer was the sound of his gun. Melanie leaped to her feet and ran. Carrie was ahead of her. It was a short sprint, and they were in place when Bjorn's gun fell silent. The light from Carrie's glove came on, bringing a high pitched screech from the demons leaving the cave mouth. Melanie's light joined in and the flow slowed to a trickle.

Rifle fire came harmlessly from the cave mouth, but it was answered by the heavy boom of the sheriff's shotgun. There were screams of pain, frustration, and rage from within the cave, but the shotgun held them back from the mouth. A few moments later Vic's voice called out.

"Melanie!"

"It's about time you showed up for work, Vic. Did you bring new toys?"

"Can you hold them for a few more minutes?"

"We can."

"Be right back."

Those in the cave tried to break out, but the sheriff used the shotgun and the general had the sheriff's automatic assault rifle. They both poured gunfire into the cave, preventing any escape attempts.

After a few minutes an ATV came chugging into the clearing and straight towards the cave. The headlights hit the cave mouth and the screams inside became intense for a moment, and then stopped. The trickle of demons stopped as well. "Give it another few minutes then it should be clear."

"Vic, talk to me."

"We modified the headlights on this thing as it was all we could get close enough to the cave mouth. It was Egg's idea. I bought the machine today thinking it might come in handy."

"Vic, I love you."

"Sorry, Mel, but I've already promised to marry your grandmother."

"Does that mean I get to call you Gramps?"

"You do and I'll shoot your ass with a tranq. It should be clear now, Mel. Hank, got your bull horn?"

"I do."

"There should be some very confused people in that cave right now."

"Roger that." A moment later the bull horn shattered the night. "Attention, you people in the cave. Throw out all your weapons and come out with your hands up."

A frail voice called from the cave. "Sheriff? Sheriff, help us. Please help us."

"Throw out your rifles and come out with your hands up. We will help you."

"Please don't shoot me," sobbed a woman's voice, as a rifle was tossed down at the cave mouth. She staggered out into the light, covered in blood.

"Step to the left and sit down where I can see you," commanded the sheriff. Falteringly, she obeyed. Several more followed her example, men women, and children. Some were wounded, others not, but all were traumatized.

"What happened to us? Why are we here? What is going to happen to us? I've been shot. How did that happen? I need help."

"Shut up, all of you," barked Melanie. "Is there anyone else in that cave."

"No. Not alive."

"I'll check anyway if you don't mind."

"Mel, catch." She looked up in time to catch the flashlight Vic tossed to her. "It's a DK."

"Thanks, Vic." Melanie cautiously entered the cave, shining the light of the DK all around the scene of carnage. Caroline was right at her shoulder, a tranq gun in one hand and a nine-millimeter in the other. There were dead bodies and badly wounded people moaning, but no signs of a demon.

A man lunged at them. "Help me."

Carrie shot him with the tranquilizer. "Wait your turn. The rest of you lie still and wait here. The paramedics will soon be here to help you."

Melanie took out her radio again. "Mel to Sheriff."

"Hank here."

"The place is clear of weapons. We have wounded and need the Medics."

"They're already on the way, Mel. Can you plug the hole?"

"Looks like they plugged it from the other side for now. Coming out."

"Roger that."

When they reached the clearing again it was nearly dawn. The sky had turned gray and it was starting to drizzle rain. The paramedics were already on the scene and getting ready to head back to the hospital with Luke and Bjorn. A hard-eyed Lizzie standing by with a gun at the ready may have had an influence on the choice of who got served first.

"Sheriff, if you moved a bunch of those vehicles we could get the ambulance a lot closer."

"You've got it, guys. All right, everybody with car keys head out and try to make a hole for the ambulance." Carrie touched Melanie's arm gently then turned to follow Hank back to the parking area.

There was enough light to see more clearly now. Melanie scanned the people in the clearing and found the man who had been in charge of the night shift. He was lying on the ground among the wounded waiting for the medics to return. She stepped up to him and nudged his foot with her boot. "What the hell happened here?"

"What happened? We got jumped, that's what happened. We were guarding the cave when all of a sudden they opened fire from behind."

"Who was watching the back trail?"

"Back trail? We were watching the cave mouth."

"Sweet baby Jesus, you idiots weren't watching the back trail?" demanded the general as he stepped up behind Melanie. "What the hell is the matter with you, soldier? How the hell did you ever get a commission in this man's army? You got sloppy, didn't post a rear guard, and got your people killed. You'd better hope you die from those wounds before you get to the court martial."

"Easy, General. I think he gets it."

The general's shoulders sagged and he sighed. "Yes, and I get it too, Rivers. I fucked up here on a grand scale. I deliberately held you back on this and now a lot of people have paid the price. That one's on me. In my own defense, let me explain something. I never believed any of this demon crap, ever. I was assigned this duty and I saw it as a test. I listened to your former team, I listened to the scientists, but all I could see with my own two eyes was a convincing dog and pony show."

"You thought you were being fed the Emperor's New Clothes story."

"Yes I did. I wanted to come watch just how far they would go with the charade. I always thought you were just another soldier who'd gone rouge, albeit it in a new and imaginative way."

"And now?"

"Now I don't know what the hell to believe. I can see dead and wounded here on the battle ground. I've been shot at and returned fire. This much is familiar to me, and I know it's not fake. I need to trust someone here and that sheriff is a real hard ass. He trusts you and I'm inclined to trust his judgement. I just wish to hell I could see what you people see."

"Wish granted," said Vic as he jabbed the general in the arm with a syringe.

"Ow. What the hell..."

"That's some special serum we've developed, General. In about half an hour you may start to see things. It won't be an hallucination; it'll be the real McCoy."

"Explain."

"Up until now there was only one way to see the demons. You had to have been attached to one at one time. However, some people got the ability through close personal trauma. Melanie is one of them. When her uncle killed himself to get rid of the demon, she gained the sight."

"Can you see them?"

"I can. I was working with the man who invented the glove lights. He had one of them attached to his back, but somehow he'd managed to render it unconscious or for reasons of its own it was helping him. I didn't believe him until I put on the glove and shone the light on his back. When I turned it on, the damn thing woke up and tried to take me over. It failed, but my world view changed that day.

"Recently I've managed to improve on that original design, and I've concocted a serum that will allow anyone to see them."

"What else? You're holding back on me."

"That tea they probably gave you at the hotel is a special blend. It prevents a demon from being able to attach itself to a human. That's all of it. I'll provide you with a full set of specs as well as the formula for the tea. I'll hand in my resignation at the same time."

"Oh? Why?"

"General, what you couldn't see when you arrived was a steady stream of demons exiting that cave. It was down to a trickle when I got here, but I'm willing to bet there were a lot before we arrived. Mel?"

Melanie was looking away towards the back trail, waiting for Carrie to return. She didn't turn back when she spoke. Her voice sounded tired and defeated. "Yeah, you're right, Vic. I'd say they were massing for an invasion. That's probably what the big mojo was all about a few days ago, making the portal a lot bigger. When we didn't close it we gave them the chance they needed."

"Jesus Christ!" exclaimed the general as he stared at a wounded man who had just been brought out of the cave. "Is that one of them?" The creature attached to the man's back writhed and struggled as it tried and failed to free itself.

"It is," replied Vic as he flicked on a light and trained it on the creature. It howled and its victim screamed in pain as it fought, but Vic held the light on it until it dissipated and the man fell unconscious.

The general was pale and shaken. "Rivers, what's your estimate on how many of these things escaped from that cave?"

"Before tonight I'd say we had about a dozen of them left on the island. Most of them showed up here with guns blazing."

"And now?"

"Conservative estimate? Hundreds, maybe more. I just hope they all headed for the mainland where our new weapons don't exist." She spotted Carrie returning and walked to meet her.

"Dr. Perez."

"General?"

"If I'm going to convince anyone in power to fund this little war I am going to have to show proof of the demon existence."

"I'll have all the specs and formulas to you before the end of day. Will you need prisoners with demons still attached?"

"No, apparently I've got a number of them back in the labs."

"General?"

"Yes?"

"Once you get all weapons into mass production..."

"I'll send you a truckload." He walked away to join Hank who was organizing the clean up of the area.

The Game Has Changed

Hank Doyle looked up as the general approached. "So, I suppose you're going to take over the show now."

"I do have that authority, but I hope I'm not that big a fool. Sheriff, I messed up and this has gone to hell because of it. I need a place to work so I can get troops here to help contain the situation. If that is even possible at this point. I'll place myself and my men at your disposal. Hopefully we will learn what we need to know to carry on this war off island."

"So you think this will spread?"

"You know it will. Once I have men and supplies we'll come to you for orders."

"Not to me, brother. If any of us are going to come out of this alive it will be due to Melanie Rivers. She's the only person I know with the grit and experience to fight these things."

"Everyone said she's the best," admitted the general. "She's a legend among the people who work on this crap." He let his shoulders droop and sighed. "I guess I'd better stop calling it crap and start calling it an invasion of unknown antagonists. What the hell are they really?"

"I have no idea, General. I asked Mel once. She said they might be aliens from another dimension, scientist from another galaxy, or demons from hell. We settled for calling them demons because their only purpose seems to be to torture humans. Why, I have no idea. I just want them gone or dead."

"I hear that. All right, Sheriff, put Rivers in charge and I'll back her to the hilt."

"Here they come now." Melanie and Caroline were approaching, hand in hand. "Mel, this whole thing has gone to shit."

"You think, Hank?"

"Yep, I surely do. Mel, the general has offered anything you need and he's giving you the lead on this one."

Melanie turned to the general and raised an eyebrow. "Oh? Seeing things differently, General?"

"Seeing things clearly. A part of me will never forgive Perez for jabbing me with that serum. However, now I can see the enemy. I have no experience at all with fighting these things, but you do. Take charge, use my resources to clear out your island and teach me how to fight these things. I can see this becoming an all-out war and I need to know how to function."

Melanie nodded slowly, thinking. "All right, General. We could use a few weapons and other equipment. We have a local militia forming to fight. They all have the vision and they all have been infected at one time. We arm the militia with the means to destroy the demons, but they'll need protection while they do. They won't want to shoot their friends and neighbors."

"How many troops do you need?"

"One squad of Rangers should do the trick. They need to know that they shoot to wound only, not to kill. If you kill the human you set the demon free to capture another. If you wound the human, the demon can't escape. That's when you can kill them."

"That's why the tranquilizer pistols were requisitioned."

"Exactly."

"All right, where can I set up to work? The Sheriff's office?"

"Hell no," grinned Hank. "Use the hotel. It's been made safe. The demons won't go near it. We didn't dare protect the office because we were using it as a place to haul the infected in for processing."

"The hotel has been made safe? How did you manage that?"

"Vic will get all the specs to you," sighed Melanie. "We won't hold anything back, General."

"Thank you, Deputy Rivers. I won't either. Not after tonight."

IT HAD TAKEN MOST OF the day to get things at the cave dealt with. In the end the scientists had been taken to the site where they cauterized the entire inside of the cave, sealing it off to the demons completely, or so they hoped.

Back at the hotel the general spent much of the day on the phone making arrangements and issuing orders. When Melanie and Carrie returned to their suite Mel headed straight for the shower. The melt down was just starting to hit her when Carrie stepped in with her, enfolding her in gentle loving arms.

Soft warm lips found Melanie's, gentle hands explored her body, and dancing fingers gave her a crashing orgasm. As she melted towards the floor, Carrie held her up, kissing her softly and cooing soothing sounds. The water stopped and Melanie was dried off then led back to the bed.

The kisses returned and she opened herself to them and the delightful distraction. After another orgasm she nestled in Carrie's arms and drifted off to sleep. As she succumbed to sleep she marvelled at how Carrie had taken her away from the massive melt-down she felt building inside her.

She was also slightly troubled at the lack of emotion in Carrie. Carrie seemed completely unaffected by the battle at the cavern. The sight of the wounded, the crying, the dying, and tortured bodies seemed to have had no affect on her at all. It was as though all emotion had been shut away and only the love for Melanie had been allowed to express itself.

Caroline Majors lay holding her lover and waiting for sleep to claim her. She was exhausted, both emotionally and physically. Melanie might wonder at her lack of emotional response, but that wasn't it.

Carrie had learned as a child to compartmentalize her responses in her mind. Yes, she was horrified at what she had seen. Yes, she had compassion for the victims. However, she also knew that a possessed human was really a demon and she truly believed all of them would prefer death to a life controlled by one of those monsters.

Once Melanie was deep in sleep Carrie reached over and took Mel's little book and pen.

"Ages have passed
Monsters hunt me still
They'll never find me."

She closed the book and replaced it. Settling down again she let her thoughts turn inside to that hidden place in her mind where she kept the fear emotions hidden. Tears flowed and she trembled as she allowed the fear and revulsion of the past night wash over her. Eventually, exhausted, she too slept.

A New Sheriff in Town

C aroline awakened alone in the bed. She swept her arm through the space where Melanie had lain and the sheet was still warm. Mel hadn't been up for long. With a yawn and a sigh, Carrie sat up, ready to face another day of the madness her life had become. Her long delicate fingers began to trace the scar on her breast, but she snatched her hand away and got out of bed. She noticed Melanie's book, open, on her side of the bed.

"I will always

Protect you

From the monsters"

Caroline smiled as she closed the book and returned it to Melanie's night table. She then went about the business of preparing for the day. She found Melanie and the remains of the others at the breakfast table. There was also a man she did not know seated with them. The conversation stopped as she entered. Melanie introduced her.

"Carrie, honey, this gentleman is Jim Hardin, Mayor of Brighton. Mr. Mayor, this beautiful lady is my partner, Caroline Majors."

"It's a pleasure to meet you, Ms. Majors."

The general cleared his throat then spoke. "All right, the gang's all here. What's on your mind, Mr. Mayor?"

"Of course, General." The mayor resumed his seat then continued. "As you all are aware, our quiet little town has seen a lot of turmoil lately." There were several snorts and guffaws at that. "Yes, well, I guess that was a bit of an understatement. What you people probably don't know is that we've lost our sheriff."

"Now wait a minute," exclaimed Melanie. "Hank Doyle is sheriff, or at least he was when I went to bed last night."

The mayor sighed as he gave her his full attention. "Yes, Ms. Rivers, he was. However, he is no longer able to hold that post. Early this morning someone broke into his house and shot him. He is in hospital in critical condition. A neighbor heard the shots and went to investigate. She found two dead bodies and Hank Doyle. He put up one hell of a fight, but I'm afraid he'll be out of the action for the foreseeable future."

Melanie had gone pale. "Will he live?"

"I'm told there's a very good chance of it. However, the loss of Hank has left the town with a crisis on our hands and no way to address it. I have come here today to bring you all up to speed and to ask the General to have the military take over the island and deal with the situation."

The general looked thoughtful for a moment then met the mayor's imploring gaze. "Denied."

The mayor began to sputter, but the general held up his hand to silence him. "You're trying to jump the chain of command, Mayor. I'm here strictly as an interested observer. I am willing to call in troops as necessary. However, that call belongs to Deputy Rivers. She is now the senior officer on the island and as such it is her call.

"Deputy Rivers, I offer you any and all assistance you may need. However, I will not interfere in your jurisdiction without your express permission. Mr. Mayor, in all honesty, Melanie Rivers is your best hope here. She has the experience and a group of dedicated people to assist her."

"Right. She's been doing a bang up job." The mayor's displeasure with events so far was quite clear.

The general grinned ruefully. "Yes, about that. She was doing a fine job, actually. The problem arose when I stuck my nose into her business. That piece of bad judgement on my part has created a serious crisis and I'm hoping Ms. Rivers can pull my ass out of the fire."

"Why should I?" grumbled Melanie. "I promised to stay as long as Hank was sheriff. Looks like that job's done for now."

"Melanie, please," began the mayor. "If, as he says, you're the one to handle this then you have to stay. Think of the town, the people..."

"You mean the people who ran my family off the island? The town that looked the other way when a bunch of assholes tried to lynch my father? The..."

Caroline was squeezing Melanie's hand. "Easy, sweetheart. For better or worse, it's our town now too." Melanie turned to her and got lost in those crystal blue eyes. "Let go of the past, lover. Focus on the now."

Melanie drew a deep breath and let it out slowly, still holding Caroline's eyes. "All right. I'll do this for you, Carrie. You and my grandmother." She turned back to the mayor. "But only if I'm left alone to do my job."

"I won't interfere, Sheriff Rivers," he replied softly. "I want you to do your job. You can start with my wife."

"What???"

"She started acting crazy last night. She tried to leave the house with my hunting rifle. I took it away from her and locked her in the bedroom. She destroyed the place. Her voice sounded different, harsh, evil, and the things she said, threatened..."

"She's possessed?" asked Melanie.

"I do believe so."

"Where is she?"

"In a jail cell," replied the mayor, studying his hands. "I didn't know what else to do with her."

"Good," sighed Melanie. "She'll be safe enough there for now. I promise we'll get her clear of the demon before this day is done."

"Thank you, Sheriff Rivers."

"Stop calling me that or I'll have to shoot you. All right people, we've got our marching orders. Council of war at the sheriff's office in two hours; Carrie, you're with me."

"Every hour of every day," grinned Carrie, as she rose and followed Melanie towards the door.

As the group broke up, Brit Majors slipped a piece of paper into the general's hand. She winked at him then disappeared into the kitchen. Opening the paper he found his IOU. Across it in a flowing feminine hand was written these words. Paid in full.

Melanie's first stop was at Ellen's house to bring them up to speed then she was off to the hospital. She found Bjorn in Luke's room with Lizzie."

"Luke?" Melanie asked softly.

"No change yet," sighed Lizzie. "They say he should make it, but it's a bit early to tell."

"Lizzie?"

"I'm battle ready, Mel. I'm good to go."

"Bjorn?"

"Leg wound, shoulder wound, neither serious. The doc has ordered me to take it easy for a few days so I don't reopen the wounds. Other than that, I'm good to go."

"Understood. Lizzie, you're assigned to protection detail. Luke is a valuable asset to the team. Your task is to keep him safe."

Tears filled the girl's eyes as she thanked her team leader. Melanie winked at her then turned back to Bjorn. "Bjorn, report to the sheriff's office. That will be our headquarters from now on. You'll be coordinating the containment efforts from there."

"Aye, Captain," he grinned as he carefully rose to his feet.

Melanie's next stop was Hank's room. He was awake, but hooked up to a battery of machines. His breathing was labored, and he look so weak tears came to her eyes. "Aw Hank…"

"You know, Mel," he wheezed, "you'd think a sheriff would know enough to lock his own damn doors."

"Aw shit, Hank. This so sucks. Now what am I supposed to do?"

"You could start by catching the fuckers who shot me."

"You already did that. Hank two, house invaders zero."

"Somehow it doesn't feel like I'm winning." He gave a wheezing chuckle at that. "Where do we stand?"

"We've got the portal closed, I've been promoted to your job on a temporary basis, and the military has offered any help we might need. I've called a council of war at the sheriff's office. I plan to arm the militia and hunt every damned demon off this island."

Hank just nodded his approval. His head began to loll and his eyes fluttered closed. "You'd better leave now," said a nurse as she gently pulled the blanket up around Hank's shoulders.

"Is he going to make it?" asked Carrie as the nurse escorted them from the room.

"The doctor sounded hopeful," she replied carefully. "Perhaps you should speak with him personally."

"I'll do that later today," promised Melanie, as she headed for the exit, Carrie right on her heel.

"Where to now?" asked Caroline, as they hurried back to the cruiser.

Melanie got behind the wheel before she replied. "Sheriff's office," she replied, as she started the engine. "Carrie, did you notice anything suspicious at the hospital?"

"No, not really."

"Me neither, and that bothers me."

"Oh?"

Melanie nodded as she pulled into the parking lot. "Yeah. Where the hell did all those demons go who escaped from the cave last night?"

"Good question, lover. They sure weren't at the hospital. Maybe some of the other folks have seen them."

They went inside to find everyone already there. Vic had brought Ellen and Egg with him. Bjorn was there chatting with the general and his scientists, and Emily was there, obviously wondering what the heck was going on. Mel swiftly brought them all up to speed.

"So, that where we stand folks," said Melanie as she finished up. "Now, here's how I want to tackle this thing. Let me run through it then if you have opinions, options, or suggestions we can hear them then. Okay?

"First, Emily, contact your militia. Take Vic and Egg with you. Vic, you guys make sure the militia is armed with the right stuff. Get them together and bring them here for a meeting.

"Vic, make sure we are armed fully with the good stuff too. Emily, once you have your people armed, keep them out of sight until we're ready.

"Carrie, the general, Vic, and I will be carrying live arms as well. We'll split into hunting groups. One or two militia with one or two regulars carrying heavy weapons. Nana, are you sure your place is safe?"

"Safest place in town, Sheriff," grinned Ellen. "You'll be needing more special tea, I take it."

"Yes. Nana, be careful. These things are using long range rifles now. That will reach well beyond the borders of your house."

"I know, Mel, I know. I'll be careful. Vic would never speak to me again if I got myself killed."

"Count on it," he grinned. "Mel, I'd feel better if Ellen had someone with her."

"Roger that, Vic. Carrie, honey, can Brit shoot half as good as you?"

"Even better. I'll call her and let her know what's up. Can I give her a weapon from here?"

"Yes, do it, honey. Get them each a vest too."

"On it, Sheriff," sang Carrie as she headed for the gun rack.

WHEN FIVE O'CLOCK ROLLED around they had all gathered back at the sheriff's office. Melanie sighed as she sank into the chair at her desk. "What the hell happened? We combed this island and found one demon? That's it?"

Bjorn chuckled from his seat in Emily's usual chair. "Looks like, Sheriff. Maybe this island was just the gateway, not the target all along."

She arched an eyebrow at him. "Yeah? So what happened to Mr. 'You will me mine, I will own you.'? Where the hell did he go?"

Carrie had just locked the high powered weapons back in the rack. She turned and went to her own desk. "Maybe we got lucky. He might have been one of the ones we killed back at the cave."

"Do you really believe that, sweetie?"

"No, I don't. No, I think they're in hiding for some reason. Yes, we combed the island, but we didn't make a hard search."

"She's right," said Emily, fingering the stunner in her hand. "We need to do a house to house search."

Melanie nodded her head slowly. "I agree. Go home. Get some rest people. First thing tomorrow we meet here to gear up then we do a house to house search. We search every house, garage, barn and shed we can find. If those bastards are still here, we need to find them."

A voice called softly from the cells at the back of the room. "Sheriff?"

"Oh, hello, Mr. Mayor. I didn't see you there."

"Can I take her home now, Melanie?" He was in the cell, holding his wife who was cuddled close. She'd obviously been crying.

Melanie rose and walked back to them, looking both of them over carefully. "They didn't have you long, did they? Have the memories come back already?"

The woman sat up slowly and swallowed. "Yes, I think so."

"All right. Sir, you'll have to watch her carefully. Have you both been drinking the tea today?"

"Yes, your man has been force feeding us the tea," replied the mayor. He was grinning and so was Bjorn.

"All right then, go on home. Be careful and call me at the first hint of anything amiss."

Melanie returned to the desk. "Go home, people. Rest. Carrie and I will visit the hospital on our way back to the hotel. Nine a.m. Tomorrow. Be here and ready for war." Chatting among themselves the warriors filed out of the office and made their way home. Melanie set the phone to forward all calls to her cell then locked the door behind them.

At the hospital they sought Luke's room first. He was awake. "Report," grinned Melanie.

"I got my ass kicked, I got shot, I blacked out. I woke up with Lizzie fussing over me like a mother hen. End report."

"You like it," giggled Lizzie.

"Yeah, I do, girl." He weakly groped for her hand, and she moved closer, protectively. Luke was awake, but still in bad shape. The concern was clear in the expression on Lizzie's face.

"You need a break, Lizzie?" asked Melanie.

"No, I got this, Mel. I'm good."

"All right then. We'll see you in the morning. Come on, Carrie. Let's check on Hank."

As they neared Hank's room a nurse suddenly blasted past them. She raced into Hank's room and screamed. "What are you doing? Get out of here? Code Blue!" A man burst out of the room, a demon on his back. Seeing the two policewomen he made a run for the stairs. Carrie brought him down with a tranq gun. He fell to the floor, halfway through the door.

Carrie almost shivered at the cold look in Melanie's eyes. She had reached for her DK, but Mel stopped her. "Not yet. I want some answers, and this one is going to give them to me." She grabbed the fallen man by the collar and dragged him back to the door of Hank's room. Inside there was a full team of medical people working frantically. One of them waved her off.

Melanie took hold of the fallen man and hoisted him to his feet. He was barely conscious and had lost control of his limbs. The demon fought to escape and/or inflict harm on Melanie, but she ignored it. Carrie took the man's other arm and together they hauled him down to the cruiser and put him inside. Melanie tossed Carrie the keys then pulled out her phone.

"Bjorn. Are you up for a bit of guard duty? Yeah, the Sheriff was attacked at the hospital again. They're working on him now. I don't want to pull Lizzie away from Luke just in case. All right, we'll wait here until you arrive." She dropped the phone back in her pocket and sighed as she leaned against the car.

"We're going to interrogate this one?" asked Caroline.

"Ah huh."

"Mel, honey, how are we going to do that?"

"I have my ways. Sweetheart, you don't have to be here for this. You should drop us both off at the office then go home to a hot bath and some of Brit's magic cooking."

Carrie shook her head. "No. You need me with you. I need to be with you."

"This will be ugly, truly ugly. I'd rather you not see me do this."

"I understand, Mel. It doesn't matter; I'm staying with you." Melanie nodded then took out her book.

"Love may be lost
In the search for truth
The price must be paid"

She closed the book and put it away as Bjorn arrived in the parking lot. He saluted on his way by, then they got in the cruiser and Carrie drove back to the sheriff's office. They half dragged, half carried the man inside to a cell then Melanie went back to lock the door again. When she returned to the cell the man was starting to come around. Carrie had secured his hands and feet.

"All right," said Melanie as she reached the cell and turned on the recorder, "I want some answers."

"Fuck you, slut..."

The man's vile response was cut short as Carrie hit him with a tazer. "Not you, asshat, that thing on your back."

Melanie had put on the glove. She turned the light on the demon for a second then removed it. Both the man and the demon screamed in rage. "Answer my questions."

"F..." another flash of the glove, longer this time. The man screamed and writhed in pain as the demon tortured every nerve ending he had. The demon howled as well. Melanie gave it a moment's relief then hit it harder with the light. When the screaming and thrashing about settled down, the man had passed out from the pain. A harsh voice came from the man's throat. "What do you want?"

"Where are they?"

"Can't find them, can you? "The demon fairly laughed until Mel hit it again with the light.

"Where are they?" She held the light on, causing the demon to writhe in torment.

"Some are near, some are not. They are everywhere now." The demon was flailing about, angrily. "Your kind will soon be ours."

"Why me? Why does the big ugly want me so bad?" The demon just laughed and Melanie hit it with the light again. It started to grow transparent so she stopped. The demon was panting and barely visible. "All right, we'll take a break then start again."

"I will kill this one that holds me," snarled the demon.

Melanie did not respond or show any emotion at all. She stood waiting until the demon had become fully visible again. Its unwilling host had recovered consciousness. He started to speak, but Caroline tranqed him. Once again he was beyond the demon's power. She had rightly guessed that the demon could not truly harm the host while it was unconscious. The demon howled in pain and rage as Melanie hit it hard with the light of the glove. "Why does it want me so badly?"

"You were the first," it gasped.

"The first what?"

"The first to escape the grasp. Morgon had you as a child, but only for a short time. He tried to reacquire you, but by then you were grown, and you'd already found the traitor's research."

"The traitor's research?"

Now that it had started talking the demon seemed willing enough to part with information. "Yes. You and only you were able to break free on your own. The traitor, Keth, was supposed to be using his host to find ways to strengthen the ties. To prevent others like you from escape. Instead he used it to plot against Morgon. That weapon you wield could only have come from Keth's research."

"I repeat, why does he want me now? The weapons already exist."

"Revenge. Had you not escaped we would have already taken much of this world."

"So, you want to take over the world. Why?"

Suddenly the man's body jerked to its feet. "Because you have physical bodies," roared the demon as its host grabbed at Melanie's throat.

Melanie thrust him back and lashed out with her foot. Her boot crushed the man's knee. As he fell Caroline turned her DK on the demon, full blast. It howled and fought, thrashing the man's head hard against the corner of the steel bunk. As the man fell dead the demon leaped free, but it was too late. Melanie had a DK trained on it as well and it shrieked in agony as it dissolved into nothingness.

They stood in silence for a moment then Caroline spoke. "I'll call the coroner."

Melanie watched as Carrie, cold and emotionless, walked back to her desk and picked up the phone. "My god, she's so cool under fire. I have to learn how she does that, and I also have to be there when she finally cracks."

Caroline returned to the cell and cut the restraints from the man's hands and feet. "He'll catch the first boat in the morning. How do you want to write this up?"

Melanie turned away from the body and shook herself. "I'll give this one to the general. Otherwise I'll be accused of murder again. He can throw a cone of silence over this thing."

Caroline dropped a blanket over the body then turned to Melanie. She saw the shaking in her hands and reached for her. "Easy sweetie, easy. Carrie's got you. We can't do this here. Let's get you home and into the shower."

"Carrie, how did you get so strong?"

"You did that, my darling girl. You did that. I was ruined, finished, ready for death, accepting of it. You reached past the fears and found me. You loved me and made me strong."

"This didn't affect you?"

"Yes and no. Yes, it had an effect, but I can't allow that. These things want to enslave our entire species. If we allow ourselves to be weak, even for a moment, we're doomed. Next time, and there will be a next time, we'll strap the victim down to a bed so they can't move."

Melanie's trembling increased. "Oh my god, we should have..."

"No Mel, there wasn't time. This man tried to murder the sheriff. He died trying to escape custody. Honey, there's no doubt at all now. We know their agenda; we know what we have to fight. We can't afford to be weak, and we can't afford compassion under fire. You're a soldier. You know this to be true."

"Yeah, I do. You're right, Carrie my love. I have to shut down until we clear this island. Then and only then can we be human beings again. Let's go home. I need a shower."

"Me too. I'll go in with you."

As Carrie drove back to the hotel, Melanie took out her book again.

"Humanity lost

Information gained

Preserve the rest."

Later, as Melanie slept, Caroline reached for the little book and read Mel's last entry. She nodded her head as she realized Melanie understood. They had to give up their humanity if they were to preserve it for everyone else. She returned the book to its place on the nightstand and drifted off to a troubled sleep.

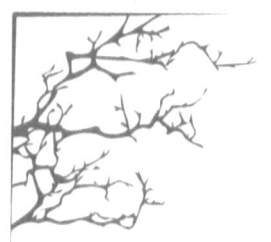

Taking Over

Caroline awakened early to find Melanie working through a series of martial arts moves, her face completely impassive. "Good morning, sexy woman."

"Good morning, my love," replied Melanie, as she turned easily and flopped onto the bed beside Carrie. "Did you get any sleep at all? I seem to remember you waking me up from nightmares."

"You had a bad dream, sweetie. That's all."

Melanie noticed the sadness in Carrie's eyes. "What is it, lover?"

"Just a memory and a dream. Nothing to worry about right now."

"Fibber. Talk to me, Carrie." Melanie gently pulled Caroline closer.

"I was remembering the way you smiled at me when we would get playful. I was dreaming of that day returning."

"Aw, I'm sorry, Carrie. I don't mean to be such a sad sack."

"No, lover. I understand. We have to go cold for a while until we reclaim our island. We can, and will, get back to the good times. But first we have a job to do."

"Yeah, you're right. Okay, I can do this. Hard-hearted Hannah, here we come. Let's get ready and go kick some demon ass off this island."

As she spoke Melanie rose and reached for her uniform. Caroline smiled as she joined her lover. The tough Melanie was back, and Caroline was delighted to see her. This was the woman who'd saved her from the demons, not once, but twice. She was also the woman who'd saved Caroline from herself and her fears. This was the woman who could lead them to victory against the demons and clear the island.

Dressed in official uniform, they entered the dining room. Bjorn was there with Brit, slowly sipping on a cup of coffee. Melanie met his eyes and her shoulders slumped. "Aw shit... Hank..."

"He didn't make it, Mel." Bjorn pushed the official sheriff's badge across the table towards her. "He wanted you to have this. His last words were, "Tell Mel to stick with it.""

Caroline reached over and picked up the badge. She took the deputy's badge from Melanie's shirt and replaced it with the sheriff's badge. "We've got a long day ahead of us, honey. We should..."

"Sit and have breakfast," declared Brit, as she rose and headed for the kitchen. She returned in a few minutes, but by that time the general and his people were gathering at the table as well. Caroline followed her back to the kitchen to help.

"Brit, I'm so sorry you got stuck..."

"Forget it, sister mine. I know you rooked me into working the B&B while you go play cops and robbers with your girlfriend. I..." Brit was leaning against the counter, her back to Caroline. She was trembling.

Carrie enfolded her sister in loving arms. "Brit, honey, what is it?"

"I'm scared, Carrie. Scared to death. I saw what those things did to you. I know what they're capable of. I know they're everywhere now and I'm scared. I need to be here, in this place where I've set up protections. Where I have access to more protections, this place with the weapons to fight them. Carrie, you need the help, and this is the only place I can feel safe. Please let me stay with you and Mel."

"Oh honey, you live here too. Even if there were no demons Mel and I would both want you to stay with us. I..."

"I can't even work, Carrie," sniffed Brit. "Where can I find a tournament now where there won't be players with demons looking over their shoulders, cheat..."

"Easy, sweetie, easy. Brit, this isn't really a B&B anymore, it's a safe house. Our family safe house. You, me and Mel. We'll get the damned demons off this island, and we'll keep them off. We will strengthen the safety nets around this house until it's like a fort against them. I promise."

Brit turned in Carrie's arms and hugged her tightly. "Carrie, I'm sorry to come apart on you like that. I..."

"Hush now, Brit. Hush. We have guests to feed. They'll be eating the tablecloth soon if we don't hurry."

Brit giggled and dried her eyes. "Okay, let's go."

They gathered up plates, filled them, then returned to the dining room. The general had just been brought up to speed by Melanie and was shaking his head. "So it's an all out war they want. Christ. I'm going to have to convince the powers that be to loosen the purse strings. We'll need to fight them on our own soil plus we'll probably have to fight off the rest of the world as well once those things take control."

"Stop and think for a minute, General," said Brit. "This hand isn't that hard to play. You're holding all the cards, now it's time to show them."

"You mean share the technology?"

"All the cards, General."

"Share the tech, the weapons and all the intel?"

Brit gave him a big smile of approval. "Think about it. If you share with the rest of the world, they'll be too busy clearing their own house to think about attacking us. That leaves you with only one battle front to worry about."

He was nodding his head slowly. "You're right, Ms. Majors. We could even run a few joint ventures with other nations, show them what they're facing and how to combat it." He turned to his three scientists. "It'll be up to you guys to provide irrefutable evidence of the danger to the politicos."

Melanie pushed the recording of the previous day's interrogation across the table to the general. "This should help."

"That the record of..."

"Yes, that's it. We have other copies. Look, General, as much as I appreciate your help here, I think you might want to start moving on the bigger picture. We've got the people and resources to clear this island. Every minute you stay here is a loss on the mainland."

"You're absolutely right, Sheriff. As soon as we finish breakfast we'll be gone. Eat up then start packing, people. We have to get moving. Sheriff, I'll stay in touch and keep you in the loop, I promise. Any new weapons we develop will be sent to you instantly."

"Thanks, General. I appreciate that. Look, folks, I hate to eat and run, but..."

"Understood," said the general. "Good hunting."

Melanie nodded then turned to Bjorn. "You'll be co-coordinating the hunt from here today. Brit can help you. Come on, Deputy Majors, we've got work to do."

As they climbed into the police cruiser, Carrie reached over to squeeze Melanie's hand. "Thank you, sweetheart."

"For?"

"For leaving Bjorn to protect Brit."

"I just felt better about him being with her. We'll stop at the hospital first. If Luke's able to move, I'll have Lizzie take him back to the B&B as well. With Lizzie and Bjorn there, an army couldn't take that place down. It's funny, you know. Before you arrived on the scene, that hotel was the last place I would ever have called safe. Now, it feels like home, a safe haven."

"It pleases me that you feel that way," smiled Caroline. "Truly it does."

They had arrived at the hospital. Melanie was barely through the door when the administrator appeared beside her. "Sheriff, thank god you're here."

"You folks have a busy night?" asked Melanie.

"Indeed we did. I see you're aware of Hank Doyle's death."

"I am. He was a good friend, and his death is a great loss to the community."

"Agreed. However, there were more disturbances. That woman you left her to stay with Agent..."

"Lizzie kept the place livened up; I take it?"

"She shot three of our staff with a tranquilizer gun. She has them locked in a room and said I should talk to you about it. May I ask what the hell is going on?"

"Sir, there's an epidemic going around."

"We've heard nothing about an epidemic."

"You're hearing now. The symptoms manifest as mental issues, sudden dramatic changes in personality or habits. Have you noticed anything like this?"

"There's been nothing like that I've been made aware of. It has a physical cause?"

Melanie nodded. "It certainly does."

"So how do we treat it? Better yet, how can your people spot it so easily and ours can't?"

"Come on, I'll show you. Call every available doctor and nurse to witness it too." He hurried away and she went looking for Lizzie. They found her beside Luke's bed, trying to keep him in it.

"At least get me some damned weapons," growled Luke as Lizzie gently pushed him back into the pillows.

"I'll see if Vic can bring some by for you," grinned Melanie.

Lizzie turned to Melanie. It was obvious the girl had faced a hard night. "Mel, make him stay in the damned bed."

"I've got a better idea. Luke, report."

"Place was a madhouse last night. Three tried to get in and Lizzie dropped them all with tranqs."

"Your physical status?"

"They want me to stay a few more days, but I can travel, and I can fight. I just can't run worth a damn."

"Very good. Check yourself out. Lizzie, take him back to the B&B. Bjorn is there and so is Brit. That place is warded, and it'll be easier to defend with the whole team together. You guys can help Bjorn coordinate the hunt from there.

"Now, Lizzie, show me where you've got the prisoners."

"They're down the hall, last room on the left before the elevator. Mel, thanks."

"Go on, girl, take him home. Come on, Carrie. Let's go give these nice folks a demonstration of the plague."

Carrie grinned as she followed Melanie to the room with the prisoners. They arrived to find the room nearly full of medical staff as well as the administrator. There were four beds in the room. Three had people held in heavy restraints. As she walked in, the administrator introduced Melanie as the new sheriff and explained what she was going to do. At the mention of a plague several people took a step back from the prisoners.

"All right, people, listen up. You need to ignore what happens and focus on these people's backs. Okay? Carrie, hit 'em with the DK. Easy now, just enough to stir them up."

Caroline flicked on her DK and all three in restraints began to struggle wildly, screaming and moaning, begging for help. "Don't touch them," commanded Melanie. "Now keep watching their backs. Tell me what you see."

"See? I see people being tortured," snarled one man. "I demanded you..."

Melanie flicked on her DK right in his face. There were moans from behind her, but he barely flinched. "What did you feel?"

"What?"

"Tell me, what did you feel when I shone the light on you?"

"Nothing. I didn't feel anything. I don't..."

He got no further as Melanie turned away and flicked the DK on, shining it into the general area of the room. The three people in restraints began to scream, howl, and thrash around, fighting the restraints. Both Melanie and Carrie could see the demons struggling wildly.

"Oh my god," exclaimed one nurse as she backed further away from the three beds, "what is that on her back? What the hell is that thing?"

"Where, what?" came another voice.

"Wait, I see it too," exclaimed another. The demon energy in the room was too strong when they were in pain. They were no longer able to remain invisible. Soon everyone could see them.

"So, can you all see them?" asked Melanie.

There was a round of yeses and affirmative nods. "All right then. We don't know exactly what these things are, or where they're from. What we do know is this. They attach themselves to an unsuspecting human and slowly take control of the mind and body. Now that you've seen them once, you will always be able to see them. For lack of a better word, we call them demons. Think of them as a giant germ.

"If the human host dies the demon is free to claim another. However, we can separate them from the host and kill them. Because of this, they will try to kill the victim so they can escape."

"They can't escape as long as the host is alive?" asked a doctor.

"Nope," replied Melanie. "As long as the human is alive the demon can be killed, and the human can recover fully. It takes a bit of time, a day or two, but the human will come back to themselves and remember everything.

"Now, Deputy Majors and I will destroy these demons, then you folks will have to keep the victims under observation for a day or two, make sure their memories are back and that they don't hurt themselves. Later today someone will arrive and deliver a few DKs to you. DK, demon killer." She held up the weapon.

"Now, here we go. Full blast, Carrie." Caroline turned her DK on full blast and the three humans in restraints went wild, screaming, moaning, and fighting the bands that held them. The demons thrashed about wildly until they faded and drifted up from their victims. Melanie turned on her DK as well and, with inhuman screeching, the demons dissolved into nothingness.

The three humans in the beds lay panting and gasping for air. "What the hell just happened?" asked one. "Where am I?"

"All right, folks, do your thing." Melanie passed her DK to the doctor as she stepped towards the door. "Keep that just in case. Works just like a flashlight. Turn it on a victim and hold it on until the demon dissolves completely."

"Thank you, Sheriff," he replied, looking at the weapon in his hand, but she was already gone.

WHEN THEY REACHED THE sheriff's office Emily was there and had the place opened up. The coffee was ready, and the militia was there in force. Vic was also there with Egg. They were handing out weapons of demonic destruction. Before Melanie could get things organized the mayor arrived. "Sheriff Rivers."

"Mayor."

"Jim, please, call me Jim. First I have to thank you. Abby is back to her old self again. Second, I presume you've heard about Hank."

"I have, Jim," sighed Melanie, a small catch in her voice.

"Look, Melanie, I know you only agreed to stay as long as Hank was sheriff, but I'm asking you officially to stay on for the rest of Hank's four year term. Melanie, we need you, the town needs you. I..."

"Save it for the voters, Jim. I'll stay and finish out what Hank and I started. It's what he wanted. We'll see how it all plays out from there."

"Oh, thank god. I honestly don't know what would happen if you left. We need this situation under control, and we need it to stay that way. As I understand it, a host of those things escaped the cave the other night. That means this will never really be over, will it?"

Melanie nodded her agreement. "No, it won't. At least not for the foreseeable future."

The mayor sighed and leaned back against a desk. "Melanie, what's our best hope?"

"Best case scenario? We kick their asses off the island then we set up a system to monitor anyone coming onto the island, stop them in their tracks before they can cause trouble. We can also monitor ourselves easily. Check this out. Vic."

She stepped back and Vic shone the light of a DK on her. "Nothing, see, easy test. If I had a monkey on my back it would have raised old holy hell when hit with that light. The hardest part of this whole thing is going to be today. It's now almost nine o'clock. Once we start the sweep of the island we don't dare stop. Is everybody ready for it?"

There was a round of *hell yeah*s from the militia. "What can I do to help?" asked the mayor.

"Go home and stand guard over your family," said Vic, as he handed the man a DK. "If you have to use that, never stop until the demon is completely destroyed. Got it?"

"Got it, and thank you. All right, I'll leave you to it, Sheriff."

With that he left and Melanie turned back to the militia. "Now, people, listen up. We could be facing high powered rifles with nothing more than tranq pistols. I'd like to see this accomplished with no loss of human life, but I seriously doubt that will happen. Think about this. Nobody will think less of you if you want to sit this one out."

One of the men stepped forward. She recognized him as the man who'd shot at her. "Sheriff, everyone here is a volunteer who has had one of those damned things on his back. We want some payback, and we want this island safe for our families. Nobody is sitting this one out."

"Fair enough. You all know what you're looking for and you know what to do when you find it. We'll start at the far end of the island and work our way back to town. We will miss some, that's a given, but we'll get the most of them and drive the others into hiding. After today we'll make a new plan for rounding up the ones we miss and how to keep the island safe in future. Right now, we go hunting.

"Everybody grab a vest and wear it. Be careful. We'll meet up at Ander's farm to start off. Carrie and I will lead us in, the rest of you spread out. Some of you search the barn and the rest make sure no one slips away. Emily is your Militia Captain, she'll divide you into teams when we get there."

They grabbed the vests and weapons then filed out of the office. A convoy of vehicles left the parking lot, led by the sheriff's cruiser. When they reached the farm the vehicles spread out and blocked every possible escape route. They were barely out of the cars when a man on an ATV broke from the barn and raced away.

Two men in a four-wheel drive gave chase and cornered him near the cliff. There were a lot of screams then the truck returned with the man lying limp in the bed of the truck. Melanie and the others emerged empty handed and helped the man out and on to his feet.

They told him to go back in the house and take it easy for a day or two. Then they all moved on to the next farm.

It was mid-afternoon by the time they reached the edge of town. They had found only one more demon and it had been summarily dispatched. Working their way into town was tougher going. Some of them went house to house while other blocked the streets. Anyone who came near or tried to leave was made to stand for a DK inspection. That turned up three more in the first block.

By this time the word was out. There was a sudden rush of people towards the hotel. That didn't work as the wards were strong and the demons' natural aversion to going near the place caused them to loosen their grip on their victims. In the midst of that confusion Lizzie and Bjorn emerged from the woods on either side of the gathered cars.

They had a DK in each hand and pandemonium broke loose. Results? Six demons dead and three fled still attached to their human hosts. Bjorn radioed that news to Melanie. Those who had fled tried to get off island, but they found the militia waiting for them at the docks. Two women with DKs were flanking the ramp to the ferry boat. No demon escaped alive.

Back in the town, darkness had fallen, and the search went on. Nothing new was turned up, the demons had stampeded. First they'd tried to capture the Hotel, then tried to flee. All to no avail. However, the searchers did find two dead bodies where the demons had forced their hosts to commit suicide to set them free. By ten p.m. It was over. The hospital was full of former hosts trying to find out what was wrong with them. The doctor had accounted for two more demons, and the last boat had left the island for the day. It was done.

When they gathered back at the sheriff's office they discovered that they'd only taken one wound. One man had suffered a gun shot, but he was bandaged up and back in action before the end of the day.

"Well, folks," sighed Melanie, as she sank into a chair at her old desk, "looks like we got away cheap today. One wound for us and two dead victims. Not the best, but a hell of a long way from the worst. Well done, people. I'm proud of every one of you."

One woman smiled and nodded to Melanie. "Melanie, I'll be the first to confess I had a fit when you came back to Brighton. Now I have to say I am damned glad you did. God only knows how long I'd had that thing stuck on my back. I'm sorry for all the times I bad mouthed you and your family, and I swear, when the election comes I'll be the first to vote for you."

"Go home, Myra," chuckled Melanie. "You're over tired and not making sense."

"I mean it, Mel."

"I know, and thanks. Look, folks, this is a new world now. What happened before we discovered the demons doesn't count anymore. Everything's all brand new. Let's continue working together to clean up the island and to make damn sure it stays that way. Back here, nine o'clock tomorrow morning?"

"We'll be here, Sheriff," grunted one of the men. They were all exhausted. They shuffled out to their cars and headed for their homes and beds for a well earned rest. Melanie nodded her approval as she noticed they all kept their DKs and tranq pistols.

"Emily, your troops worked wonders today," grinned Melanie.

"Thanks Sheriff Rivers. First thing tomorrow I'll help you clear out the inner office and get you set up in there."

"Em..."

"No. He's gone, Mel, and no matter what we do we can't bring him back. All we can do is make sure we do the job in a way that would make him proud."

She burst into tears and Caroline was right there to take the distraught woman in her arms. "We all liked Hank, Emily. We did. Hold it together now. Just as soon as we have this situation under control we can give him a proper send off. We can and will mourn him then."

"I know, I know," sniffed Emily. "I guess I'm just overtired too. I'll see you guys in the morning."

"Good night, Em. Make sure you have a DK with you."

"Right here, Mel. Thanks."

Once Emily was through the door Caroline sighed then turned to Melanie. "You all right, lover?"

"I am, sweetie. I am. I need a shower and a bed to sleep in and I'll be right as rain in the morning."

"Yeah, me too. Say, how about a warm girl to snuggle with in that bed?"

"Good idea," grinned Melanie as she gathered her gear and headed for the door. "Know where I might find one?"

"First place I'd look would be right beside you."

Settling Into New Lives

Melanie was first in the shower. She'd been there long enough for the shakes and the emotions to put her down, but it hadn't happened. For some reason, that concerned her. In the past, when she spent the day fighting for her life, seeing dead bodies, witnessing tortured people, and actually killing someone she'd always felt a full range of emotions. Powerful emotions. Emotions that battered at her, tore at her sanity, and drained her completely.

This time she was oddly serene. Caroline joined her and Melanie smiled as she pulled her lover into her arms and kissed her deeply. Carrie moaned and melted under the fire of that kiss. As their lips slowly parted she whispered in Melanie's ear. "Are you okay?"

"Better than, hush now, I'm busy exploring. If you distract me I might have to start all over." As she spoke, Melanie placed soft hungry kisses along Carrie's jaw line and down her throat.

"Oh gods, we wouldn't want that," grinned Caroline, as she leaned back against the wall of the shower and released herself to her lover's kisses and the warm cascading water.

Melanie's lips nibbled at Carrie's nipples while her hands explored the long lines of that delicious athletic body. The finger tips delicately traced the lines of the long scars they found and Caroline stiffened slightly. She relaxed again as warm lips took over from the fingers and traced the scars with soft kisses.

Hands with strong fingers gripped Caroline's buttocks and pulled gently, forcing her hips away from the wall slightly as Melanie knelt before her and continued with her explorations. Caroline

203

groaned with pleasure as she tangled her fingers in Melanie's hair, pulling her closer.

Warm kisses traced the lines of Carrie's inner thighs, gently nuzzling them further apart. Caroline moaned and ground her hips against the hungry mouth that brought her closer and closer to the edge of reality. Suddenly the hands on her buttocks gripped tighter and forced her closer to the hungry lips and flicking tongue. The sudden onslaught pushed Caroline over the edge into oblivion. Loving arms caught and held her as her body convulsed several times to absorb the shattering orgasm.

The warm cascade of water and Melanie's gently kisses slowly brought Carrie back to the world, a sigh of pure delight on her lips. "My god, Mel, that was amazing."

"I'm happy you enjoyed it, sweetie. You are truly delicious, you know that?"

"So you keep telling me. I know you'd never lie to me, so it must be true."

"It is true, my delight. I have tested the theory several times and each time it proves to be true. You are truly delicious."

"And you're truly a sweet nut. Let's get out of this water before it gets cold. I want to dry your hair then tuck you into bed properly."

"Take me away, lover. I'm all yours."

"And don't you forget it."

Melanie just chuckled and turned off the water. "Perish the thought, my love. Perish the thought."

CAROLINE AWOKE LATE the next day. She sat up with a start. "Oh crap, I am so late. What happened to the alarm?" There was a piece of paper lying atop the clock. She recognized Melanie's flowing script. "Relax, beautiful lady. You've got the day off. Go play in your studio. I love you. Mel."

Carrie flopped back onto the pillows. "What a sweetheart. I wonder just what it'll take for her to have a day off." She snuggled down again, then noticed Melanie's little book beside the bed. She must have forgotten it.

Picking up the book Caroline realized the book was left behind because it was full. Melanie must have taken a fresh one with her. Carrie opened the book to the last page.

"Humanity lost, but

Lust remains

Love remains."

"She must have left it out for me to read," smiled Carrie. "She wanted me to know she is okay, even though she didn't release the emotions last night. Hmm, maybe we just found a better way for her to release." That thought brought back a delightful memory of the previous night. Carrie stretched luxuriously then allowed her agile fingers to explore her body and bring the memory back into sharper focus.

It was much later when she arrived in the dining room where she found Brit working at her laptop.

Brit looked up then grinned. "I'm sorry, Ma'am, but this is a B&B. We don't serve lunch."

"Ha ha ha, very funny. Fine then, I'll just see what I can find in the kitchen."

"Sit down, silly woman. Mel said to let you sleep so I saved you some breakfast. Grab yourself a coffee and I'll be right back."

A few minutes later Caroline pushed away her plate and took the last swig from her coffee. "Brit, that was perfect," she smiled, as she rose and took her dishes to the kitchen.

Brit followed her in. "Hey, lady, there will be no stealing my job." She took Carrie's plate and put it in the sink. "You have a job. Today is your day off. Shouldn't you be playing in your studio?"

Caroline took her sister by the shoulders and turned her around, then hugged her gently. "Brit, what's going on?"

"Nothing."

"Bullshit."

"Fine. I'm sorry, Carrie. I guess I'm still scared."

"And you're still in love with Melanie."

"That easy to read, am I? Is everybody having a good laugh?"

"No, honey, you're still the best poker player there is, but I'm your sister. I know you too well."

Brit burst into tears and buried her face in her sister's shoulder. "I'm so sorry, Carrie. It's a lot harder to let go of her than I thought it would be. Please don't be angry. Please don't send me away."

"Stop this, silly sister," cooed Caroline. "Stop it now. I'm not angry and I'm not going to send you away. No one is, this is your home."

"But..."

"No buts. Melanie and I talked about this. She loves you too, always has. Brit, she chose me, swore to be faithful to me, and I trust that. I also know you would never do anything to come between Melanie and me, or you and me.

"Honey, Melanie is a big part of the mess we're all in and she knows it. She fell for both of us. Life got in the way and forced her to make a decision she didn't want to make. Mel wanted to take time and let everything evolve, enjoy flirting with us both, and slowly sorting out her feelings while we sorted out ours.

"Life got in the way and none of us had the chance to get our feelings explored. The demons showed up and forced Melanie's attention back to her old job, her old war, the one she tried to leave behind. Meanwhile, we forced her to make a decision she wasn't ready to make. Being Mel, she made it rather than lose us both.

"Honey, we both believe love and lust are different things, you know that. Mel believes the same thing. She wants you here because she loves you. I want you here because I love you. You love both of us, so you have to stay."

"Okay, so are you saying I am allowed to love the both of you?"

"I insist."

"Are you going to share the lusty part too?"

"Oh, hell no."

"Damn."

Caroline laughed and hugged Brit tighter. "I have no idea how Mel would react to that suggestion. Give it time and I'll talk to her, who knows?"

"Carrie, thank you. I really didn't think you'd be willing to..."

Caroline kissed her forehead and smiled. How she did love her sister. "Honey, are you okay now?"

"Yeah. Carrie, I can get this thing settled. I can shift my feelings for Mel to sisterly love, I can. I just need to know you're not angry and will help me, give me the time I need."

"Oh, Brit, you know I will, but you may not have to."

"Okay, then I guess I should get back to work and finish the dishes. You go play in your studio."

"Brit, what else is going on?"

"Carrie, you're the deputy sheriff now. I'm the B&B staff. I know you planned to be the deputy just for a week or so until this thing with the demons was under control."

"But..."

Brit's shoulders sagged. "Mel will shoot me."

"Brit, what's happened?"

"I've been watching the news feeds on the net and the general sent me an update. Honey, I think you'll be wanting to keep that job for a while longer."

"Is it that bad?"

"And getting worse. Look, things on the island are quiet right now. Mel said to make sure you relaxed today and to not show you the news."

"She's still trying to protect me."

"Yeah, she still hasn't figured out that you're the strong one."

"It's because I wasn't when she first got to know me. I'd been crushed and at my lowest ebb in my entire life. I just hope she likes the real me too."

"Oh she does, girl," grinned Brit. "She likes this new super woman far better. She told me so this morning. Carrie, Melanie truly does love you, never doubt that. You go play now, I'll come up with more coffee as soon as I finish here."

Carrie nodded, kissed her forehead again, then left the kitchen. She returned to her suite, changed out of her uniform and into jeans with a loose smock, and then ran up the stairs to the studio. She was still moving things around and unpacking her supplies when Brit arrived with the coffee.

MELANIE REACHED THE sheriff's office to find Bjorn, Luke, and Lizzie already there. The militia was there too. Luke was laying out a plan to keep the island clear of demons. He grinned and gave Melanie a quick run down. The plan was to have the militia use DKs to monitor all vehicles arriving on the island. They would also run regular patrols. Vic was working on new and better weapons. Tea would be mandatory for all members.

Melanie grinned and nodded her approval. "Emily, looks like Luke has stolen your job."

"I gave it to him, Mel. I'm the office girl and dispatcher. I'm supposed to make this office run smoothly, not go running around playing super soldier."

"I don't know, girl. You did a fine job though. I think you like giving the orders."

"I do, way too much. That's why Luke is taking over the militia. Lizzie is his second in command, and Bjorn is going to be a deputy sheriff."

"Excuse me?"

"Mel, we have it in the budget to hire two deputies. Bjorn says he's quit his old job and needs a new one."

"That right, Bjorn old buddy? This wouldn't have anything to do with a tall blonde working at the B&B would it?"

He just grinned. "Maybe, maybe not. I'll let you know when I have more intel. So, how about it? Got a job for me?"

"You're serious."

"I am."

"You're hired. Welcome aboard. Emily, Bjorn will be the force detective, no uniform required. Badge and weapons only."

"Thanks for that, Mel."

"I know how you hate wearing a uniform," chuckled Melanie. "Luke, report."

"I have new orders from the general. I am to remain on this island with whatever personnel I need from my former team, and coordinate with the local populace and law enforcement. Since Lizzie is all I have left on my team I'm keeping her with me."

"Lizzie, you okay with that?"

"I'll manage, Mel."

"Atta girl, tough it out. All right, people, you seem to have things under control. I guess all I have to do today is enjoy some coffee, maybe even a doughnut."

Emily shook a finger at her. "There will be none of that until after we finish the move."

"Move?"

"You know damn well what move, Sheriff. Mel, I'm sorry. I really don't want to do this either, but we have to. We have to clear out his things and move you into that office. You're the sheriff now."

"So I have to look like it, do I? All right, slave driver. Throw this motley crew out and we'll get to work."

There was a round of laughter at her expense as the militia filed out, Luke and Lizzie in the lead. Bjorn leaned back in his chair and put his feet on the desk. Melanie arched an eyebrow at him. "Is that it? Don't you have work to do? Go detect something."

Bjorn picked up his coffee mug and gazed into it. "Hmm, I detect a severe lack of the medicinal herb in this mug. As the official detective for this office, I will take it upon myself to rectify the situation." Melanie just rolled her eyes and groaned.

Together, Melanie and Emily entered the inner office. At first glance there wasn't a sign of the man who'd occupied this office when Melanie had first returned to Brighton. This was Hank Doyle's office and it had been for longer than Melanie had been alive. Pictures of siblings and their families hung on the walls as well as a number of awards for service and memorials of great events in the town's history.

Hank had never married. He'd lost his one true love to a car accident when he was a teenager and had lived alone for the rest of his life. Teary eyes, Emily produced a cardboard box and began to take down the pictures and pack them away. The sad reminders of a life of service.

Melanie began to clean out the desk. The cases Hank had been working on she put to one side. All his personal effects she passed to Emily. One fairly new journal caught her eye and she flipped it open. There in Hank's strong handwriting, was the answer to a question she'd wanted. She had been refused release from the secret service several times, but the last time they had practically thrown her out. No one would tell her why. The journal read:

"I'm seeing strange things again. People suddenly acting out of character, turning nasty, brutal, mean. I don't like it. It reminds me too much of when Rivers went crazy years ago."

Several entries were the same, then one caught her eye. "It's getting a lot worse. I can't convince that mainland jackass of a thing. He just calls me an old fool. Damn, I should never have retired.

"Last night I called in a favor from an old army buddy. Told him my suspicions. He said he knew what was up and he had the answer. He said his best super agent was an old friend of mine. Melanie Rivers. She wants out to come home. We need her here desperately. He said he'd make it happen, but I'd have to play straight with her. I remember her as a strong kid. I hope he's right about this. I'll keep an eye out for her."

Melanie sighed and closed the journal. "Hank, you old bugger, you set me up."

She chuckled and showed the passages to Emily. "So, you're a super agent, are you? I'm not surprised, Mel. You always were the go-to girl, the one who could get things done. Mel, I'm glad you're back, I'm glad we're friends again, and I'm glad you're the sheriff now. I'll miss Hank like my own dad, but I believe you can handle the job, Hank believed it, and I'll do whatever I can to help you."

"I'll miss him too, Em. Hank Doyle was always good to me, he helped me, and he believed in me. Maybe this is where I belong after all. I was at loose ends when I got home. Hank gave me a job, a direction, and support when nobody else would. I promise I'll try to be worthy of his faith in me. Your job is to make sure I don't screw it up."

Emily laughed and shook her head. "Mel, you always said that to me and it always scared me. It's good to have you back. Oh, I guess you should have this too." She passed Melanie a pearl handled revolver. Melanie cocked an eyebrow at her. "It belonged to the original sheriff of Brighton. It's been passed down from one to the next until now."

Melanie checked the weapon. It was empty, but well cared for and fully functional. "Hank loved that silly old thing. He used to take it out to the range once a week."

"Yeah? Well, it's a bit heavy for my liking," sighed Melanie. "I'll take it to a trophy shop and have it set up for a display. We can find a home for it on the wall.

"Well, that looks like all of it, Em. Not a lot to show for a lifetime of dedicated service, is it?"

"This is just stuff, Mel. It's the people of this town and the good memories of him that testify to Hank's lifetime of service."

"You're right, Em. Hank's left big boots to fill. Hope I'm up to the job."

Emily didn't reply. She just nodded then picked up the box and turned to go. "I'll take care of this for you. You gather your stuff from that desk out there and move in. I'll get, Bjorn is it? I'll get him settled in."

Melanie nodded and let her gaze return to the old oak desk before her. She let her fingers slowly trace the outline of the blotter. "Big boots to fill, for sure." She sank slowly into the faded leather chair. "Sadly, I'm not too sure I really want to. Even if I am, can I really do it? I'm more of a warrior by training, not a peacekeeper. Peacekeeper is what this job requires."

She was still sitting there, lost in thought when Emily returned a while later. A fresh cup of coffee was placed at her right hand and a new box dropped on her desk. "Your stuff, Sheriff. Get to work."

Melanie shook her head and chuckled. "I'm a police officer now. Coffee first."

She barely had a sip when a loud voice from the outer office shattered the air. "I demand to see the sheriff."

"Oh bugger. I guess I'm up." The coffee was left to go cold.

Calm Before the Storm

Melanie arrived home at the end of the day to a silent B&B. She called out, but got no answer. With a shrug she entered the suite she shared with Carrie and tossed her hat in the general direction of the hangar. She was out of the shower and dressed in her sweats when Brit popped her head through the door.

"Hey, Mel, I thought I heard you come in. Dinner is nearly ready. Go on up to the studio and see what your honey has been up to today."

She stepped back and looked away, but Melanie had caught the look in her eyes. She stepped through the door and caught Brit by the arm, turned her, and pulled her into a hug. "Hey, you. That wasn't much of a poker face."

"Melanie, I am so sorry," sniffed Brit, as she hugged Melanie tightly, fiercely. "I know..."

"Stop that right now. Brit, I never thought of you as second best, nor do I love you less than I love Carrie."

"But we made you choose?"

"Yes, you did. You didn't take the time to get sick of me or turned off by my craziness..."

"That would never happen, Mel. I'm ashamed to say I'm not dealing with this very well."

"None of us are, sweet sister. Life stepped in and buggered everything up in a hurry. Now we all have to figure out how to live with it. Brit, I do love you too and it will kill me if you pull back from me, from us. Carrie is worried about that, I know she is. She's afraid she's losing her sister."

"Oh, god, Mel, that will never happen..."

"So go put dinner on the back burner for a few minutes and we can go up to fetch her together."

"Oh, Mel, that might..."

"Life is what it is, Brit. Now, just like at the hospital, put on your game face and let's go. You're running on what might be and you need to know what really is. It's time to ante up and call."

"Can't I fold?"

"Oh, hell no."

Brit gazed into Melanie's eyes for a long moment. "God, you don't make things easy. It was me, wasn't it?"

"Carrie knows, Brit."

"You chose her to bring her back, even though you knew how hard it would be with me around. You did that for Carrie and you did it for me, so I wouldn't lose my sister. She knows it too, but she loves you and is willing to accept that."

"Go put the food on the back burner now, Brit. We'll go up together. Carrie needs to know we're okay and that you won't leave or pull away from her. Yes, she loves me. I really do love her, too. However, make no mistake here, Carrie's love for her sister is stronger. The only way she can be truly happy is if you stay."

Brit grabbed Melanie's hand and dragged her into the kitchen which was filled with wonderful smells. "Melanie Rivers, I could never leave. My biggest fear was I would have to go so you guys could be happy."

She turned the heat off then took Mel's hand again and led her towards the stairs. "It's just not bloody fair you know, you greedy bag."

"What?"

"You got both girls after all." She squeezed Melanie's hand then they stepped into the studio.

Melanie gave a long slow whistle as she took in the sight before her. Carrie had her hair tied up in a sloppy bun, her loose smock was covered in paint, and a fresh canvass was well under way. Melanie could see the view from the window appearing on the canvass. Carrie looked up and instantly noticed the clasped hands.

A bright smile of delight spread across her face. She jumped up and pulled them both into a tight hug. "I love you both, you know that?"

"We do, sweetie," whispered Brit, "and we plan to make sure it stays that way."

THEY WERE ALL GATHERED at the table, relaxing after the meal, Melanie, Brit, Caroline, Bjorn, Lizzie, and Luke. Carrie smiled lovingly at Melanie. "Hey, Sheriff, tell me all about your day. What did I miss?"

Melanie smiled and shook her head. "Not much, Deputy Majors. I got to work, Emily informed me we had enough in the budget for another deputy, she hired Bjorn on the spot, then she drove me into the back office and locked me in. She didn't let me out again until quitting time."

"She made you clean out Hank's desk, huh? That can't have been easy, love."

"It wasn't. I did learn something new, though. Hank and my old boss knew each other. My request for release had been refused several times. It wasn't until Hank asked his old buddy for a favor that I was cut loose."

"Oh?"

"Yeah, Hank was retired, but still a cop. He could see something was wrong, but couldn't convince the new guy to take it seriously.

Hank called his buddy, and I was cut loose with nowhere to go but home."

"Hank set you up?"

"Apparently so. It was what I wanted anyway. I wanted to come home and Hank needed someone to believe him. I just wish I'd been able to..."

"Hey, none of that at the dinner table," said Brit as she patted Melanie's hand. "Tell us what else happened."

"Nothing, as far as I know. The Militia patrolled the island, Emily manned the phones, Bjorn investigated the case of a vandalizing dog, and I spent the day shuffling paper. Now, time for all you guys to share. I know you had a more exciting day than I did. Luke, report."

"Hmm, let's see. Lizzie and I joined the militia. We set up watch points across the island. We set up shift rotations for scanning the passengers of the ferry boats as they landed. What else did we do, Lizzie?"

"Oh, let me think, we decided to move in together and sneaked away to find an apartment. Does that count?"

"Well, it's about time," grinned Melanie. "Bjorn, report."

"I signed on with the local police force, drank some fairly decent coffee, investigated a vandalism, caught the perp and took him home where he was promptly put in chains. I also took a long look at the room above the office. I plan to move in there, with your permission, at least until we're sure this current situation is completely under control."

"You don't think it is?" asked Caroline.

"No, I don't, Carrie. It was just too easy. That thing has a big hate on for Mel; I just don't see it giving up anytime soon."

"So, you're leaving me?"

"Brit, I'll miss your cooking more than you know."

He gave her a smile, but it wasn't convincing. Bjorn was no fool, he could see where her heart lay, and he was ready to move on to save his own. "You've got this place so well protected it's like a fort, so is Ellen's place. No, I expect that thing to come after Mel again and I expect it to come in heavy. The sheriff's office is the most likely place for the action to start. I want to be there when it does."

Brit gave him a sad smile and patted his hand. "Don't be a stranger."

"I'll come by every time I get sick of my own cooking. You'll see lots of me."

"So, looks like we'll be on our own, girls..." Melanie got no further as a knock came to the door then Ellen stepped inside.

"Anybody home?"

"Just us chickens," called Mel, as she rose to go to her grandmother. "Come on in."

Ellen entered followed by Vic and Egg. Both men were loaded down with gear. Melanie gave Ellen a hug then turned to Vic. "So, whatcha got there, Vic? New toys?"

"Oh yeah, you're going to love this stuff. We've got another dozen DKs and these babies. Vic held up a floodlight with a speaker wired to the top.

"What the heck is that thing?"

"My invention," grinned Egg. "I built the first one myself."

"What does it do, Egg?" asked Caroline as she joined them.

"This is great, Ms Majors. First there were the gloves, but their range was limited and tightly focused. Vic invented the DKs, like the one you used to set me free. Now this is the new L-bomb."

"L-bomb?"

"Yes, ma'am, a light bomb. It's a floodlight that can reach half a mile and the speaker will project the sound with it. It also can cover a wider range than a DK. We've rigged up the headlights on Vic's car to do the same thing."

"My sorcerer's apprentice here has rigged one of these up on the house," grinned Vic. "We can set it on sweep and it will wash over the surrounding area all night long. Mel, it has roughly the same effective range as a rifle. With one of these sweeping the area it would take a real sniper to get to you. We want to set this one up on your roof."

"Guys, that's awesome. Go for it." Melanie grinned as Brit led them up the stairs. She turned and took Ellen's arm and led her to the living room. The others followed.

"What's on your mind, Nana?" Melanie asked as soon as everyone was settled.

"It's Egg. His folks are leaving the island, they think it'll be a lot safer somewhere else. We know better than that. He's a great kid and he'll be a lot safer here than anywhere else."

"And, you want the sheriff to have a talk with them, is that it?"

"Pretty much. Now that you've moved out we have a spare room. He could stay with us."

"Yeah, about that, Nana. What's this I hear about you and Vic getting married?"

"That'll never happen, Melanie. You know that. I wouldn't marry your grandfather and I won't marry Vic."

"But you will shack up with him, as you call it."

"Of course. I'm a traditionalist after all."

"Nana, you're such a hippie."

"And damned proud of it," replied Ellen. "I brought you folks more tea. It's out in the car."

"Thanks, Nana. So, what's in the tea?"

"You're the sheriff. I'm not telling you a damn thing. Just drink the tea, three cups a day."

"Yes, ma'am," grinned Melanie.

At that point the boys returned from the roof. "All set and working," smiled Vic, as he sat beside Ellen and put his arm around her shoulders. Egg ran out to the car then returned with a big bag of loose tea which he handed off to Brit. He sat on the sofa beside Vic and looked hopefully at Melanie.

"Oh, stop with the puppy dog eyes. I'll talk to them, but I make no promises. The decision with be theirs to make."

"Thanks, Sheriff. I appreciate it." The rest of the evening passed in pleasant conversation. Melanie fairly glowed as she enjoyed a family style gathering of all her favorite people. That had been missing for far too long in her life.

AS THEY PREPARED FOR bed Melanie took Carrie in her arms and kissed her. Carrie melted into that embrace, but there was a sadness to her response and Melanie felt it. She pulled back slightly and kissed Carrie softly on the forehead. "What is it lover?"

"Nothing."

"Liar, liar, pants on fire. What is it?"

"Nothing, Mel, honey. I'm so sorry."

"Is this about Brit and me holding hands when we came into your studio?"

"No. I'm just afraid that you're wishing you were kissing Brit and not me."

"Caroline Majors, when I kiss you it is because I want to kiss you. When I'm kissing you I am fully aware of who I'm kissing and that's who I focus on. When I kiss you, ma'am, it is you I kiss because I want to, and you are the only woman I think about when I do it."

"Thanks for that, lover, but I know you have feelings for Brit. I know it is her you truly love. I don't understand why you didn't choose her."

"Oh sweet Jesus, Mary, and Joseph," sighed Melanie as she turned away and threw herself on the bed. "I chose you because I wanted you. If faced with the same decision again I would still make the same choice for the same reasons."

Carrie sat on the edge of the bed and tentatively reached for Melanie's hand. She laced their fingers together and squeezed gently. "You love Brit more than me, Mel. I know that."

"Bullshit, Carrie. Pure bullshit. I love Brit as much as I love you, I admit that, but that's all I'll admit. Look, under normal circumstances we all would have had the time to sort this out before any decisions were made. However, these are not normal times."

"We forced you to make a decision you weren't ready to make, didn't we?"

"Yes you did, but that doesn't matter now. My decision is made, I love you to distraction, I am besotted with you, and I've never been happier in my life."

"But..."

"No buts, Carrie. No buts. I was forced to make that decision once. I will not make it again. I love you, I chose you, and I will never part with you until you force me to go. Seeing as how I'm the sheriff, that's going to be a hard order to enforce."

In spite of herself, Caroline giggled. "Dammit, Mel, you're a complete nut, you know that?"

"So I've been told, and recently. Carrie, honey, come here to me. I want to kiss you again." Carrie obliged by lying close and bringing her kips to Mel's for the kiss. It was a soft, gentle, loving kiss. "Now that's Carrie's kiss," sighed Melanie as their lips slowly parted.

"Just what does that mean?" asked a puzzled Caroline.

"That's your kiss. You guys both kiss different, that's how I can stay focused. You see Brit..."

Melanie got no further as Caroline swept up a pillow and began to beat her with it. "You beast, you rotten, miserable beast," exclaimed Carrie, as she emphasized each phrase with a blow from the pillow. Melanie giggled and tried to protect herself from the attack. "That's it for you, Melanie Rivers. Now you're going to get it."

"Oh good. I've been wanting it all day."

That got her another swat with the pillow. Carrie tried to glare at her, but failed and burst into giggles then hit Melanie again. She then tossed aside the pillow and grabbed the front of Melanie's night gown, puling her into another kiss. She kissed her hard then pushed her back. "Gods, you're such a brat." She pulled Mel into another fiery kiss.

Much later they lay in each others arms, their passions spent and the bed practically destroyed. Carrie was resting her head on Melanie's breasts, listening to her breathe. "Mel, honey?"

"Mmm?"

"It's okay if you love Brit too."

"Thanks, sweetie. I do love Brit and always will, but, make no mistake here. You're my woman, and I will never be unfaithful to you, end of story."

"Even though I'm a mass of insecurity?"

"Yeah, even then."

"How is it you knew exactly what to do when I came unglued?"

"Same way you did for me, sweetie. Carrie, you knew what to do when you found me in the shower having a meltdown. You knew because you've been through hell even worse than me."

"That's how you knew what to do for me too, wasn't it? Gods Mel, I'm so sorry we forced you into that decision so quickly."

"Don't be, lover. I'd have made the same choice anyway."

"Oh?"

"Carrie, I love Brit and she loves me. I love you and you love me. The tipping point here is our past experiences. You and I have a far greater understanding of our deeper wounds, our unseen scars. I don't think Brit could ever understand me the way you do."

Caroline snuggled closer. "Gods, Mel, we're such a mess, the three of us. What are we going to do?"

"Love each other as hard as we can, all three of us. Time will sort out the rest for us."

"I like this plan, sweetheart. I like this plan."

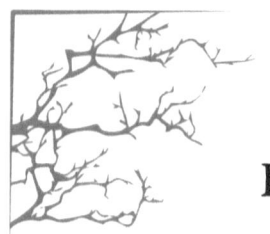

Fairly Warned

Over the next few days they sorted themselves out. Luke and Lizzie moved in together, Bjorn moved into the room above the sheriff's office, and the girls spent as much time as possible together, hoping the togetherness might smooth things out between them. It sort of did, and it really didn't. In the end, Brit went up to her suite alone every night. They could see the sadness in her eyes and they both felt guilty about it.

For her part, Melanie was tormented. The more time she spent with Carrie, the deeper in love she became. Goddam stupid laws anyway; why the hell couldn't she have both women? She snorted at herself in derision. "Yeah, like that would work." Melanie sighed and told herself that if this was her only problem in life, she'd be a lucky woman.

"What's the matter, honey? Can't sleep? Thinking about Brit? About all of us?"

"Tell me you aren't taking up mind reading for a hobby," sighed Melanie.

"It wasn't so hard to figure out," said Caroline as she snuggled closer. "Are you wanting to change your mind? Do you regret your decision?"

"No, and you're not allowed to say anything like that again. Not ever, you hear me? Never again. No, my love, sadly, it's just the opposite. The more time you and I have together the more in love I am. I still love Brit too, but somehow this isn't working out. I want her to be happy, like we are. I'm lost here and I don't know what to do about any of this."

"There is an option you may not have considered, at least not seriously."

"And that is?"

"We could move Brit in with us."

"What??? What the hell are you suggesting?"

"Actually, it was Ellen's suggestion, and I've been mulling it over. It makes sense to me." Melanie just stared at her with wide eyes. "Honey, Brit and I had a tough childhood. We had to share everything. We're used to that sharing, we need that sharing and closeness. I know that's why you chose me in the first place. The shape I was in wasn't good and you knew Brit could never be happy unless I was too."

"Carrie..."

"No dear, it's all good. I love you more for what you did there, but, as you say, it's not working out completely. And it needs to. Brit and I have shared a lover before, but never a woman. I don't see a problem here, and I'm sure Brit won't either. Neither of us is trying to own you, Mel. We just want to share completely in your life. Both of us do."

"Sweet baby Jesus, and my grandmother suggested this?"

"Yes she did," laughed Carrie. "She told Brit it was the perfect solution. She said it was what they would have done back in the sixties."

"My grandmother is a bad woman," sighed Melanie. "She's the one who jumped all over me to make a decision in the first place. Why the hell didn't she say something to me back then?"

"Mel, how would you have reacted to that coming from her?"

Melanie sighed and shook her head. "I'd have told her she was bad and laughed it off. Brit told me herself I couldn't have both girls. She's the one who forced the decision. She..."

"She loves you, and she's hurting."

"Carrie, I don't truly understand here. Are you really suggesting I bring Brit down here to share our bed?"

"Yes, that and more. I want you to make love to her the way you do to me, then when she's just a puddle of happy I want to take you myself. I love you both to bits, Melanie Rivers. I believe I have enough room in my heart for both of you. I know Brit does too. The only question here is can you get past your initial reactions? Do you have enough love in your heart for both of us? Can you?"

"Oh great, so here we go again. Life as I know it is about to explode all over the place, and I'm the one who has to make the decision? Is that what life with you, both of you would be like? Would I have to make all the decisions?"

"Of course, dear, but we'll always tell you what decision to make."

"That's it, woman, you're getting a beating." Melanie seized up a pillow and began to beat Carrie gently with it. Carrie giggled and tried to hide under the covers. Finally Melanie stopped and gathered Carrie into her arms. "You're a crazy woman."

"Come on, Mel, you know you wanted both girls all along."

"You guys aren't going to gang up on me are you?"

"Of course we are. Was that a yes?"

"That was a maybe. If you're truly serious I want to talk to Brit myself about it. Actually I want to talk to the both of you about it. I'll know if it's not one hundred percent right."

"Thank you, sweetheart. I know this is really testing you. The thing is, why can't we be allowed to love more than one person at the same time?"

"Because we're not supposed to, that's why."

"Who says so?"

"All the religious guys who want to control everybody, I guess. Carrie, we can't ever let the townsfolk know about this."

"Scared of losing your job?" she teased.

"Yeah, a bit. I'm just not quite ready to let it go. I have this deep feeling that we're not finished with the demon thing yet. That big bugger still wants my hide, and I don't get the sense he's the type to give up easily."

"I agree, but you're not allowed to think about that right now. You're about to be married to two exceptional women. Think about that instead."

"I am. Now I'm really scared." This time it was Melanie who got the beating with the pillow.

The next morning Melanie was having trouble meeting Brit's eyes at breakfast. "What's up, Mel?"

"Huh? Oh nothing."

"Bullshit." Melanie just sighed and looked away, blushing to her roots. "Carrie had the talk with you last night, didn't she?"

"Indeed I did," smiled Caroline, as she appeared and joined them at the table. "Brit honey, our poor Melanie will need a while to adjust to her good fortune."

Melanie gazed at them both. Carrie was smiling with pure delight. Brit was looking hopeful, begging Melanie with her eyes. "Brit, are you certain about this?"

Brit slid into Melanie's lap and kissed her deeply, softly, and yet hungrily. When their lips finally parted, Melanie sighed and hugged Brit tightly. "Man, that really fogged up my eyeballs." Her eyes weren't foggy though, they were crystal clear and boring into Carrie's. Caroline's grin of delight never wavered for a second.

Finally she nodded and relaxed her arms around Brit. "So there truly is no jealousy between you."

"There never has been, sweetheart," replied Carrie.

"And there never will be," added Brit. "The thing here is, can you handle the two of us?"

"Probably not. It will most likely be the death of me, but at least I'll die happy. If you're both hellbent on this we'll move in together after work today."

"Upstairs or down?" grinned Carrie.

"Who's got the biggest bed?"

"I do," laughed Brit. "It's a king size."

"Works for me," sighed Melanie, a bemused smile on her face as she rose to her feet. "Carrie, why don't you take the day off."

"And do all the heavy lifting before you get home?" Caroline arched an eyebrow at Melanie.

"It was worth a shot," Melanie sighed elaborately. "All right, Deputy Majors. Let's get to work before Emily fires the both of us." Carrie winked at Brit, kissed her cheek, then ran for the door.

ELLEN AND VIC WERE at the sheriff's office waiting for Melanie to arrive. As soon as they walked through the door Caroline grinned and Melanie blushed. Ellen gazed into her eyes for a moment then winked. "Thank god that's been resolved. Not you can get focused on your job."

"Nana..."

"I know, I'm a bad woman. Just your cross to bear, Mel."

"Beast," chuckled Melanie, as she gave her grandmother a hug. "You're awful. You're just lucky you're related to the sheriff."

Vic was chuckling and waiting for Melanie to have a moment. "What's up, Vic? You're looking pretty smug."

"I am, Mel. That kid is a slave driver, but he's good. Between us we've mounted anti-demon floodlights at the ferry dock as well as the Fisherman's Wharf. We've got the top of our house and yours as well as the hospital and school. Egg is home building more. He wants to mount them just above Sandy Cove Beach and Albert's Beach. The militia has agreed to man them around the clock. The only way..." The ringing phone interrupted him.

Emily picked up the intrusive instrument. "Brighton Sheriff's office. What? Who? Just a moment General." She handed the phone to Melanie.

Melanie poked a button with her finger to put it on speaker then spoke. "Morning General."

"Sheriff, I have bad news and good."

"Gimme the good first."

"There's a shipment of weapons headed your way. Stronger tranquilizer pistols and a few tranq rifles. There's also tazers and newly designed DKs. On top of that is a crate of the tea. You can tell Ellen we know what's really in it and we don't give a tinker's damn. We're just thrilled that it works."

"That's great, General. Now hit me with the bad."

"Melanie, the Navy has just admitted they've lost a team of Navy SEALs. This is a five man team of highly trained infiltrators. They vanished from a base near you about four days ago. We believe they're coming your way."

"What makes you think that?"

"They've stolen a boat and weapons. Assume they're possessed by demons and headed your way. If not, then great. If they are, and we do believe they are, then you can be waiting for them."

"Thanks for the heads up, General. We'll be ready if they show up here."

"Melanie, I can't stress enough that these are highly trained people. They are not to be taken lightly."

"Understood, General."

"Good luck, Sheriff." The line went dead.

"Well crap, there goes my day off," sighed Emily. "I had a date for a picnic too."

"Oh yeah?"

"Yeah. Ah well. I'll call Luke and we'll get the militia on this one."

"Call a council of war for this afternoon," sighed Melanie. "Vic, you got any more magic up your sleeve?"

"Yeah, I do, but I don't think the general's supplies will show up here in time to be of any help."

"What makes you think that?"

"Has it ever been that easy before?"

"No, it's never easy," sighed Melanie.

"I'll get right to it, Mel. Come on, Ellen, we've got work to do."

"Work? Are you crazy? I'm a hippie. I don't work, I sing and dance with flowers in my hair."

"Okay," laughed Vic, "you dance, I'll watch, and Egg can do the work."

"Now you're talking. Mel, thanks for bringing this guy to the island. He's the best old man I've ever had."

"Flatter me all you want, pretty lady, but you still have to cook supper. I've got weapons to build. See you later, Mel."

Melanie sighed as the door closed behind them. She leaned against a desk and faced Bjorn. "Tell me this isn't as bad as I think it is."

He snorted and shook his head. "What's your take on it, Mel?"

"As I see it this could go two ways. One: these people are possessed by demons and we hit them with everything we've got. That one we can handle. We can win that. Two: These people are not possessed, but acting on orders from someone who is. In this scenario, I'm as good as dead." Caroline sucked in her breath.

"I've never known you to give up that easy, Mel," grinned Bjorn.

"So tell me I'm wrong. Hell, tell me there's another possibility."

"If there is, I can't see it. We have to prepare for worst and hope for the best."

"Yes we do." Melanie rose and began pacing about the room. Caroline took a step towards her, but Bjorn shook his head. Better to let her think. Caroline looked closer, there was no sign of fear on Melanie's face. Whatever was coming she would face it head on. Carrie's heart swelled with pride and admiration.

Finally, Melanie stopped pacing and faced the room again. "All right, here's how I see it. If they come they will try to take me in some secluded place. Most likely at home in the night. That's not going to happen. I want to face them in a place of my own choosing. We need to know the minute they hit the ground. If we're lucky we can hit them when they reach the beach. Bring them down before they can hurt anybody."

Emily set the phone back in the cradle. "Sorry Mel, it's too late for that."

"Em?"

"The man watching the beach was just found unconscious and tied up. There's a strange boat pulled up and covered with brush. The militia found them."

"Ah crap. Em, call Luke. Get the entire militia in here as quickly as possible. Tell them to avoid the intruders at all cost. Do not engage. We'll make a plan from here."

Emily was instantly on the phone again. Melanie noticed Caroline giving her a hard look. "What?"

"You're not going to try to keep me out of this are you?"

"I'd love to, honey, but I can't. I'd like to keep the militia out of it too, but that won't be possible either. If we fail here, everybody is doomed." Melanie had opened a cabinet and pulled out a bullet proof vest. She tossed one to Carrie. "Em, give Vic and Brit a heads up. Send Brit over to Nana's house. Tell them all to hunker down until we give the all-clear." Emily nodded and continued making calls.

"What are we doing, Sheriff?" asked Caroline.

"Sadly, my love, we're putting ourselves in harm's way. Bjorn, can you see the cafe from the roof?"

"Clear as day," he grinned. "I'm on sniper duty?"

"Yep. Carrie and I are going to hang out at the coffee shop for a while, then we'll wander over to the hardware store, and after that we'll stay visible where you can cover us from the roof. We'll be carrying, tranqs, DKs, and side arms."

"Okay, am I using tranq rifles or live rounds?"

"Live rounds, old buddy. You know what we're facing here. Trained assassins controlled by demons are bad enough, but if these guys are unhindered and acting on orders we dare not take any chances.

"Emily, as soon as the militia gets here fill them in then start sending them to the cafe one or two at a time. If we're lucky nothing will happen until after dark, but I do want the SEALs to know where to find me. I also want that cafe filled with armed militia, both as customers and as staff by the time sundown arrives."

"I'm on it, Sheriff. Gods, Mel, you sound so much like Hank. He'd be proud of you."

"Thanks, Em, I just hope he has to wait a long time to tell me in person. All right, Deputy Majors. Let's go step into the jaws of hell and taunt fate for a while." She glanced down Caroline's weapons then back up to meet her eyes. "Two side arms? Where's the tranq Pistol?"

"In the weapon's locker. There's no doubt in my mind that these people are possessed and are after you. I also doubt a tranq dart will stop a Navy Seal in time. I'm not screwing around with this. If somebody comes at you tonight I'm putting them down. I really don't care if the demon can escape. The DKs can handle that."

Melanie looked thoughtful for a moment then nodded. "All right, love, let's go. I'll buy the coffee."

"And the Danish?"

"You're buying the Danish."

Emily smiled and shook her head as the door closed behind them. Bjorn grinned at her as he took a long range rifle with a scope and ammunition from the weapon's locker. He winked at her as he headed for the stairs to the roof. "We'll do that picnic just as soon as this is over, Em. Don't worry." With that he disappeared up the stairs.

"Don't worry," she muttered, as she went back to the phone calls. "Don't worry he says. How am I supposed to not worry when the whole world is crawling with demons trying to possess everybody? Hello, Jimmy..."

"MORNING SHERIFF, WHAT'LL it be this morning?"

Melanie smiled at the cheerful server. It was the same girl who'd brought her a burger on her first day back on the island. They placed the order then glanced around the room. There were several nods of greeting and Melanie relaxed in her chair. Caroline gave her a questioning look. "In spite of what's going on, I'm actually pleased, Carrie. When I first got home a few months ago things were a bit different for me."

"I remember the first ferry trip we made together. I can see the change too. You've made a big difference in this town in a very short time, Mel honey. People have begun to see the real you and not the upset teenager they remember. They look up to you now. It's a good feeling for me too."

"Oh?"

"The first few days I was back on the island my scars were like a neon sign. People stared openly. Some even pulled their children away. Teenagers snickered behind my back and a room would go quiet when I walked in. Now things are different for me too. People don't see the scars anymore, just the uniform. I like that. Except for the demons, I like the changes."

"Yeah, me too, honey, me too."

The conversation stopped as the girl returned with their order. As she set down Melanie's plate, Mel slipped a note into her hand and shook her head. The girl nodded then disappeared into the kitchen to read the note. "Demons coming. Militia will trade places with all of you. Go home and wait for the all-clear."

A while later a different woman approached their table. "Want a refill on the coffee, Sheriff?" It was one of the Militia. Melanie grinned and held out her mug. When she walked away, Melanie took a sip of her coffee then pulled out her little book.

"Change is life
Life is change
Embrace it."

Melanie and Carrie finished their leisurely coffee then left the cafe to wander around the block, checking in with a few stores then returning to the cafe for lunch. By late afternoon the staff and customers at the cafe had all been replaced with militia carrying tranquilizer weapons and DKs. It was well known around town now that the sheriff would be spending the evening at the cafe, hanging out with friends.

"It's starting to get dark, Mel. What do you say? Shall we have dinner at the cafe tonight?"

Melanie grinned at Carrie and nodded. "Sounds like a fine idea to me. Let's lock her up and go for dinner. You all right on your own here, Bjorn?"

"I'll be just fine." He grinned as he patted the rifle with a night vision scope on it. As they left the office he jogged up the stairs to the roof once again.

Melanie finished locking up the office and turned to find Carrie frowning at her phone. "What it is, sweetie?"

"I just called Brit to make sure they were okay. She sounded fine, but said they were in position. That tells me they aren't where they're supposed to be."

"Aw, dammit it anyway. Crap, I hope they stay out of the line of fire. I know Vic well. He's probably up to something, but he wouldn't risk, Nana, Brit, or Egg unnecessarily. I just hope he doesn't leave them somewhere vulnerable to come help us."

"Well, there's nothing we can do right now, but I plan to have a word or two with my little sister when this is over."

"Uh-oh."

"Oh forget that, Melanie my darling, you'll still be stuck with both of us. You'll just have to duck for cover when the fur starts to fly."

"Fairly warned," sighed Melanie. "What the heck have I gotten myself into?"

"Stop whining, you wanted both girls, now live with that dream come true."

Melanie chuckled as she held the cafe door open for Caroline. "I plan to, girl, and I can't wait."

"Beast. Just for that, you're buying dinner."

"Sure. I just hope Luke isn't cooking." Carrie was still giggling as they reached an empty table.

"YOU SURE YOU GOT THOSE relays right?" Vic asked, as Egg finished tying the wires together.

"Yes, master," grinned the boy. "For the tenth time, I'm sure. Use you night vision glasses. Check light number one." Vic raised the field glasses to his eyes as the boy began to work a remote control with his thumb. The big search light swung easily back and forth. He turned to the second light, it moved as well. So did the third. "Sorry, Egg. I just don't like having Brit and Ellen here with us."

"There was no safe place to leave them, and you know that," replied the boy, still fussing with his remote. "Besides, I get the feeling that lady is pretty good with that tranquilizer rifle. She seems right at home with it in her hands."

"You should see her with a deck of cards. That's when she's really scary."

"I heard that," came Brit's voice. Egg snickered and focused on the lump of darkness that indicated the location of the stolen boat on the beach. He carefully set the search lights to pinpoint that area. "Are we ready?"

"All set," replied Vic. "Ellen?"

"Just finishing up," she replied, as she returned to the hiding place on the hill. They were well protected by a rock outcropping, yet had a full view of the end of the beach where the boat had been hidden. Ellen had scattered some of her anti demon potion along the ground. There was no way to approach them without passing over it and no demon in a hurry would attempt that. "All right, I'm done. It's up to you wizards and sharpshooters now."

"So now we wait and watch," said Vic, as he made himself comfortable.

The night was fully dark when they heard the car coming at speed. The headlights had been disabled. It raced down to the beach, then two people leaped out and ran towards the hidden boat. Suddenly a searchlight lanced out, shattering the darkness and engulfing the two men.

The men began to scream and writhe as the demons felt the pain of the light and sound. One man managed to get control long enough to shoot out the light, but instantly another came on from a different position. The man with the rifle yelped as a dart struck his neck then another hit him in the shoulder.

The second man had managed to get the cover off the boat and push it part way into the water, but a dart hit him in the back of the leg. He struggled on under the pain of the light, but a second dart struck him, and then a third finally brought him down.

Vic raced to the beach, Brit and Egg hard on his heels as the second man fell. Vic dragged that one from the water to keep him from drowning. Brit trained the rifle she'd taken from the fallen man on the two captives. "Brit?"

"No, Vic, these guys are way too dangerous. If they twitch I'm gonna put them down. Tranqs are fine from a distance, but up close with these guys? Nope, all bets are off."

"Understood," he agreed. "All right, you keep them covered. Ready, Egg, We'll both work a single demon at the same time. We finish one then we do the other."

"Got it, Vic. Your guy first?"

Vic nodded then he and Egg trained their DKs on the fallen man. Even with all that drug in him the pain inflicted by the dying demon woke him up, but it abandoned him before Brit had to shoot.

The man rolled on his back as the demon left him. He watched through foggy eyes as the demon was destroyed. "What the fuck? What was that? Who are you people?"

"Shut up and don't move," commanded Brit, as she trained the rifle on him. "Don't think about testing me, mister. You're full of tranquilizer and I'm a crack shot. Just shut up, watch, and learn. Do it Vic."

Vic and Egg turned their DKs on the other unconscious man. The first man watched in horror as his friend was tortured by the demon before it was finally driven out of his body and killed. The first man sat very still, trying to absorb what just happened. Finally he turned his eyes to Brit. "Relax, woman. I won't try anything. I just want to know what happened, where I am, and how I got here."

"There will be a full briefing later," said Vic, as he propped the other groggy man up against a log. "For now, tell me what you just saw."

"I have no idea what the hell I just saw, and I hope I never see one again."

"Sadly, you are going to see a lot of that in the near future," replied Brit, as she leaned the rifle against a rock and sat beside him. "What you saw was a demon. Your friend was possessed by one. So were you. We killed the demons. Now I'm just hoping the rest of your team hasn't killed my lover and sister."

"What???"

"Your team was taken over by demons," said Vic. "You went AWOL, stole a boat, and came here to kill or capture our sheriff. For some reason the big boss demon seems to want her bad."

"You're serious."

"I am. You should also know there's another sniper up in the rocks. Do anything stupid and..."

"Relax, buddy, relax. You had the chance to kill us and didn't. I'm not doing anything until I'm sure of what the hell has happened and this mess is cleared up. Okay? Truce. Just let me clear my head. Christ, what did you shoot me with?"

"Enough tranq to bring down a rhino," grinned Vic. "Brit wasn't taking any chances."

"Just be happy it wasn't my sister up there," grinned Brit. "She would have used live rounds."

"Then I'm more than happy it was you," groaned the big man as he carefully adjusted his position then lay back on the sand. Neither man made a threatening move, they just sat and fought the tranquilizer until Melanie showed up to collect them.

DARKNESS HAD FALLEN and the tension in the cafe was building. Melanie worried that if it didn't happen soon one or more of the militia would crack under the strain. Suddenly Carrie tapped her toe under the table. A car with three strangers had just arrived in the parking lot. Dammit, the general had said it was a five man team. She guessed the other two were already outside somewhere.

The three men approaching the door looked dangerous. They wore long coats even though the night wasn't cold. Melanie guessed they were carrying weapons and night vision goggles under the loose coats. They were well prepared for that. She almost grinned as the adrenalin began to course through her veins. She tapped the table three times with her knuckles. Everyone in the room stiffened.

The three men then made a simple mistake. They entered the cafe and sat to a table, ordering coffee. Everyone knew their exact location. They gazed around the room, their eyes lingering on Melanie and Carrie who were still in uniform. Finally one of them cleared his throat loudly. The lights went out.

Instantly the room was lit up by flashlights, DKs. The three men were the focus of the lights as the militia pulled away from them, holding them in the light. The men screamed and fought as the tranquilizer darts pierced their clothing. Two of the demons were driven from their victims and killed, but the third had managed to escape the cafe. He didn't get far. The parking lot was lit up by floodlights armed as DKs. There was no hope there.

Melanie and Carrie chased after the escapee to find him in the parking lot, writhing on the ground, Bjorn standing over him with a DK focused right on him. "Mel, two got away."

"Shit. That isn't good. Let's haul this bugger off to a cell then finish him. I don't like being out here in the open with two of them on the loose." The militia was now bringing out the two bemused and groggy men from the cafe. "Take those two to the hospital and get them patched up. Stay with them and keep your DKs ready just in case."

The militia men nodded and helped the two men into a car then several joined them. In all, four cars left for the hospital. Bjorn fairly carried the man down the street, Carrie's DK trained on him the whole time, but something was wrong. He wasn't struggling hard enough, and the demon wasn't putting up much of a fight, and yet it would not let go of the victim.

Once they were inside, things changed. The man slipped out of Bjorn's grasp and knocked him down. He spun like lightning and lashed out. Carrie tried to block the kick, but it sent her against the wall, knocking the breath from her body. She sank to the floor, gasping.

Melanie landed a solid kick to the back of the man's knee, taking him down. She was horrified as the demon fully showed itself. She and Bjorn focused their DKs on it, but it rose from the man, a sinister laugh echoing from its twisted mouth. "So, at last I have you."

Melanie stepped back, reaching for her side arm, but, she'd lost it in the fight. It was on the floor beside the fallen man. "Yes, now you see my full power, my full strength. I no longer need a host. I can enter or leave any host I desire whenever I desire. Your foolish toys can no longer hurt me."

"So, you guys don't need hosts anymore," grunted Bjorn, as he levered himself back to his feet.

"No, they all do," roared the demon. "Only I can assume full manifestation in this realm. Only I have the true power."

"So, you can become solid," grinned Bjorn, as he opened fire with his pistol. "Good to know."

The demon shook off the bullets and roared with something akin to rage and laughter. Melanie attacked from behind, but it tossed her away easily. "Don't be so hasty," the thing chuckled as it turned to face her. "I will get to you in a moment."

"What the hell do you want here?" asked Melanie. She was trying to distract the demon. She'd seen Carrie loading a shotgun.

"I want vengeance on you. I will possess you then use your body to reopen the portal. I will leave your mind free to enjoy the task of protecting the portal while my legions pour through and enslave your species."

The thing turned to face Carrie. "Foolish human, you escaped me once, but not again. You should know by now those things cannot harm me."

"Wanna bet?" Carrie snarled as she fired the shotgun at point blank range. She continued to pump the action until the gun was empty.

"You see," began the demon, and then it stopped. "What have you done?"

"Fucked you up nasty," replied Caroline as she turned her DK on it. The demon's shrieks and howls of pain and rage filled the room. Melanie and Bjorn scattered as the demon flailed about in agony, trying to escape Caroline. When they got clear they added their DKs to her's.

The battle raged on for some time, but the demon continued to weaken. Somehow the shotgun had made a difference and now the DKs were being effective once again. It howled, pleaded, threatened, and fought, but all to no avail. In the end, it was completely dissolved into the ether.

Melanie sighed and gazed around at the wreckage of her office. "Carrie, you okay? Bjorn?"

"I'm fine, sweetie," replied Carrie. "I'll have a few bruises, but I'll be fine."

"I'll live," grunted Bjorn, as he hauled the Navy SEAL back to his feet. "Can you stand?"

"Probably shouldn't," replied the man, as he reached for an overturned chair. Bjorn helped him right it and eased him into the seat. "What happened to me? What happened here? Where is here? How..."

"Easy mister," grinned Bjorn. "Wait a bit until all the tranquilizer has worn off then I'll brief you fully."

Carrie snapped her phone shut and dropped it back in her pocket. "Brit says her team has capture the two who got away, Mel."

"I told them to stay at Nana's house and be safe."

"Bad news, honey. Ellen was the ring leader on that one."

"The hell she was. I know Vic all too well. Ah, it doesn't matter. They're safe and they got the bad guys. Life is good. We'll drop this guy off at the hospital and go gather up the two Brit caught."

She turned her full attention to the man in the chair. "All right, soldier, I mean sailor, on your feet. We'll take you to the hospital to get patched up. I fully expect to find you there in the morning. Once you and your team has slept off the effects of the tranqs there will be a full briefing."

"Thanks, Sheriff. Sheriff, I don't understand a bit of what happened here, but I do know I'm not on foreign soil. Tell me my team didn't hurt anybody."

"You tried, but we beat you. Nobody was hurt bad, not us and not you."

"What the hell was that thing?"

"That thing was a demon. It had taken control of you. Your whole team was possessed as well. Actually, I am happy about that. I don't think I want to face you guys when you're in control of your own bodies. The demons made mistakes you never would have. Now, that's all until the debriefing."

"Yes ma'am, and thank you. My guys are okay?"

"Two are at the infirmary and we'll bring in the last two soon. Relax now and let that drug wear off."

Melanie turned to Caroline. "Speaking of drugs, what the hell was in that shotgun. Bullets didn't hurt that monster any."

"Vic brought some special loads yesterday. He said Ellen had made them special just in case."

"Another one of Nana's magic potions."

"Yup."

"My grandmother is a dangerous woman."

Caroline chuckled as she opened the back of the cruiser for the captive and Bjorn. They left them at the hospital then headed for the beach to collect the last two sailors.

Melanie pulled the cruiser right up to the edge of the sand, the headlights aimed at the group by the fire. Everybody put up their hands to block the lights until she switched off the car. "Well this is a fine thing to find," she said, as she approached and sat on a log beside Brit. Carrie sat on her other side.

There was a small fire going and the whole gang was warming themselves beside it, roasting marshmallows and drinking from plastic cups. "I see you've secured the prisoners." Egg snickered at that and looked away. "Vic, report."

"We arrived at the suspected departure point of the incursion team, Sheriff. Egg and I set up augmented search lights at three separate vantage points. The lights were controlled with a remote devise. Brit and Ellen established a defensible position at yet another location with a clear view of the beach.

"We settled in to wait and when the remains of the invaders returned we hit them with the lights. They shot out one, but the other served well. Brit brought them down with the tranquilizer rifle. Egg and I moved in with personal DKs and finished off the demons. Once we'd freed the sailors from the demons we lit a fire and Ellen broke out the marshmallows."

Melanie was shaking her head. "Nana, what the hell were you thinking? Coming out here when you were far safer at home."

"Nobody will be safe anywhere if those damned things get a foothold on this island, Mel. You know that. I brought food and tea for the troops, laid down some repellent in case things went sour, then settled in to make sure Vic didn't get up to any mischief. We're together now, we have to watch out for each other."

"How about you guys," Caroline asked the sailors. "Still groggy?"

"I will be for a month," sighed the heavily muscled man lying back against a log. "Brit tried to put me in a coma."

"It's your own fault," grinned Brit. "You wouldn't just lay down and let us win. We had to stop you and get that monkey off your back."

"Yeah, about that. I owe you big time. The memories are starting to filter in like you said they would. It's enough to make you sick. How about I buy you dinner by way of thanks?"

"Sorry, big fella, but I'm taken," grinned Brit, as she kissed Melanie on the cheek.

"Too bad, that. How about you, Deputy. Are you single?"

"Nope, sorry," grinned Caroline, as she leaned against Melanie and kissed her other cheek.

"Both of you and the sheriff?" asked the big man, a grin on his face for the first time.

"Yes indeed," replied Brit, a bright smile aimed at Melanie who was blushing furiously.

The big man chuckled. "Sheriff, that's not only wrong on so many levels, it's just plain greedy."

"Okay, that it," growled Melanie, trying not to blush harder or smile. "I'm hauling you two off to jail then taking my wives home. It's been a long day." She tossed Carrie the keys then got in the back of the cruiser with the two men. Brit got in the front with Caroline.

"Hospital?" asked Carrie, as she backed the car onto the road.

"Hospital," replied Melanie. She noticed the arched eyebrow of the smaller sailor. "The rest of your team is there getting patched up now. We'll drop you guys off and then sort out the rest of it all in the morning. Most of your memories will have returned by then. "

"Sheriff, you knew we were coming. How?"

"When your team went AWOL, I was contacted. The big badass demon was after my hide, so we figured you would come for me. We set up a trap, killed the demons, freed the slaves, and nobody was hurt badly."

"Yeah, about that, why not use live rounds? That would be the simplest way."

"Not really," sighed Melanie. "For one thing, if you kill the victim the demon can escape. Keep the victim alive and the demon is stuck to him. You can kill the demon and free the slave, but they go through a lot of pain. It's not a perfect system, but it's well ahead of what we had a few months ago. Back then only one in four managed to survive."

"God bless tech improvements," agreed the larger man. "So, what do you think will happen to us now? Will we end up with a court-martial?"

"No, I expect you'll be trained as demon hunters now. Once you've been through this, you will always be able to see them. They can't hide from you anymore."

"I like the sound of that."

"Yeah," agreed the other man, "payback time. Bring it on. I'd be happy to hunt those suckers down."

"Hospital," announced Carrie, as she pulled up to the emergency doors. They took the men inside, reunited them with the rest of their people then left them in the care of the medical staff and headed home.

On the way home she took out her book.

"Monster evolved

More deadly

And yet dead.

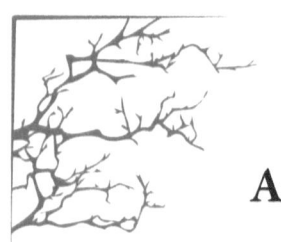

After the Battle

Melanie was quiet as they all rode home together. Brit unlocked the door then took Mel by the hand and led her towards the stairs. Carrie locked up and followed them up to Brit's suite. She saw as Brit tried to pull Melanie into a kiss, but Mel stepped away, her hands shaking. Brit's world fell apart as Melanie pulled back. "Mel?"

"That thing," Melanie said, her voice breaking. "That thing. It wanted me. It wanted to make me..." her hands were shaking badly as she fought her way out of her clothes. "Shower..." she almost ran to the bathroom and started the water.

Tears ran down Brit's face as she watched her go. She noticed Carrie stripping off as well. "Hurry, Brit. She needs us now. Hurry." Stung into action, Brit swiftly shed her clothes. When they found her, Melanie was cowering in the corner of the shower trying to scrub her own skin off. "That thing," she kept repeating. "That thing..."

Caroline gently took the brush from Melanie's hand. "Let me, lover," she said as she moved aside to let Brit into the shower too. "Brit will hold you and I'll wash it all away."

Brit reached for Melanie again and this time Mel came to her, burying her face in Brit's shoulder and sobbing like her body would shake itself apart. Caroline put the brush aside and enfolded the both of them in her arms. Together the sisters held Melanie until the storm passed. They dried her off and wrapped her in a fuzzy robe while they dried themselves.

Once dry, they led her to the huge bed and tucked her in, one of them on each side. They held her until she drifted off to sleep. Her eyes fluttered open and she gazed at Brit. "I'm so sorry about that. I..."

"Hush now, sweet thing. I didn't know, that's all."

"I didn't mean to hurt you..."

"I'm not hurt, Mel. I'm fine. We're fine. Go to sleep now. There'll be time for talk when you're rested."

Melanie's hand groped until it found Carrie's hand then lightly squeezed. "Carrie?"

"I'm fine, love, I'm fine. You sleep now. Brit and I will hold you and keep you safe while you sleep."

"It's nice to feel safe," she replied sleepily. "I love you guys."

"We know, sweetheart," smiled Brit, as she tightened her arms around Melanie. "We know. We love you too. Go to sleep now." She did, almost before Brit finished speaking. Caroline's fingers sought Brit's hand and together they held Melanie and faded into the land of dreams themselves.

Melanie awakened to sunshine streaming through the window and Caroline's blonde hair tickling her nose. She was lying on Carrie's shoulder and for a moment, that was all that mattered in her world. She lightly kissed that scarred shoulder then carefully rose to make her way to the bathroom. It wasn't where it was supposed to be.

Memory came flooding back as Melanie came fully awake. "Oh crap, Brit's room, and she's not here. Shit, I pushed her away and melted down. She had no idea what the hell was happening, or why." Melanie sat to relieve the pressure in her bladder, quickly washed her hands and face then hurried out and down the stairs looking for Brit. She found her in the kitchen, cooking breakfast.

Brit looked up as Melanie burst through the door. She turned back the burner and stepped up to Melanie, her eyes searching the face of the woman she so deeply loved. Melanie started to speak, but Brit placed a finger on her lips to silence her. "Hush, Mel. Let me look at you. Are you all right? Did you sleep? Are you..." She got no further as Melanie pulled her close and kissed her deeply, hungry for her, holding her tightly as though in fear she might run away.

There was no need for her to worry about that. Brit enthusiastically returned the embrace and the kiss. As their lips parted, Melanie hugged Brit fiercely, still afraid she might bolt. "Brit, lover, I am so sorry about last night. I..."

"It's all right, sweetheart," breathed Brit, as she kissed Melanie's lips softly, lovingly. "It's all right. Yes, I was scared, frightened that you'd suddenly changed your mind..."

"Never," replied Melanie, responding to Brit's kiss with soft kisses of her own, "never change my mind."

"I might have known," came Caroline's voice from the doorway. "Breakfast is burning while you two stand here making out before I even get a cup of coffee."

Brit's laugh was full and rich as she gave Melanie one last kiss then stepped out of her arms and back to her place at the stove. "Carrie, you take over kissing Mel while I finish cooking breakfast."

Melanie looked at Carrie carefully, looking for any sign of hurt or jealousy. She found none, only that bright loving smile she had grown accustomed to waking up beside. "Carrie..."

She got no further as she was pulled close and kissed deeply once again, this time by Caroline. As their lips parted Caroline began to nibble on her ear lobe. "Relax, lover, you'll get used to it after a while. Honey, I'm not jealous. I love you both. I want you both to be happy and I want to share in that happiness. Brit feels the same and I know you do too. This is the only way for that to work out."

"Come on, girls," smiled Brit, as she kissed each of them on the cheek. "Breakfast is ready. Save some of that for later."

They ate at the small table in the kitchen, stealing glances at each other, smiling and blushing and enjoying the thrill of their first real morning as a trio. Eventually Brit shooed the two police officers off to work with a kiss on the cheek for each. Caroline smiled with delight as she started the car and waited for Melanie to collect another kiss from Brit. The haunted look was gone from her sister's eyes, and Melanie seemed more relaxed.

"You're looking pretty pleased with yourself, Lady." Melanie was poking Caroline gently with a finger.

"I am," laughed Carrie, as she pulled away from the exploring finger that was searching for a ticklish spot. "Stop that or I'll tell the sheriff."

"You planned this whole thing, didn't you?"

"What whole thing?"

"The three of us together?"

"Okay, yes I did. I know the feelings I had for you, and I could see past Brit's poker face easy enough. We both love you, Mel, and it was pretty easy to see that you love the both of us. I could also see what making that decision between us cost you. I saw it the day you made it. So did Brit. She tried to live with it, but I've been plotting against the both of you ever since.

"Yes, some people might play the martyr and step aside so both people they love could be happy, but I'm too damn selfish for that. I want to be happy too."

"So you set us up."

"Indeed I did. Mad at me?"

"Madly in love with you, sweet woman. Now, we have to stop this. We're at the office and we have to put on our tough cop faces for the day."

"Gotcha, Sheriff Rivers," giggled Caroline.

The parking lot was a busy place. A military truck was parked outside, and the militia was emptying the contents out and carrying it inside. The supplies had arrived. Inside, Emily was surrounded by men and beaming her delight as she enjoyed being the center of their attention.

Bjorn was grinning at Emily, and she blushed then shook a finger at him. Melanie gave her a sly wink as she and Carrie entered. "Bjorn, report."

"Morning Sheriff. Military supplies arrived on the first boat. Militia is off-loading now. Captives from last night's invasion are in custody."

"Custody? Looks to me like they're just sitting around drinking all the coffee."

"I'll make a fresh pot, Sheriff," grinned the big sailor that had held the big bad demon. He rose and went about the task. "I've got enough of my wits back this morning to be functional. Allow me to introduce myself. I'm Captain Alex Duncan. Me and my men are fit to travel and thought we'd hitch a ride back to a military base with the army. That is, unless you have charges to levy. If you do, we'll stay. Your call."

"Got your memories back?"

"Yeah, for the most part. Your deputy here has given us a full briefing. That thing that had me sure wanted your hide. Any idea why?"

"I shook him off years ago then went on the hunt for them," replied Melanie, as she leaned back against Emily's desk. "Nobody else has ever been able to do that. I think he took it personally. Whatever the reason, he made a bad mistake last night. Deputy Majors blew his ass to Mars. I have to say it is a big relief to have that thing dead."

"No more looking over your shoulder?"

"No more looking over my shoulder. You're good to go, Captain. You guys were the victims here, not the bad guys." She turned to Emily. "I suppose you're going to make me do paperwork all day."

"Of course, Sheriff Rivers," replied Emily, a twinkle in her eye. "Reports have to be written, amends made, the cafe was a mess, they will be making a claim, the mayor will want an update..."

"Okay, okay, I get it," Melanie sighed elaborately, winking at the Captain. He chuckled and looked away. "However, I'm not doing a damn thing until I get some of that coffee I smell brewing."

By mid-afternoon things had settled down a bit. The town was quiet and so was the office. Carrie and Bjorn were finishing up the last of their reports, Emily was doing the last of the filing on the new supplies, and Melanie was standing in the doorway of her inner office, smiling.

The Mayor came through the door and he too was smiling. "The town seem unusually quiet today," he said as he leaned against the desk. "Nice for a change after all the madness of the past few months."

"Yes, it is," said Melanie, as she stepped further into the room and sat on the edge of Caroline's desk, "and I have a plan to keep it that way."

"I'd love to hear it."

"All right, Mr. Mayor, I was about to unload it on the staff anyway, so you might as well sit in. Here's the plan folks. As of right now, police officers on this island will carry only DKs and tranq pistols as side arms. Heavy vests will not be worn unless in an emergency situation. Anti-demon weapons only in evidence, all anti-human weapons to be under lock and key until needed."

"Is that wise, Melanie?" The mayor seemed genuinely surprised.

"Jim, the people of this town aren't the enemy, and I want them to know that. I want them to feel they can approach us without fear for their lives. The demons are the enemy, and we'll go about armed and ready to face that threat. We're here to serve and protect the citizens of this island and I want it to be well understood that is our prime focus."

"So what will you do if a fight breaks out or..."

"The tranqs can deal with most anything we might face and there will be loaded weapons locked in the trunk of both cruisers if we need them. Look around, Jim. Look at the militia Emily built to work hand in hand with us. Look how well they did. I plan to keep them all armed with anti-demon weapons too. I plan to keep them active."

The mayor grinned and shook his head. "Melanie, I will admit I had a fit when Hank said he was hiring you as his deputy. He made it clear there was no other option as far as he was concerned. I can see now how right he was. Please tell me you will stay on for a full term."

"I'll stay, Jim, and I'll run for the next term when the time comes. I'm starting to like this job."

"Then I'm a happy man," he grinned, as he straightened up and stepped toward the door, "and I'll let you get back to work, Sheriff Rivers."

Once the mayor was out the door, Bjorn spoke up. "Actually, I have a better idea than the mayor. Why don't you take the rest of the day off and all of tomorrow."

"Bjorn?"

"Look, for the first time in weeks things are under control here. You have a new family situation to explore, and I want a few hours alone with Emily. I'll hold the fort for a day or two. You go play."

To everyone's surprise Melanie stepped up and hugged him. "Thanks, old friend, but I'm all right. I had my meltdown last night. I'm all good now, but I do appreciate the thought. However, I will take you up on the offer." She patted his shoulder as she stepped away and reached for her hat.

Caroline followed her out and the drove away. "What do you think, honey, would Brit like to go out to dinner instead of cooking?"

"I'm sure she would, honey. Mel, it's okay to relax and enjoy yourself."

"Huh?"

"I know you, woman. You're still tense about the three of us. There's a part of you that's afraid if you let yourself relax and enjoy it, it will somehow get ripped away from you. I promise you, that will never happen. I know you're afraid that if you show too much affection for one of us the other will get jealous. Won't happen. We have always taken pleasure from each others happiness and always will.

"Yes we will have problems, the odd spat, and get on each others' nerves from time to time, but that doesn't mean anything. What is important is that we all love each other and we will all work together to make this a loving relationship that will last forever."

"Thanks for that, Carrie. I did need to hear it, and I will from time to time in the future."

They arrived home to a warm hug for Carrie and a deep kiss for Melanie. A few hours later Melanie once again walked into the cafe, every bit as apprehensive as she had been that first day back on the island. However, unlike the first time she ate there, this time she had a dazzling blonde on each arm, she was greeted with welcoming smiles and warm greetings. "Evening Sheriff, ladies."

For the moment, life for Melanie Rivers was good. Yes, there might be demons to fight in the future, or worse, for the future is always unknown, but for the moment, her life was good, and she meant to enjoy it. Who knows, with Brit and Carrie around, life just seemed to be getting better. Maybe that trend would continue. As they waited for their meal to arrive she took her small book from her handbag.

"Darkness shattered
Love shining through
Possibilities endless."

Melanie had thoroughly enjoyed the meal and her partners being accepted in public, but as they returned home, her nervousness began to show. It didn't have time to cause trouble, her phone did that for them.

"Melanie."

"Sheriff Rivers, it's the general. Can you get off the island right now?"

"No."

"I can send a chopper for you."

"General, what's up?"

"I'm at the Secretary's home right now. The place is surrounded by secret service and security."

"So?"

"So the secretary has a monkey on his back. He's planning to withdraw all attempts to fight the demons. Instead he wants to declare a state of emergency, citing mass hysteria."

"Oh shit."

"Look, I can't order any troops here or I'll be over ridden and relieved of command. I'm desperate here, Melanie. I need you and your people right now. Sheriff? Are you there?"

"I'm here. All right, send the chopper. I'll need lots of tranq ammo..."

"Melanie, these people will be using live ammo."

"Understood. Send the chopper."

He replied, but she'd already shut off the phone. Brit was driving and she pulled into the parking lot at the B&B and stopped. She turned to Melanie and sighed. "So, what's the plan, Mel?"

"The plan, my darlings, I go in alone. One person has a chance to infiltrate this place, but a full crew will draw too much attention."

"Bullshit."

"Dammit, Brit..."

"No, Melanie. It's bullshit and you know it. You need a small team, but Bjorn still isn't up to speed, neither is Luke. Vic is too old for this kind of action, and you won't part Luke and Lizzie. I'm going with you."

"Brit, no..."

"Melanie, yes. Look, I won't try to get into the mix up, but I will act as sniper. I can peg off the guards with the tranq rifle, clear a path so you guys can get inside. I can keep that path clear until you're finished."

"Guys?"

"You really don't think you're leaving Carrie behind, do you?"

Tears filled Melanie's eyes as she gripped both their hands. "Please listen to me, both of you. Don't do this. These people are all trained agents, fully armed and using live rounds. They don't know we're the good guys. One slip and I'm as good as dead or worse."

"Mel..."

"No, dammit, listen. You two magical women have given me more love than I've dreamed possible. This will probably go down ugly, and I can't bear the thought of either of you getting hurt. Please, please, please, listen to me, just this once..."

Caroline pulled Melanie's chin around so she could kiss her. "Silly woman, do you think either of us could live with ourselves if we did that? Do you think we could live without you now? Stop trying to be a martyr and get busy. We don't have a lot of time to prepare."

Brit pulled Melanie the other way and kissed her deeply. "Don't you dare ever think about leaving me behind again," she breathed as their lips parted. "Now that I've got you, I'm not letting you out of my sight."

"Girls, please, these guys are trained..."

"That last bunch was Navy Seals," grinned Brit. "They weren't tough?"

"Enough of this," declared Carrie. She threw the car door open and stepped out. "We're wasting time. Let's go."

"Brit opened her door as well. "You heard the woman, Rivers. Move it."

"Oh, now I see the downside," grumbled Melanie as she scooted over and out of the car. "I get hen pecked in stereo too."

Carrie laughed and linked her arm through Melanie's. "Count on it lover." Brit took Mel's other arm and together they marched her into the house to get ready.

The chopper landed in the parking lot. "I hope nobody gets wind of this," mutter the pilot as he waited for his passengers. "It's one thing to do a friend a favor, but another to get tried for treason." The sight of his approaching passengers did nothing to relieve his mind. The three women were dressed in black with hoods up to hide their faces. They were armed to the teeth.

The one hour flight was quiet. Finally the pilot spoke. "We'll be there in about five minutes."

"Drop us out of sight and out of range," said a cold voice behind him. Once we're on the ground, go home and forget all about this."

"About what?"

"Good man." Melanie relaxed back in her seat.

A few minutes later the helicopter landed, but he kept the motor running. "Down that road, five minutes by car. Fence is juiced. Gate's locked and guarded." The woman nodded her thanks and leaped to the ground to join her companions. The chopper rose into the air and left.

Melanie led them out at an easy jog. They stopped to rest once then continued. A few moments later the saw the gates through the trees. One man paced before the open gate, another was in the gate house. Suddenly the man pacing yelped and slapped at his chest. As he began to fall his fellow guardsman came running out to him. Jim..." he got no further as the sting of the dart stopped him speech. He reached for the alarm, but collapsed before he could reach it.

He saw three black clad, hooded figures slip past him just before his world faded into darkness.

Caroline boosted Brit to the top of the gatehouse and tossed up the tranq rifle as well as an extra box of ammunition. Melanie was already halfway to the house when the first security man stepped out. He fell before he could challenge the person running towards him. He groaned as he fell and another came to investigate. She fell as well, clutching at the tranquilizer dart in her neck. A third appeared and met the same fate. Melanie waved for Brit to join them.

"That was damn fine shootin' Tex," grinned Melanie as Brit joined them beside the door. "Ready ladies?"

They both nodded then Melanie leaped through the door with Carrie close behind her. Both had tranq pistols at the ready. Melanie flinched as the sound of a tranq pistol popped beside her. Down the hall a man sank to the floor. Brit grinned and winked. Melanie shook her head then led the way further into the house. They brought down two more security people before they found the General and three other men sitting at a games table playing poker.

One man had a huge demon on his back. Before they could act he pulled a gun and fired. With a yelp, Carrie grabbed her arm and fell. Melanie was on him, knocking the gun from his hand and sending him crashing to the floor. Two of the men leaped on Melanie, but the general grabbed one and hauled him off then broke his nose. Melanie stopped the other with a hard kick to the groin. She turned at the scream behind her.

What she saw made Melanie's heart soar as well as leap to her throat. Brit was on the man with the demon, her DK aimed right in the creature's face. The man tried to fight, but she had already tranquilized him, and she battered aside his feeble attempts to stop her. As the demon fought, the man became aware of what was happening and what was trying to escape from him. He felt the creature's hooks tearing at him and he began to scream as he thrashed about.

The door flew open and two men with guns leaped inside. The sight of the demon stopped them for a second, then they looked down at the darts sticking in their legs. Before they could further react, Melanie was on them, stripping away the guns and letting them fall to the floor.

The battle with the demon was over. Brit Majors stood over the groaning man, still shining her DK on him to make sure it was completely gone. Melanie took her by the arms and gently pulled her off. The general knelt beside the man and gave him an injection. "Ow, what???

"You've been hit with a tranquilizer dart, Mr. Secretary. This is the antidote. You head will clear in a moment. Let me help you up into a chair." As the man complied he watched Melanie fussing over Caroline's flesh wound and Brit watching the door, her weapons at the ready.

Caroline lightly kissed Melanie's cheek. "Mel, honey, Brit going to need some fresh air. Better take her outside. I'll stay here and help the general explain the facts of life to the secretary." Melanie nodded and took Brit by the arm. "Come on, sweetie, Carrie's got this."

"Carrie..."

"I'm fine, Brit, just a scratch. I probably won't even get a new scar from it. You and Mel go watch the main doors."

Melanie led Brit outside. The people she'd shot with the tranq rifle were still down. Brit slowly allowed her shoulders to relax then she started to tremble. "Oh crap," she groaned as she leaned heavily against Melanie.

"Adrenalin downer," whispered Melanie as she took Brit in her arms and held her tight. "Still think I have an exciting life?"

"You will once I get you home, you bag. Teasing me at a time like this..." Melanie grinned then kissed her softly, sweetly, holding the kiss until the girl melted fully into her arms. "If you think that is going to get you out of trouble," breathed Brit, "you're probably right." Suddenly she was hugging Melanie tightly. "I love you, Melanie Rivers. I love you so much it almost hurts. Thank you for loving me back. I don't think I could live without you."

"You don't have to, sweetheart, and you never will."

"Save some of that until we get home," came Carrie's voice from behind them. "The general says to start waking these folks up. He's sent for a taxi to get us home."

"Everything okay in there?" asked Melanie.

"Yeah, the secretary has a headache, but now he's on side. The General will have full command of this war and the secretary's full support to wage it. You okay, Brit?"

"Yeah, I am, Sis. You?"

"I am. Come on, let's get them up before the chopper gets here."

The sun was just beginning to rise as Melanie drifted off to sleep, Brit resting her head on Melanie's shoulder and Carrie snuggled close to her other side. Melanie's little book lay open on the night table.

"More strength lies in Beauty
than the Darkness knows
I am doubly blessed

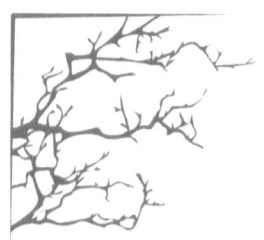

The End

About the Author:

I live on a small island, just off a larger island, off the coast of North America where I write romance, sci-fi, and fantasy/adventure for a wide audience.

What's my superpower? I'm a storyteller, an entertainer. As you begin to read my words the stress of the day, nay, the stress of everyday, begins to magically fade away. Transported into another world, your worries and troubles are forgotten for a time as you share adventures with me and my friends. My art, my power is as old as humankind, for the magic of the storyteller has ever been with us and it will always be.

Okay, I'll confess, I've been busted. I was accused of once being a life coach and hiding some of those techniques in my books, disguised as adventure.

Guilty as charged. Sigh.

I was also accused of lightly touching on a number of taboo subjects in my books, trying to shine a different light on things.

Guilty as charged again.

As a result of these transgressions, I have been labeled an underground writer. Oh the shame of it all. (Hangs head and moves slowly towards penalty box.)

I'M A SPIRITUAL SEEKER, dog trainer, Reiki Master, and Interior designer who has turned her hand to writing. I am also an avid World of Warcraft player, not a great one, but an avid one. I bake, I build, I knit, and I tell great stories.

I have roamed far and wide for over seventy years in this realm, and I have seen much; some I wish I hadn't, and a great deal that I would love to see again. Some days I feel like Bilbo Baggins, for I have been there and come back again.

No, I haven't written a book about my wanderings, at least not yet, but much I have experienced, observed, learned, surmised, or imagined, is woven into the tales I have written.

NOW LET'S TAKE A LOOK at another adventure:

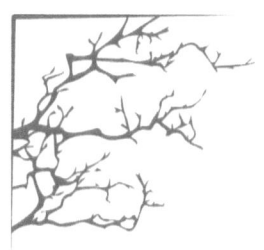

Dragonae

by

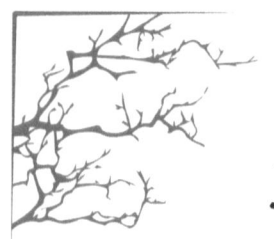

J.L. Crandall

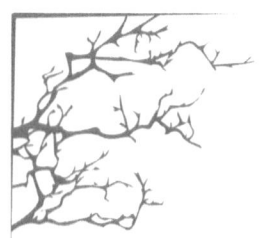

Raven's Field

It was the call of the ravens that brought him back. How long the warrior had stood drawing great heaving breaths into his lungs was unknown to him. Raising a weary arm, he unhooked the strap then pushed off the helmet, allowing it to fall to the gore bespattered ground at his feet.

Despite the fatigue that tried to hold him still, he straightened up and gazed all around. As far as he could see, the only living things in this valley, besides himself, were the ravens feasting on the dead. Thousands lay dead, both of the Southern Legions, and of the king's army.

A heavy sigh escaped his lips as, leaning on his great sword for support, he reached down and scooped up his helmet. With a visible effort he managed to get the sword into the scabbard that rode at his back. Only then did he turn around to see the fate of the king.

The king lay dead, along with his two sons, mere paces from where he stood. "They called me the Dragonae, the warrior who cannot be killed, the one man who could protect them, keep them alive." He paused to gaze at them for a moment. "I guess they were half right."

He took the fallen king's sword from his hand and stuck it in the ground, lifted the broken crown and hung it on the pommel, then sadly turned away.

"I wonder, am I truly the only survivor, or could you have managed to save yourself. Let's see." He gave a piercing whistle, which was answered by a bugling call in the distance.

A smile of delighted relief creased his weary face at that call. "Come to me, my fine bold lad." He whistled again, then saw the movement as the huge warhorse made its way toward him.

When the horse reached him, he hung his helmet on the pommel, then used the last of his strength to swing into the saddle. "Lucky it is that dragon scale makes light armor, at least for me." A light touch on the reins set the beast in motion.

He leaned over to pat the horse on the neck. "We'll go northwest as my brothers did, Stump. That accursed Empire has already eaten everything to the south and east. Come, my fierce warrior, let's go exploring. There's no point returning to the palace, the Second Legion out-flanked us. There'll be nothing left there but rubble and signs of carted off slaves. No, it's the unknown lands of the northwest for us."

The big horse gave a snort of agreement then set out at an easy trot. As the warrior rode away the camp followers and others moved out of the nearby forest and onto the field to begin looting the bodies or looking for their dead.

Don't miss out!

Visit the website below and you can sign up to receive emails whenever Prudence MacLeod publishes a new book. There's no charge and no obligation.

https://books2read.com/r/B-A-ZKBBB-AIEBD

BOOKS 2 READ

Connecting independent readers to independent writers.

Also by Prudence MacLeod

Children of the Goddess
Lady Blue
Fallen Angel
Lady Justice
Lady Shadow
Lady Seeker
Watcher and Warrior
Shadow Ascending

Children of the Wild
Immortal Tigress
Children of the Wolf
Vampire's Lair
The Hawk and the Wolf
The Oregon Incident
Race the Wind
Heir to the Throne

Elvish Chronicles
Rise of the Queen

The Road Home
A Winter Seige

Forgotten Worlds
Suvi
Echo of the Past
Survivors
Ship
Fleet
Unite
IGEN
T.E.N.

Nova series
Novan Witch
Novan Witch
Assassin of Nova
Beyond Nova
Claimstake
Red Nova

Standalone
The Second
Hell Comes Home

Watch for more at https://www.prudencemacleod.com/.

Telling a story is like knitting a sweater. Start with a ball of possibilities, pull out one small thread and begin. With luck and patience you will create something quite wonderful.

About the Author

On a far off windswept island Jennifer Crandall sits with her dogs and cats creating fantastic stories for all to enjoy. She publishes as JL Crandall, Prudence MacLeod, and Jenni Leigh.

Read more at https://www.prudencemacleod.com/.

www.ingramcontent.com/pod-product-compliance
Lightning Source LLC
Chambersburg PA
CBHW020737250626
47155CB00003B/800